Freefall into Us

urbanepublications.com

"I am more interested in human beings than in writing, more interested in lovemaking than in writing, more interested in living than in writing. More interested in becoming a work of art than in creating one."

Anaïs Nin

In loving memory

Of

David Ruiz

Who said I could, and I should

So I did.

First published in Great Britain in 2015
by Urbane Publications Ltd
Suite 3, Brown Europe House,
33/34 Gleamingwood Drive,
Chatham, Kent ME5 8RZ

A CIP catalogue record for this book is available
from the British Library.

Paperback ISBN 978-1-909273-26-9
mobi ISBN 978-1-909273-84-9
epub ISBN 978-1-909273-83-2

Cover design and typeset
by Chandler Book Design

Printed in Great Britain by
CPI Antony Rowe,
Chippenham, Wiltshire

urbanepublications.com

The publisher supports the Forest Stewardship Council® (FSC®), the leading
international forest-certification organisation. This book is made from acid-free
paper from an FSC®-certified provider. FSC is the only forest-certification scheme
supported by the leading environmental organisations, including Greenpeace.

CONTENTS

Acknowledgements

THANK YOU, GRACIAS, MERCI, DANKE, GRAZIE, ARIGATO, ASANTE, CHEERS!

I start with the boys from the Bronx.

Thank you to the beautiful Paul LaRosa. For being my pivot, my muse, my journey, for most of this book. Without you, it never would have been written. You put the mirror in front of me, helping me see who I really am. You will forever rock my world.

Thank you Eugene Duffy. For letting me cry, laugh and scream at will. "It's too, not to...And it's you're, not your!" Thank you for your divine, unconditional friendship. "Breathe....and let the magic exhale." ~Eugene Duffy

Thank you Ian Lowell Blankfeld. For always taking my phone calls at the drop of a hat.

You've always been there for me and I love you for that. Of all the Bronx boys, your NY accent is the most believable.

Thank you Louis Romano, for being my greatest cheerleader. Your humor, wit and passion for writing got me through my darkest days. You were always my light at the end of the tunnel. I love the messages you left on my phone and I will never, ever delete them. Jesus....I'm speechless. Thanks for always treating me like a queen whenever I am in NY.

Life would not be the same without you, Terrence McCauley. You are one bad ass boy that I never want to cross. Thank you for extending your hand, helping me jump the puddles, and your heart as you held mine when it was breaking in two. Incredible, that is you.

Thank you Denise Carns, for anxiously reading every word I wrote. You started this journey with me. Look where we ended up. Love you.

Thank you to my work family. Your support, enthusiasm and love always kept me going. I am grateful for the gypsies in my life.

There are so many of you, I can't begin to list you all. You know who you are. I love you with all that I am. Also, thank you, wine, for being such a wonderful beverage.

To the following coffee shops, where I spent hours on end. You were all so gracious, asking me how the book was coming. Thank you for letting me plant my ass for so many months:

Starbucks, #439 Redmond, (friendliest baristas)

Roy Street Coffee, Capitol Hill, Seattle (spectacular ambiance)

Starbucks on 74th (Bayridge) Brooklyn (It's NY, nuf ' said)

Starbucks, #3414, Rose Hill, Kirkland (love the re-model)

Thank you Susan Wolfin. Your courage, strength, love and friendship shoots me to the moon and back. You are truly one of the most inspirational women I have ever known. Watching you kick breast cancer was simply bad ass as hell.

The moment I set foot in New York I felt I had come home. Thank you Lois Colucci, for letting me stay over and over again in what I call 'my Brooklyn house'. I am in love with that house and I hold many fond memories there. Not having internet forced me to write without distractions. I am forever grateful to you.

All of my love to Janice & Edo Vanni, Mike Albritton, Bridgette Gubernatis, Samuel Bussey, Lucy & Russ Stuefloten, Lissa Ongman, Jelena Raco, Floyd Jenkins, Heaven Muxworthy, Tom & Fran Underhill, Alisa & Zach King, Randy Pope, Autumn Moore, Rob Desch, Lorraine Perez, Wendy Paylor & Ryan Colvin, Steven "Esteban" Calbaum, Ben Gutierrez, Linda Orlandi, Katelyn Peil, Lanii Chapman, Mark Svectos, Breauna Stockton, Judith Garner, Juliana Loken, Rich Troiani, Amber Morse, Bruce Lyon, Laraine Corneilson, Heidi Dillard, Maria Ramos, Karri McGough, Brittany Graham, Shawna Canova, Katrina Shull, Rob Baker, Tabitha & Larry Kurofsky, Mindy Peek, Tony Nilsson, Jeff Vileta, Victor May, Natalie Joy Nemeth, Leishawn Hayward, Andrew Cimburek, Dillon Bulette, Sarah Butterfield, Elijah DiStefano, Stacy Albright, Paul Vilsack, Stephanie Crowder, Kristie Polito,

Nicole Sesar, Victoria Oestreich, Colleen
Baumgardner, Chase Harden, Lou Hunter,
Courtney Elliott, Mike Wilson, Carolyn Cobler
Moore, Nick Hunter, Colleen Graham, Charene
Herrera, Chris Castleman, Ami Schneider, Dylan
Wiemer, Nicole Iovino, Brian Schutt, Tuan
Lam, Alex Lisette Vela, Seth Goldberg, Sophia
Moreno, Izzy Moreno, Kerri & Paul Lucchese and
David Wood, for being whom you are. Amazing,
wonderful, selfless people that have been a constant
hum in my life in one way or another.

A special kiss and hug to my first love and high
school boyfriend of four years, J.D. Parkman.

Thank you Jack Graham, owner of the UPS store
on Novelty Hill. Your kindness
and smile always made me feel so good. You are the
supreme of customer service.

Thank you JoAnne Averett, my therapist, for
throwing me a line before I got to the deep end of
the pool (I never did learn how to swim properly).
I love you so much.

A huge hug and kiss to the poet, S.E. Lucas, a
beautiful man with a beautiful soul. I couldn't have

gotten through these past few months without you. Not possible. I love you.

Thank you Gina Fiserova for your invaluable help with early drafts. Never have I seen anyone work so diligently, swiftly and hard as you.

Thank you to my beautiful daughters. So glad you chose me to be your mother. Thanks for putting up with my oddities and lack of direction all these years. I am proud of the beautiful, strong, intelligent women you have become. I love you both to no end.

Thank you to the bitches that threw my painted rocks into the street when I was selling them door-to-door. Thanks to the bitch that stole my journal and read it aloud in class. Thanks to the bitches that locked me in armoires, closets and pitch black basements. Thanks to the bitch that slept with my boyfriend when visiting me from Montana. Thanks to the bitches that called me names in high school in the hallways, making me cringe and sulk for hours. Thanks to the bitch that pushed me down, causing a serious knee injury because she thought I stole her boyfriend. You all helped mold me into what I am today and I say, "THANKS BITCHES!"

Thank you to the wonderfulness that is Urbane Publishing. Matthew, not only are you dashing and handsome with a killer British accent, but you single-handedly made my dreams a reality. Your wit, charm, humor and vast knowledge of the publishing world gave me faith that my words would make it to paper and illuminate. Heeerrreee weeeeeeee goooooo!!

Thank you mommy and daddy, for your love, support and belief in me. You have always been there for me. I love you both incredibly so and none of this would have been possible if not for you.

Freedom

poem

When will they learn I am not a servant?
I don't care about their breast-fed lies,
Spooned to me on their heaped plates
Alongside Cornish game hens and split peas.
When will they learn
I don't give a fuck about their rigid
Conforming of me, their molding of me,
As they pluck my truths and whore-like nightmares
From my body
As they would pluck a peacock of its rainbow
And unparalleled plumes.
When will they learn my words combat theirs
And I leave them drooling and slobbering like idiots
From their slack mouths.

When will they learn I don't want what they have,
Their bedpans and open sores,
The wounds that never heal.
When will they learn that their lies and absurdity
Give me a god-like strength to mow them down
As they stand naked, stupid, and ignorant
In a field of poppies.
When will they learn they cannot take from me
What it is I have.
When will they learn they cannot see through their
muddied goggles
And cataract-blind eyes.
When will they learn that my pain,
My suffering of myself,
Has given me
FREEDOM!

Easy for a Girl

poem

It's easy for a girl
To get it
Whenever she wants.
I know this.
Everyone knows this.
Certainly the boys in the bar
Know this.
Real fucking easy.
It was my intention
To play the slut role,
The whore character,
One time only,
At my will, my choice, my discretion.
My doing, my command.

There is something about
Walking into a bar, alone.
Can they see that I am on the hunt
As I place my sweet ass on a barstool?
They know the truth.
WOMEN DON'T DRINK ALONE.
I feel their eyes on me wondering
When will I turn around,
My eyes hunting for my prey?
They stare at my back,
Pretending not to notice
My eyes searching in the mirror placed against
The bar,
Reflecting not only
Campari, Seagrams, Stolichnaya,
But
The cowboy with his bull-legged saunter
As he shoots the number three ball
Into the
Corner pocket.
The sports enthusiast, his football jersey
Graced with a team emblem
That I don't give a fuck about.
The bearded man, disheveled, scotch in hand, eyes
dark and sad.

I would have my choice of men,

Picking them among a line-up of sorts.

I go for the blonde, seated two

Stools away from me.

His body, lean in his 501's.

His hair, shaggy,

Surfer-type.

Dimples punctuate his pretty lips,

His feet graced in denim Van's.

Our eyes meet, we smile.

He knows what I want.

What I seek.

What I am all about.

Don't worry, my eyes say,

I don't want you to buy me a drink.

TAKE

ME

HOME.

And he did, and it was

Mellifluous

Breathtaking

Exuberant

Pleasurable.

I waited for him to fall asleep,

Laying in his arms.

Will I see you again, he asked?

Of course, I replied.

What do you

Think I am,

A

ONE NIGHT STAND?

He laughed, holding me tight.

His eyes then closed, his snores ensued.

I dressed, and climbed out the window

Into the night.

Smiling at how it's

EASY

FOR

A

GIRL.

Gone Awry

short story

I had never seen my daddy cry. My mother told me she had seen him cry once, the day I was born. Tears of joy. Apparently my arrival into the world, his world, had moved him to tears.

Now, my departure from this world had warranted this emotion, causing tears to roll down his cheeks. Tears not of joy, but from the deepest anguish possible for a parent; the loss of a child. They were supposed to go first. Everyone knows that. A parent burying a child...well, that's the cruelest of cruel.

My daddy had survived my first tooth, bike ride, period, date, drivers' ed, kegger, loss of virginity and high school graduation without so much as a hiccup. Now he stood, disheveled and bent over, his eyes swollen and red, holding onto my mother as though he were standing on the edge of a cliff, teetering over the abyss. My mother spoke for the both of them in the dimly lit cold room of the Flathead County Morgue.

As she whispered "Yes, it is my daughter" (audible only to my father and the soft-spoken, consoling John Petesch, county coroner), the light above them flickered. Did they know that was me? Did my daddy feel my lips move about his cheek, telling him not to cry, it will be okay? Did they know I was trying to tell them I felt no pain during my dance with death?

They would never believe that by looking at the cruel black, blue, and yellow marks around my slim neck. They would find out later there was not a struggle. They would find out later that my vagina was full of semen. They would find out later from some of my friends that I was 'hooking' online, to pay for my college tuition, books, make-up, clothes, and a new pair of Frye boots.

I had managed to get through my freshman year without a worry or care. Sure, I attended an occasional party, smoked a few joints, and drank some, but for the most part I was a good girl. Early to bed, early to rise. I spent most weekends in my dorm room, studying. Mom and Dad pretty much took care of all of my expenses. That was the deal, study hard, get good grades, we've got your back. Well, for my first year. My second year, I was expected to pull my weight and get a job. Options. A barista at Starbucks. A sales girl at Forever 21. I had heard that job was hideous, full of long hours, shit pay, and bitches for bosses. Starbucks looked good, offering employees good pay, health insurance, even helping with tuition. The problem, it seemed, was everyone was vying for that, and, if someone left, there were twenty call backs on a wait list holding their breath. Then, of course, there were the usual fast food jobbies and 'bag girl' at the supermarket. A girl had standards, dammit. I remember first hearing about Operation PMS during a study session at the Grizzly Union.

My roomie's best friend from high school was asking me and a couple of other girls at our table if we were interested in making some incredible cash for just a couple of hours of work. One seemed interested, the other didn't, and I didn't hear the whole spiel as I was running late for a class. Now, almost a year later, I was back at the union, searching for the red head. As if I had willed her, there she was. The well-dressed, statuesque… dang…. I was trying desperately to remember her name. J…J…Jane. That's it! I remember because sometimes I would make a quick rhyme with someone's name so I wouldn't forget it. Plain Jane. She was anything but. She was stunning.

"Jane!" I shouted, suddenly realizing I shouldn't have. At least twenty people turned, giving me 'the stink eye'. Either way, she saw me and started walking towards me, her silky red hair and pert breasts bouncing right along with her step. Plain Jane. I laughed to myself, more out of nervousness than anything.

"Forgive me," she said, as she got closer. "You're Bridge's roomie, but I've forgotten your name."

"Ruby. Ruby Martino."

"Yes, yes, Ruby. That's right. How's school going for you? This is your second year, right?"

"Yes. Second year. Things are going well, but I'm having a tough time finding a job. I remember you talking about a job last year, and I was wondering if that was still available. Operation PMS, I believe?" She looked me up and down, then grabbed my arm, leading me outside. We walked across the street, stopping under a large maple that was frequented by students as a quiet place to read. Oddly, it was unoccupied as if by magic.

"Look, I will just come out with it. It's not a typical job. Nothing close. PMS stands for Professional Men for Sex. So, basically, your name, age, photo, clean bill of health, and class schedule go into a confidential website. The men browse whenever they get the urge, and bam. The minimum is $500. I get $150. The deal is you're on call. Aside from classes, you have to show up." She said all of this so matter of factly.

"Um, okay," I said, not sure what else to say.

"Look, it's all fairly simple. The men are clean, professional, attractive, and loaded. Most of them are married, and wifey either won't put out anymore or they want something a little kinky." She must have seen my fear after that statement. "Oh, we have rules as well. No S & M, whips, or handcuffs. Blindfolds and tying up are okay. There are about twenty-five girls currently on the list.

It seems as though they all average about twice a week. Of course, some men have their favorites like anything else. You'll do fine, I am quite sure," she said, glancing at my breasts. I felt degraded, but then, this would probably not be the first time, the circumstances being what they were. "Oh, and when you want out, you're out," she added, tossing her hair. "You can't get back in."

Suddenly, I was looking down at my shoes, kicking some dirt that wasn't really there. She seemed suddenly to be irritated with me. I felt like I was being scolded, and I didn't know why. She noticed the silence in me. "Look, I gotta run. If you want to....." I quickly cut her off.

"No, I'm interested," I said quickly, not wanting to have this conversation again. Her demeanour changed.

"Great! Okay, jot down your email here," she said, thrusting the back cover of a notebook at me. "Let me just find a pen." She began to toss through her oversized Chanel backpack. I wondered if it was one of her rewards she had decided she deserved for taking it up the ass from some sweaty, grunting sixty-year-old.

"Here," she said, thrusting a pen into my open palm. "I will send you the link tonight. Just sign in with a user name and password to sign up. You will go through a short questionnaire. It takes about twenty-four hours when everything is said and done." She pulled out a piece of paper, scrawling a number down. "Oh, and here's my number in case you have any questions."

"Um, ok," I said, not sure of anything at the moment. Before I could say anything else she was already almost across the road, her red hair flying in the wind. I glanced at her scrawl then shoved it into my pocket, making my way back to my dorm.

As promised, the link came through at about 7 p.m. just as I was returning from the cafeteria with Bridgette, the burger I had consumed laying heavily in my stomach. I jumped on my computer, deciding if I didn't do this now, I would chicken out given too much time to think about it. As I began to fill out the questionnaire, Bridgette announced that she was going to go down and shower. As she shut the door, I debated telling her. I decided to tell her if and when I made the decision that I would stick with it.

Two days later, I got my first 'John'. His name was Derek, according to Jane. I was to be outside my dorm at 9 p.m.

"Do you own an umbrella?" she had asked.

"Of course."

"Good. Be under it. He will be driving a forest green Jeep Wrangler. Questions?"

No, I told her. Wondering why she had all of a sudden turned into a total bitch, I hung up the phone. It was seven p.m. I had two hours. I did an hour's worth of homework, and then I went and showered. I was nervous. I made sure I was extra clean, going over everything twice. I shaved again for the second time that day. As I brushed my hair in the mirror, my eyes spoke volumes. They said 'Don't do this, Ruby. There are other ways to make money. Your parents would die a thousand deaths if they knew what you were about to do, Ruby'.

Shut the fuck up! I shut my eyes, continuing to brush my hair. I just had to pretend I was on a date. It would be a date that would end in sex, that's all. Oh, and I'd get paid for it. What's all the ruckus about? I wore a black dress with black heels. I left the dorm a tad early, umbrella in tow. I was surprised I didn't run into anyone. Five-to-nine. I closed my eyes again then took a slow breath in. Then slow breath out. I opened my eyes. Was everyone staring out their dorm window? Maybe, but I felt hidden. The umbrella made sense now. Then, the green jeep pulled up, at precisely 9 p.m. I got in.

"Hi, I'm Ruby." I sounded like a little girl.

"Ruby, nice to meet you. I'm Derek." He put out his right hand, pulling it from the steering wheel which he seemed to be gripping tightly. I barely saw his face, afraid to take him in.

"Are you nervous?" he asked, his hand still on mine.

"Yeah, it's my first time," I said, then giggled a bit. "I mean, not my FIRST time, but..."

He cut me off. "I know what you mean, Ruby. Well, if it's any consolation, it's my first time as well."

This is when I looked at him. He appeared to be mid-to-late 40s. Blondish hair. Spitting image of Kiefer

Sutherland. My dad had started watching 24 again, and, on my last visit home, I started watching it with him. I was hooked. I quickly looked away, thinking this was too good to be true. Hell, I'd lay with him without pay.

"Ready?" he asked, putting the Jeep in gear.

"Uh huh," I said, putting my seatbelt on. We drove in silence for about five minutes. Then he began, quietly.

"I won't ask you a bunch of personal questions nor will you ask me about myself. I don't live here. I fly in every two weeks or so. If things go well tonight, you will be contacted in the same manner as tonight and picked up the same way. Sound good?"

"Yes," I said, feeling nervous again. My hand felt sweaty in my lap. He sensed my trepidation.

"I don't bite, promise," he said, pulling up to a red light. I didn't answer back, my head was spinning. Again, Ruby, like we discussed before, just pretend you are on a date but you're getting paid for it. Besides, look at him. He is sexy and beautiful as hell. Live a little.

After about five minutes of silence, he turned up the radio. It was Radiohead's 'Creep.'

"I love this song," I said, grateful for the distracting power of music. I was thankful he turned it up, and we rode on without speaking. About twenty minutes later, we pulled into a Residence Inn. The place was huge, looking like a large compound. We drove by Units A and B then pulled into a parking spot in front of Unit D. I wondered what happened to C. He turned off the lights but not the car. I was nervous again. He pulled a card key out of his pocket. D24 was in bold black on the side. 24...I thought of Kiefer Sutherland again. Odd coincidence. He handed me the key then turned his body toward me. I saw him more full on, his face now brightly lit by the street lamp. God, he was attractive. He had that 'hadn't shaved in a couple days' light beard stubble. Strong jaw and gorgeous blue eyes, his blond hair strewn about in different directions; disheveled but with purpose. He was wearing dark blue dress pants, a lighter blue, button down oxford, like he had just stepped out of a board meeting. I could feel my heart beating faster in my chest, this time out of anticipation not fear.

"Give me about fifteen minutes. I need to check e-mails and a couple of voice messages." He turned the car off, pulling the keys out and handing them to me. "When you step out of the car, just lock it. My room is up those stairs," and he pointed out the window, "second from the landing."

"Sounds good," I said for lack of anything better to say.

"Great, see you in fifteen." With that, he got out, shutting me in with a few minutes to breathe. I immediately put the key back in the ignition and turned it slightly so that only the music came on. Caveman's 'In the City' was playing. As I sang along, I flipped down the visor, the little light coming on. Eyeliner still on. No smudging. Thank God no zits had reared their ugly heads. Hahaha, I laughed to myself, liking my pun. Hair, check. Blush, good. I flipped the visor back up. I turned up the song, thinking of the video with Julia Stiles. She was beautiful. I loved the red dress she wore. The video was so weird, but I loved it. Kinda dark. No, really dark. I fished my light pink lip gloss out of my purse. I flipped the visor mirror back down again. God, he was probably watching me through the window, thinking I was vain as hell. Nah, the room was on the other side. I pulled the brush out, painting a light coat over the bottom lip, then rubbing the top into the bottom. Someone told me one puts gloss or lipstick on the same way as their mother, from watching her as a child. For some reason little girls love watching mommy put on make-up, wishing they could have a little bit, too.

I remembered how I would giggle when my mother would turn from the mirror, giving my cheeks a light dusting with her blush. More mommy, please, put on more! Put your lips out, she would say. I would pucker them, pushing my face towards her and closing my eyes. I could still feel the lipstick run ever so lightly over my lips, her hands so tender and careful. There's my beautiful girl, she would say.

I flipped the mirror back up and closed the lip gloss, dropping it back into my purse. I got out of the car, locking it behind me. I walked across the dewy lawn instead of the walkway, keeping my shoes silenced. There was a tinge of chill in the air; soon, the leaves would start to fall. I walked up the concrete stairs, stopping midway to take off my heels, my feet grateful for their release. As I neared the top,

I could see D21 to my right. Past D23. I stopped in front of D24, sliding the card key. It flashed red, then nothing. I slid it again. Red flash, then nothing. I tried it a third time. Three's a charm don't you know! Nothing. I took it as a sign and begin to walk away.

I stopped, turned around, slid it through again. It flashed green. Green means go. I walked in, closing the door quietly behind me. I stopped. The place was huge, more like a suite. I walked past the kitchen, noticing an open bottle of wine, still full. There was a roomy living space in front of me with a giant computer on the desk. I stopped, putting my shoes and purse down next to me.

I looked to my left, into a bedroom. He was lying on the bed, still dressed, his hands underneath his head which is on the pillow.

"There's some wine on the kitchen counter if you so desire," he says, glancing out the window. He turns back to look at me. "If you pour yourself a glass, would you mind pouring one for me as well?"

"Of course," I say, pleased that he has broken the ice this way. "I really could use a couple sips, just to settle my nerves a bit."

"Me too," he says, turning off the lamp next to the bed. As I pour the wine, I wonder what it is he does for a living. Is he married? Children? Where does he live? No questions, he told me. I walk slowly with the wine glasses towards him, his eyes on me the whole time. I walk towards his side of the bed, handing him a glass. He takes it from me, still looking into my eyes.

"You look like Kiefer Sutherland", I say, then suddenly regretting it. Oh, God, how stupid did that sound?

"I get that a lot, Ruby. I take it as a compliment. Thank you." He lifts his head from the pillow, taking a large sip. Okay, maybe it wasn't that stupid.

"My dad is into 24, and I watched a couple episodes with him." I take a big gulp of the wine before lying on my stomach next to him.

"Yea, I love that show as well. I heard they were going to bring it back in May for twelve episodes, something like that," he said, taking another sip, placing it on the bedside table, and then moving onto his side, propping his head up with his left hand. He began to play with my hair very lightly. God, it felt so good. As I took another sip of wine, he pressed it to my lips then took the glass from my hand, putting it next to his on the bedside table. He began to kiss me, his mouth so soft and sensual, and I reciprocated, almost hungrily. He was wearing a t-shirt under his dress shirt, which was still tucked into his dress slacks. There was something so sexy about this, about him. I stopped, my face just above his. He smiled at me, the cleft in his chin so prominent. I hadn't noticed it before. I laid my head on his chest for a moment, just taking in his sensuality. His hand went back to my hair, pulling and wrapping it around and through his fingers. He lifted my face from his chest, kissing me lightly then more forcefully, lightly biting at my lower lip. He moved his hand down over my breasts, stopping at the nipple and encircling it with his finger. I felt it harden instantly. He then moved his body on top of mine and slowly began to move lightly back and forth over me. I could feel his hardness through his pants, his cock firmly brushing over my clothed body. I had a flashback to my first boyfriend and how I was introduced to the art of dry humping by him, although it was not an art, more like a playground wrestling match. This was fine art, truly. This was a grown man in a suit minus the jacket who was making this act extremely erotic and sensuous. I could feel my wetness soaking into my panties.

"Do you like this?" he asked quietly, into my ear.

"Yes, very much," I said with a whisper.

"Tell me if I hurt you or feel heavy on you," he said, kissing my neck and rolling his tongue on my skin.

"Mm...hmm..." was all I could muster. What he was doing was electrifying my body, sending small shudders down my back, striking into my pussy. He was at my mouth again, his lips soft and melding into mine as he continued to air fuck me. His soft moans, his mouth, the way his body moved, and his sensuality were like nothing I had ever experienced. I could feel my orgasm coming, my own moaning loud in my ears. He unzipped his pants then, pulling his cock out and looked at me as if asking if it were okay or not. I knew what he was asking. I pushed my dress up, just underneath my breasts, my stomach exposed.

"Cum on me, Derek, please." He closed his eyes then, drawing himself in close to my body, kissing me. I could feel his hand moving faster and faster, his moans low, guttural. He moved away again, and he came on my stomach, staring into my eyes. We lay there, my head resting on his chest.

"That was wonderful, truly," I said, lightly rubbing the top of his chest.

"Mmm. I need to get you back home; I have an early flight."

I got up quickly from the bed, thinking maybe I shouldn't have said that. Wait. I was sure I shouldn't have said that. That was something you say in a relationship not a business transaction.

"Do you mind grabbing the Jeep keys and waiting in the car for me?" he asked, getting up from the bed.

"No, not at all," I said, grabbing my shoes. "See you in a sec," and, with that, I walked out, grateful for the fresh air. I climbed into the Jeep, immediately turning the ignition on so I could listen to music. About ten minutes later he got in and without a word, drove me back to the dorm. Before I got out, he handed me a wad of cash.

"Goodnight, Ruby." I stepped out of the Jeep, still barefoot, holding the straps of my heels.

"Night Derek," I said, shutting the car door.

He smiled at me then drove off. Over the course of the next two months, I worked about five nights a week for only a couple hours, making ludicrous amounts of money. Most of the guys seemed pretty typical. The average age was about 58. The sex was pretty straight, nothing kinky. One just liked to hold me; that was it. It was easy money. I did end up telling Bridge about it, swearing her to secrecy. I had decided I was only going to do it for a couple more months then bow out. I had lied to my parents, telling them I was working at a friend of a friend's coffee shop and that the tips were great. I had managed to save up a significant amount of money, buying myself time not to have to look for a real job until summer. I had seen Derek a total of about four times. The second time we were together was very similar to the first. The third and fourth time, we actually fucked, and it was incredible - as I knew it would be.

I found myself falling for him hard. He was always very quiet, speaking to me through his body and the way he made love to me. I wondered many times why he chose to pay for sex. Was he married, single, divorced, gay, bisexual? If he was married, did he love her? Why not just have an affair? He could have any woman of his choosing, this I knew. Maybe he liked them young. Did they fall for him? I had. Maybe he didn't want the emotion of a relationship. Was this his fantasy, his turn on? A woman who didn't ask him how his day was or what he was thinking. No fancy dinners, no flowers, no jewelry. Whatever it was, whatever he was, I was happy with it. Fuck, who was I kidding? The questions still went on and on in my brain. Did he see others?

He knew I did. Was he jealous of the other men? Did he wonder where I was, what I was doing when I wasn't with him? Did he lie in bed at night, thinking of them kissing my breasts, my hair, my lips, my sex? Did it make him toss and turn? God, so many questions I wanted to ask him.

But none of it was my business. I thought of hookers, prostitutes, escorts, call girls, and strippers. How far would a woman go to feed her family? How many hours away would she need to spend away from her children just to put food on the table or pay the light bill? If roles were reversed, you know damn well men would be prostituting themselves.

Judge all you want, but I got it now. I understood it. I would easily spend two hours on my back, making in one day what a minimum wage job paid in a month, especially if it were for my family. I thought of what my Grammy always use to say, 'You never truly understand someone until you've walked a mile in their shoes'.

Yeah, a considerable amount of money in a short time, allowing for time with children, college, or perhaps caring for a dying family member. Did they too get 'wrapped up' in a 'John'? Fall in love? I suspected so, that it had happened thousands of times. Well, the questions would go on and on. In the meantime, it is what I had signed up for, agreed to. I hated it but not with Derek. Oh, God, the high I would get when he would pull up in the Jeep, my heart beating quickly as we drove to the same hotel, usually in silence, and I would stay in the car, listening to the radio, waiting for him to get settled, counting the minutes, anxious to be in his arms, enjoying his sensuous body.

The night I died was like all the others. I waited in the Jeep, the radio on. The song 'In The City' was playing, just like the first time I had been with Derek. I thought of Julia Stiles in the hotel room bed, her husband lying next to her. After she fell asleep, the man who was hiding behind the curtain crept out, cutting her with his knife. I wondered why she didn't wake. How can you be cut, hell, even touched for that matter, without waking? Why did she think her husband was cutting her? Did she? The whole video was bizarre. That's the whole idea, dummy, it's just a video!

I grabbed the card key Derek had placed in my lap, deciding to leave my bag and shoes in the car this time. I would only be a couple of hours. I got out of the car, locked it, and made my way to room B14 this time. I was having déjà-vu. I hadn't been in B14 yet, this I knew. I started thinking of deja-vu, the oddity of it, no one really being able to explain it. I looked up then and saw Derek in the window, just standing there and looking at me, a quick wave and a smile. Looking just like Kiefer.

I didn't use the card key. Derek was standing there in the doorway, waiting for me, holding the most beautiful orange tulips. Passing them to me he picked me up then, carrying me to the bed. I was thankful the déjà-vu had stopped. He placed me on the bed, my head slightly hitting the headboard.

"Oh, God, Ruby, I am so sorry," he said, kissing the top of my head. I laughed a little, placing the tulips on the bedside cabinet.

"It didn't even hurt, silly. It's okay." He began kissing me, his lips so soft, his tongue twining itself with mine. I felt my body come alive instantly as it always did the moment he touched me. I started to unzip my dress.

"No. Keep it on. Ruby, have you ever done anything kinky?" he asked with trepidation in his voice.

"What do you mean by kinky? Whips, chains?" I asked, knowing the rules specifically said nothing kinky.

"No, no, like this." He put his hands lightly around my throat, pressing softly. It felt good, really good. I immediately liked it.

"That's not really kinky, Derek. Some of my friends have talked about being choked. I have never done it before."

"Do you want to Ruby? I would never ever hurt you. You can tell me if you don't feel comfortable or if you want me to stop."

He looked like a little boy, explaining to his mother that he was sick today and couldn't go to school merely because he wanted to spend the day with her, watching TV and playing board games. I couldn't resist his eyes. I couldn't resist anything about him, including some kinky desire he had to choke me. I decided to ask him a question, since he had opened the door to questions.

"Have you ever done it before?"

"Yes, and she really liked it," he said, his eyes still locked on mine. I didn't want to know anymore. I had no desire to hear him speak of anyone else. I lifted my head off of the pillow, kissing him. He reciprocated, putting his hand on the back of my head, resting it back on the pillow. His mouth on my neck, kissing and slightly biting me. I felt his hand under my dress, slowly pulling my underwear down past my thighs. I maneuvered them the rest of the way down my legs and over my feet. I felt his hand, his finger, moving back and forth over my clit. I wanted him to go slower, but I couldn't wait for him to penetrate me either. He tugged at his pants, pushing them and his underwear down over his ass. I could feel his cock so hard against my leg. He entered me then and, at almost the same time, he put his hands around my neck. With each thrust, he squeezed my neck. It was turning me on so much, and I felt my orgasm building. He knew I was about to cum, knowing my body well enough to know I was close. He fucked me feverishly, and I began to orgasm, my body arching, his hands tight around my neck. I held my breath as my orgasm shuddered through me. I felt his body cumming with mine; we seemed in unison always.

But I couldn't breathe. No, it wasn't that. I couldn't catch my breath. I sucked in nothing. Empty.

As I tried to take a breath in, I felt a lightning bolt of pain in my head. It was excruciating. Then everything stopped, and I saw Julia Stiles in her red dress. She looked so beautiful and happy getting out of the cab, her blonde hair bouncing around her head. The pain was gone. I was floating now. The room had a mist, a slight film as if I were seeing everything through a fog. I went upwards, feeling my body, but it was without joints, muscles, bones, or blood. I felt so peaceful, euphoric, so alive! Then I heard Derek. Derek screaming.

"Ruby! Oh, God, Ruby! Oh, dear God, what have I done? Ruby!"

I was high above, my back against the ceiling, as though I were a chandelier. Derek was over my body, shaking me, pleading with me to wake up, to breathe, to open my eyes. I began to scream at him, telling him I was okay. The screaming so loud in my ears, echoing through the room, though it is not a room anymore but a stage, and I am in a performance, the audience sitting in their chairs, their hands over their mouths, aghast at what they have just witnessed. My untimely death, my demise, my end. The end. Everyone is dressed in black except for Julia Stiles, who is seated in the front row, wearing her beautiful red dress. She is the only one clapping. 'Encore, encore!' she screams as though I had just given the performance of my life. My life. What of it? Is it over? What is this? Oh, no, not like this. This can't possibly be. Wait, no! Not like this, oh, God, not like this! Please! So many people are whispering in my ear. Voices from far away. I hear my grandmother, telling me how pretty I look.

Derek is talking to me now. It is so loud and fast. It comes at me at once. All the questions being answered in a flurry of whispers and shouts. He is married, going through a nasty divorce. She has everything wrong. She is a gold digger. His wife wants sole custody of his three-year-old twin girls, claiming him unfit, always out of town, a womanizer. None of this is true. Women come on to him. His wife's friends have sided with her. They make up lies about him. They say he has come onto them, that he is a cheater, that they have seen him at restaurants and bars with other women. She will take all his money and run because that is what women do. She will take his girls away; he will never see them again. He just wanted to be with a woman with no questions, no emotions. It could only be when he was out of town; that had been his rule. No one would see him. It was his only solace. His only quiet. I was his only peace and quiet! His two hours of joy with no attachment. I watch him cry. I feel his pain, his sadness.

He kept asking himself what have I done over and over again. Jesus, what have I done? What have I done? What have I fucking done?

"Derek!" I shout at him. You have done nothing wrong. Nothing. I wanted you. You wanted me. You asked if this would be okay with me, I said 'Yes.' You didn't kill me, Derek. Oh, God, you think that you did! You do! But you didn't Derek! Please, stop crying. Please. I can't bear to watch you cry.

He pulls his pants up, buttoning them. He puts on his socks and shoes. I see my body now that he has moved away from it, my hair splayed out on the pillow, my mouth slightly open as if about to speak. No words to be heard now. There are garish marks about my neck. Why? He didn't do it that hard. No. It didn't hurt, not my neck. Only my head. He sits back down on the edge of the bed next to me, his body shaking and sweating, pale as hell. He rubs his palms down his legs, a nervous gesture, a frantic movement, over and over again. He stares at me for the longest time, touching my face, smoothing down my hair, as if I am a sacred doll, unbreakable, but now clearly broken, beyond repair, no glue will fix me.

He cared about me. He loved our time together. He is so angry with himself. Why did I do that to her? Why did I kill her? Had she struggled for breath, and I hadn't noticed? Had she tried pulling my hands from her neck? Poor Derek. His thoughts are everywhere in the room. They are crowding me, pushing at me, begging to be answered. I try to answer him. He can't fucking hear me! You didn't kill me Derek. I don't know what happened, but you didn't kill me!

He is panicking now. No one can find out about this. He will be ruined forever. He will never see his daughters again. He will rot in prison. He would rather die than live with this guilt. His daughters would know their father was a twisted, kinky fuck who hired whores and murdered them. No, Derek. No. You are not. Not twisted, not kinky. It was just a mistake. An idea gone awry. His thoughts now are moving so swiftly through the air, bouncing this way and that, jumbled and coming at me so quickly I just can't keep track of them. He is going to call Jane. She will know what to do. I watch him fish his cell from his pants pocket. He goes into the bathroom, shutting the door. I am sitting on the bed now, next to my body. My skin is so pale, no sign of life. Dead. What now? I think of my parents. Oh, God, no, no, no! This will kill them, cut them in half. Especially my daddy. Why does it have to be like this, this way? Not like this! I frantically lay on top of my body, willing myself back in. Pleading with whatever God is out there to give me a second chance. Please, just this once. Unite us, body and soul. I promise to stop hooking. I promise to get a real fucking job. Please spare my parents from this heartache. Please. Please. Please.

Nothing. I could hear Derek, his voice shaking and muffled. He came out of the bathroom, his face pale, tears running down his cheeks. The empathy I felt was something I had never experienced. Not like this. I was so much more aware of emotions. Mine and his. They were 3-D, standing out on their own, like a building, a structure. He began searching the room, frantically.

"No, Derek, my shoes and purse aren't here. They are in the Jeep. Derek, go to the Jeep!"

He grabbed the card key from the kitchen counter and left. Had he heard me? Oh, God, could he hear me?

I went to the window watching him run across the lawn to the Jeep, opening the passenger side door. He then shut the door quickly, running back across the lawn. Within seconds, he was back in the room again. Jane had told him what to do. She had told him to calm the fuck down and listen to her. What he did next was beyond beautiful, beyond moving. He lay down next to me, placing two tulips on my chest, then grabbed my hand and wept. I could read no thoughts, his mind void of everything except for extreme sadness and heartache. He lay there with me for two hours, staring at the ceiling. Every so often, he would bring my hand to his face, brushing his tears away with my fingers then softly kissing my palm.

At around three a.m. he got up and looked out the window. Everyone is sleeping now. No one will see us. He picked me up, and, cradling my body like a small child, my head on his chest, he carried me out the door, down the stairs, and across the lawn. He put me into the Jeep and pulled the seatbelt across my chest, clicking it into place, the tulips in my lap. He shut the door, going around to the driver's side, stopping before he opened the door. He looked around, seeing no one watching us. He got in, looked over at me, and then started the engine. He began to weep again. I turned the radio up, unable to bear hearing his sobs. He looked at it strangely. I had done that. I had done that! Derek, I know what you are going to do. Don't do it. Please. Drive my body to the hospital; explain what happened. Derek, please don't do this! I screamed this at him. He couldn't hear me. His thoughts were quickly coming at me again, they were all over the place.

Samantha will take the girls far, far away. I will rot in prison. My parents will be disgraced and shunned by their neighbors. People will say I was such a nice man, a successful man, a family man. Where did he go wrong? Derek pulled up to an abandoned warehouse covered with graffiti, the windows broken out. As he put the jeep in park, the song 'In The City' came on.

Derek, I love this song. Have you seen the video, Derek? It's the beautiful Julia Stiles in a red dress. God, she is pretty, Derek. Don't you agree?

He turned towards me again, kissing the top of my head. I am so sorry, Ruby. Oh, God, Ruby, I am so sorry. He got out of the Jeep, making his way to my side. He undid my seatbelt, catching my body as it began to slump further. He grabbed my purse from the floor, putting it over his shoulder. He then grabbed my shoes, placing them in my lap with the tulips, and with that, picked me up again, carrying me towards the abandoned building. No, Derek, please, don't do this, Derek. This isn't the right thing to do.

He pushed the door open with his foot. A couple of rats ran across our path. Derek let out a low groan. He stopped for a moment, panting, his face sweating. His beautiful face was gone. Desperation, fear, and sadness ran across it now. The sparkle in his eyes dimmed by heartache.

He was afraid. No, fucking petrified. He spotted a corner made somewhat cozy by a couple of abandoned blankets. He carefully put my hands on top of each other over my heart, tucking the tulips under my hands, the tops almost touching my nose as if I was smelling them.

Ruby. Beautiful Ruby, I am so, so sorry for all of this. Derek began to cry again, bending down, lightly kissing my cold lips. He got up and began to walk away.

"No, Derek. Please, don't leave me here. Please. Derek! Please, don't leave me here!"

He stopped, turning around. Had he heard me again?

"I have no other choice, Ruby. I don't. I am so sorry."

He walked away, leaving me in the dark warehouse. I tried to follow him, but I couldn't. I tried to go through the door, but I only made it to the window, watching the Jeep drive away. Derek! He was gone. I was alone, and my gaze went from the window to my body as Derek had placed me, looking peaceful, the blankets tucked around me, the tulips pushed underneath my hands. I sat there on the window sill for I don't know how long just staring at my body. Would someone take it? Where do I go? I was afraid to go near me, afraid of the death, my death, my lifeless self. I was alone, no voices. Nothing. Trapped. Someone, show me, help me. Grammy wasn't even here. What now?

I stayed there, alone. Two days later, a homeless man came inside seeking shelter, and found me. He went back outside, flagging down a motorist to call 911. Within a half hour, my body was taken from the cold warehouse to the city morgue.

My ID and cell phone were retrieved from my bag, and my parents were called to come and identify me. Watching them shuffle in, my mother's arm around my father's back as if holding him up, was heart wrenching. They moved so slowly, as if putting off the inevitable by a few moments would soften the blow. I couldn't watch this. I shut my eyes tightly, shutting out the sadness, their pain and suffering. Home. I want to be in my home, in my bed, snuggled under my blankets, listening to my iPod and watching the willow tree branches brush against my window in the moonlight.

And there I was. As quickly as I had envisioned it, I was back in my childhood home, standing in the living room, the tick-tock of the grandfather clock loud in my ears. Everything was so big, so...the view master. I thought of the box of old toys my mother pulled out of storage when she thought we were old enough to take care with them, one of them being a view master. You put the little round disc in, pushing down a little lever on the right. You looked through a miniature square lens, and an image would appear. Everything 3-D. Yes! My world was a giant view master. I began to sort through my new reality. I was dead, that I knew. But how? Something sudden had happened, something in my head.

I lay down on our old, white leather couch, covering myself with my grandmother's beige chenille blanket, her smell still trapped within the fibers. What had I done? A bad choice had resulted in my death. Was this a trick, a lesson? But I didn't do anything wrong. Ultimately, my parents were paying the price. They would never be the same. Would they ever smile again? Laugh? Oh, God, what had I done? Derek. Poor Derek. Distraught Derek. I shut my eyes tightly. The smell had changed. Gone was my grandmother's chenille blanket, the faint odor of Jergen's lotion. I smelled now the aromatic sweetness of freshly baked chocolate chip cookies. Mmmmm, I could taste them now, their ooey-gooey goodness melting in my mouth.

I opened my eyes to two beautiful twin girls, their blonde curls wisping around their cherubic faces, their blue eyes dancing as they giggled. They were seated at an island counter in the middle of a beautiful spacious kitchen. Then I spotted him. He was crouched down, playing peek-a-boo with them. He was wearing a pink tutu over his jeans, his blond head graced with a crown that said 'Princess'. He had a wand in one hand, the hand wearing a long white glove. In his other white-gloved hand, he held up an Elmo doll that he had just tripped over, making the girls roar with laughter, milk coming out of their noses.

He was smiling and laughing but only for their benefit, to hide from them the slow death he was dying inside. The outrageous turmoil that was causing him to thin, his hair to begin falling out, his sudden bursts of anger, bouts of unending tears. His thoughts were all over the room, staring at me in big bold letters. They were jumbled, hitting me at once.

Ruby... help, Oh God... I will lose my babies... My job... A trial where I will be found guilty... Death... Electric Chair... worse yet... will rot in prison... I can't go through that... my daughters can never know... but Samantha will tell them... What will she say? Ruby, I am so sorry... Ruby, please help... the cops are closing in Ruby, I want to die Ruby... I am so sorry, Ruby, why did this happen to us, to me... We are good people. I felt safe with you Ruby, happy!

I shut my eyes tightly, pushing his thoughts from me, and just as quickly as I had arrived, I was gone, back home again, snuggled under Grammy's chenille blanket, the Jergen's lotion smell strong in my nose. Then I heard them, my parents, their sobs cutting into the darkness. I went into their room. They were lying on their bed, still clothed, not having the energy to do anything but collapse on the bed, quivering and shaking in the darkness. I kissed them; I lay with them; I cried with them; I told them I was okay. I am OK! They held each other tightly. Their anguish was more than I could bear. I got up, standing in the doorway, their thoughts crowding the room, stifling, making it unbearable.

Oh, dear Lord, not our baby, please, not our baby, take us now. Who did this? What monster in hell could kill a beautiful young girl, our girl? ... Her body cold, dead, gone! I want to die too! I can't take this pain! I can't. ... I will find the son of a bitch that did this and fucking gut him like the pig that he is … this fucking monster, not my baby!

I shut my eyes tightly, blocking them out. Suddenly I couldn't hear them anymore and realized I was standing in the morgue with my body which had been placed on a table, my brown hair splayed about, my skin a bluish pallor, my lips shriveled. I was naked. I wanted to cover myself but realized how ludicrous that thought was. Showing modesty when dead is, well, isn't that why I ended up here in the first place? For my lack of modesty? Joining John the coroner was his buddy Adam Stevenson, pathologist. They both held knives in their gloved hands. They worked together when a criminal autopsy was called for as they had done for years.

"Sad case this one, huh, John?"

"Yep, sad 'nuff, I s'pose, but I've seen it all. Stopped cryin' years ago."

"You golfin' this weekend out at Bender?"

"Doc Grady gonna be there?"

"I dunno; why?"

"'Cause I can't stand the son of a bitch. He's got a fuckin' comment about every shot I take. Just can't take it no more. Motherfuckin' cocksucker. I'd love to shove my nine iron up his godforsaken asshole."

"I hear you on that one."

"Let's move quicker than normal tonight, I've got a hemorrhoid that's itchin' like lice in pubic hair."

They were comical, these two, and though I wanted to hangout just for the conversation alone, I shut my eyes tightly just as they were ready to make the first incision. I was suddenly back in my dorm room with Bridgette. Poor Bridge. The police had just left the dorm, seizing my computer and some personal items. She was packing, intent on going home for a few days to grieve and be with her parents. She had told the police about the hooking, and it would be only a matter of time before they had contacted Jane and had a list of the 'Johns.' She seemed to be void of any emotion, or I was just unable to draw much from her. I sensed fear more than anything else. She was already arranging to move out of the dorms and in with some friends that had a house. Best friends or not, she was angry at Jane for this whole hooking thing, not liking it from the get-go. I sensed after all was said and done, this would kill the relationship between Bridge and Jane. In fact, I already knew Jane would lose a lot of friends and be outcast from many circles. She would eventually get her 'come upins'.

I sat down on my bed, looking up at my bulletin board full of pictures, concert tickets, and a couple of birthday cards. I tried retrieving a photo of Bridge and me, not realizing how hard it would be for me. In the process, the whole thing came crashing down. Crap. What had I done? Poor Bridge almost jumped out of her skin at the sound of the bulletin board hitting the floor, pictures and papers askew. She turned, staring at me for what seemed an eternity.

Could she see me? She then left the room quickly, forgetting to shut the door. She had seen me. I was sure of it. A few minutes later she came in with Chelsea, our R.A.

"She was there, right there, I am sure of it," said Bridge. Her face had gone pale, her breathing heavy. She was pointing to the exact spot I had been standing. Chelsea began picking up the debris from the fallen bulletin board.

"Honey, I don't see anything. What time are your parents picking you up?" asked Chelsea, placing the items on my bed.

"About a half hour," said Bridgette, still looking around, visibly shaken. I had stepped behind the door just in case.

"Just grab your stuff. Come wait in my room," said Chelsea. I intentionally came out from behind the door, standing in front of the girls. Without a word, Bridge grabbed her stuff and they both left, locking the door behind them. Neither one of them had seen me. I grabbed the photo of Bridge and me and shut my eyes tightly, and I was back home. The cops had just left my parents' house, telling them of the coroner's report. They had more information for my parents, but that would come later. They wanted them to get through the initial shock of the autopsy findings before they dumped any more on them. They were seated at the kitchen table, across from each other. The cops had seen themselves out, my parents still digesting what they had just heard. Our daughter wasn't murdered? She had suffered a brain aneurysm? Who was she with? In a hotel room? Why? She let a man choke her? We didn't raise her like that! She hadn't suffered. It was quick, said the police. Where is the man who did this?

Then the anger came, their thoughts being thrown around the room. Mostly they were my mother's thoughts, my father looking sullen, somber, and numb. Would he get through this? At what cost? His health, his happiness?

I sat down at the table with them. I had had a brain aneurysm that ruptured, resulting in a subarachnoid hemorrhage. The cops said that it could have happened anywhere, in the grocery store, putting on make-up, driving down the road. Derek simply had the bad luck of being with me when it did. Brain aneurysm? It made sense to me. I had been suffering some weird headaches as of late, downing way too much ibuprofen. I guessed the 'bearing down' during orgasm had something to do with it, causing the hemorrhage. That explained the quick flash of pain I had felt in my head. I knew Derek had not hurt me. Just a fluke thing. I shut my eyes tightly. I was back in the warehouse where Derek had placed me.

The entire site had been covered with yellow 'crime scene' tape. The blankets were gone as were the two orange tulips. I sat down in the spot Derek had laid me, grateful to be free of the noise from everyone's thoughts coming at me. I sat for a long time; then I heard crying, sobbing. I shut my eyes tightly, following the sadness. I opened my eyes, and I was standing in my dorm room. It was Bridge, and she was sitting on her bed, staring at what was once a lively, colorfully-decorated, girl's college dorm room. Now it was empty, my things gone, retrieved by my aunt, my parents unable to cope at the moment, if ever. She looked around, tears streaming down her face, at the gray walls, the bleakness. I sat down on my bed, across from her. Bridge, don't be afraid, honey. I'm ok. It will all be ok. I love you, Bridge. She looked straight at me as I said this. Straight at me. She could see me. I knew it.

"Bridge, don't be afraid," I said, getting up from my bed and sitting next to her on her mattress, devoid of the pink sheets and floral comforter that once graced it. Her eyes followed me.

"It's you, Ruby. Isn't it?"

Her voice so soft, quivering, trying to summon some sort of strength. She hadn't believed in ghosts. Until now, until me. I was a ghost. Fuck. That was a hard pill to swallow. Who could see me? The chosen few? Is that lucky, not lucky? Who knew?

"I can't stay long, Bridge. I can't be here much longer, that I know. It will all be okay, honey. You will get through this. Please. If not for yourself, for me. Live for me, love for me. This is the best time of your life." I put my arm around her. She began to really sob.

"Ruby, it isn't fair. Why is this happening?"

"I don't have those answers for you, honey. You need

to find them for yourself. I can only love you and tell you that I love you. Here."

I handed her the picture of us together, taken the day we moved into the dorms, our innocent faces smiling in the sunlight.

"Oh, my God, I looked for this everywhere. I saw you the day the bulletin board crashed down. I thought I saw you, but then thought I just imagined it. But I did. Thank you Ruby."

I got up from the bed, holding her hand. I felt a strong pull, knowing right away I needed to be somewhere else, quickly.

"Bridge, I have to go now. Be strong. You can; I know it. I love you."

"I love you, Ruby. I love you, Ruby."

I shut my eyes tightly, still hearing I love you, Ruby, I love you, Ruby loudly in my ears. I opened them, and I was in the cold graffiti-laden warehouse again. I wasn't alone. Sitting in the corner where my body had once lain was Derek. His face was twisted in anguish and sadness. His mind was void of any thoughts except for one blaring one. As I moved closer to him, I saw he held two orange tulips in one hand. In the other was a gun.

"NOOOOOOOOOOOOO!"

I realized I had screamed this. He looked up, not believing he was seeing me. "Derek, don't do this baby. Talk to the police, Derek. I know you have been questioned, but you did nothing wrong. It's all coming out now, Derek.

I died from a brain hemorrhage. The cops said it could have happened anywhere, anytime. I was a ticking time bomb."

He stared at me, blankly, not believing what he was seeing or hearing, deeming it impossible. He blinked. Once, twice, and then closed his eyes. I saw his body take a deep breath in and exhale slowly. He opened his eyes.

"Ruby, God, Ruby. I am so sorry. I can't do this. I can't. I can't face anyone."

My words came spilling out of my mouth, shocking me. "Shut the fuck up, Derek. What kind of a man takes the easy way out? What kind of a man robs two beautiful, little girls of someone they are so in love with? You know what you would do to them? I love my daddy. And no matter what he did or I did, I would love him. I saw his face at the morgue as he looked at my dead body. Don't do that to your girls. They will understand a lot of things, but I guarantee they would not understand you taking your own life. No family ever understands that, ever. Don't make them suffer that way. Please. Think about your own parents. Now stop your fucking, pansy-ass whining. Go to the cops; tell them that you were with me. They know that anyway. Come clean. Face the music for your daughters' sake. I can't be with my daddy anymore. Don't do that to your girls, please, honey. Promise me. You're a beautiful, wonderful man. Okay, you made a bad decision. Big fucking deal."

Derek put the gun down, kicking it across the room. "Ruby, I am sorry this happened. But I am not sorry I was with you, not for a moment. You made me happy; you made me feel good inside." He handed me a tulip.

"I can't take it with me," I said with a smile.

"I get it," Derek said, laughing. "That is funny. I'm sorry Ru…"

I cut him off. "Ssshhhhh….enough. I know. Now go. Everything will be fine."

"But what about you? Where will you go? Are you afraid? How will I know if you're okay?" He asked, his face beginning to soften again.

"Come on, silly, you've seen enough ghost movies to know that when my work here is done, I move on. I will be fine, that I already know." I kissed him softly.

"Goodbye Derek." And with that I shut my eyes tightly. I was back in my house again, lying underneath my Grammy's chenille blanket. She was calling for me. I could hear her louder every moment. Grammy, just give me a little more time. I closed my eyes, this time not going anywhere.

* * *

I stayed around long enough to find out that Derek had indeed gone to the police. No charges were filed.

Bridgette moved into a beautiful Victorian house with a group of friends. She had framed the photograph of us together, placing it on her bedside stand. She no longer spoke to Jane. Needless to say, the cops shut down PMS.

Jane was expelled from school. My funeral was to take place in the next couple of days. It was time for me to go. Time heals all, this I knew. My parents were seated at the dinner table. I sat with them, watching them move their food around their plates. I couldn't read their thoughts anymore. I was giving myself over slowly, crossing over to another plane. I got up from the table, going over to my mother and kissing her softly, saying goodbye. I went over to my daddy. I stared at him for the longest time, and then I touched his face softly. He brushed his cheek with his hand. He had felt me. I whispered in his ear. I love you, daddy. He turned his head, looking right at me. He stared at me, a tear rolling down his cheek. Did he see me; could he see me?

I love you, Daddy. Goodbye, Daddy. I love you pumpkin. It was the last thought I read.

Derek didn't attend the funeral, but he stayed in town until it was over. I watched him pay his respects late at night after everyone was gone. He held a bundle of orange tulips. I couldn't bear to go near. I didn't want to see my grave. I waited for him by the Jeep. Derek got in and started the car. 'In The City' was playing on the car radio. I smiled.

"Goodbye, my Ruby. Rest in peace."

"Goodbye, Derek," I said, and I shut my eyes tightly for the last time.

Pablo the boy

poem

He enters the room with his tobacco air.
I've seen him before in a world long ago.
Not this one where he wears his silk tie and suit
But in a past so distant, inhabited by
His youth and carefree ways.
His notebook in hand, his beautiful, brown eyes,
He finds a chair and readies himself
With his youthful casualness.
He scribbles his poems; his writings come forth.
Glancing to the front door to see who enters,
Not taking the chance on his thoughts
Being permeated.
He attends diligently to his work at hand,
Proudly reading and re-reading his prose.

Did he get it right?
The nervous crossing and uncrossing of his legs.
His pencil, dangling from his mouth
As he reflects on the words
He wants to choose.
His mind, full of substance and
Thoughts of meaning.
Well, to him anyway.
Yes, I have seen him before, but I
Am not sure where.
But my yearning to know him now
Rides heavy in my mind...
But mostly in my heart.

Saving Jack

short story

Apartment 210 is vacant. I know this because the old woman who once occupied it died a few days ago. I was told about her death, three days after I saw an ambulance in front of the building, a common sight in these parts. I did not think much of it until I peeked out the window, and a body shrouded in a blanket was loaded into the ambulance. I quickly closed the drape, going back to writing my column, not wanting to deal with death so close to my door. Life goes on. I didn't know her. I had only lived here just shy of four months. My friend, Juliana, fleeing Brooklyn and going back to the confines of her mundane ho-hum life in dreadful North Dakota, told me to apply for her space before she had even given notice. I moved in as she moved out.

I think the old woman's name was Sylvie. No, maybe it had been Sarah. I can't remember which but I needed to find out so I could give my condolences to her granddaughter.

I assumed this was the young woman I had seen on occasion, exiting and entering apartment 210 with flowers or groceries, me just a few doors down. A 'hi' was exchanged by us but that was the extent of our acquaintance. I constantly feel I am rushed for time, barely able to get in a good flossing.

During the day I work at The Concupiscent Concubine, a woman's magazine in midtown Manhattan. I write a column called 'The Standing O'. It's not what you think. O stands for orgasm. I interned at the 'Conc' while finishing up my last year at Columbia. Now, I am no expert when it comes to sex and/or orgasms, but it seemed the editor loved my snarkiness and sense of humor regarding the topic. After submitting some of my work with a bunch of other intern hopefuls, I was offered the job. My own column. At night I wait tables at The Shattered Plate, serving the hipster set in SoHo. The job comes naturally to me, as I have done it since age 14. The money is good and makes up for the lack of it from The Concubine. Most everyone I know works two jobs. It's NY for fuck's sake.

I know death all too well, having lost my brother only a year before. It was then I decided to leave my small town and strike out. It was one of the things he had always hoped I would do. Pack my bag of talents and head for the city. I revisited the last time I saw him. I had played it over and over so many times in my mind. This time I did it without crying. This time I did it with a smile. We were standing in line, waiting for our coffee. As children, we always held hands. He was always my protector, as I was younger by 13 months. As I stood behind him, smelling his faint cologne, he grabbed my hand, turned towards me saying, '*I hope you know how much I love you*'.

It was sudden the way he did it. As if he knew it would be his last chance to speak to me before leaving our earth forever. He died a month later, a virus had settled in his heart. I was knocked senseless by his death. The wailing sound that came out of me was like nothing I had ever heard before. Complete anguish. I believed I could hear my heart bleeding, the blood gushing from it in a torrent of sadness. I don't know what I would have done without my friends to hold and console me.

Stop Stella. You will run your mascara down your face and surely be late for the R train. I brushed my teeth quickly and decided on another quick piss before I hit the subway. I grabbed my bag and cell, heading out the door. As I was turning my key in the lock I heard a soft male voice behind me.

"Excuse me miss, sorry to bother you. It looks like you're in a hurry but I......" He stopped midsentence.

I was startled by his voice into dropping my keys. Before I could bend down to retrieve them I felt a slight woosh of air against my cheek. Then I saw his eyes. The most beautiful dark eyes I had ever seen. The sadness of them caught me by surprise.

"Thank you," I muttered as he dropped my keys onto my outstretched palm. God, those eyes, his smell, I even knew that cologne, Lagerfeld. I had an old boyfriend who used to wear it. He kept it in the glove compartment of his truck. Whenever he got out to pump gas, or run into a 7-11, I would quickly retrieve it, pulling the top off and inhaling the smell. It was incredible stuff.

"Hey, did you by chance know my grandmother, Sylvana?" He asked, sounding hopeful.

Ah, so that was it, Sylvana. What a beautiful name. I felt the shame pass over me. The shame for closing my drapes so quickly as her body was hauled down the brownstone steps, the last time she would ever go down those stairs, leaving life as my brother had done. I looked into his eyes, now realizing the resemblance between him and the beautiful girl I had seen entering apartment 210. Sister and brother no doubt.

"No, I'm sorry, I haven't lived here long. I had every intention of meeting my neighbors," I said quickly as if consoling myself. My usual acts of divination had not lent me a hand this time.

"Well, forgive me, I am Jack Leavenworth. Sylvana was my grandmother. Honestly, I didn't visit her as much as my sister Deirdre did. Do you know Deirdre by chance?" Again with that hopeful voice.

"No, but I see the resemblance. Your sister is very beautiful. I saw her at times with groceries and flowers. I am so sorry about your grandmother, Jack, very sorry." I saw him wince. "Oh, I am Estella Robbins," I quickly added, jutting out my hand, my keys dangling from my thumb. Instead of shaking it, he moved his mouth towards it, awkwardly kissing the top of my hand. I was taken aback. I had only seen this in the movies and was certain I had never had a man actually perform this genteel gesture. I liked it, and him, right away. His wavy black hair, the paleness of his skin, made him stand out as unusual. As he looked back up at me, I saw a vastness in those eyes, a sobering emptiness I felt had nothing to do with the death of his grandmother. I had this strange urge to hold him. He was thin, but not rock star skinny. He seemed uncomfortable, but quite congenial.

"Well, Estella Robbins, the pleasure is mine," he said, releasing my hand. "You said you have not lived here long. Where do you hail from?"

He was clearly hoping for a conversation and I was wishing I had left my apartment earlier as I normally did, instead of running late. Today of all days. I wanted to plop down on the stoop, with him setting next to me, the denim of his jeans touching my bare arm as we sat close, his Lagerfeld cologne strong in my nose. I wanted to watch his lips move over his beautiful straight white teeth as he chatted, his voice dark and smoky.

"Jack," I suddenly blurted out. "I have to dash to work. I would love to talk more, but….." He cut me off.

"Well, if that is the case, then how about tomorrow, coffee?" And as he asked, he insecurely ran a couple of fingers through his hair, shifting from one leg to the other. He seemed a bit embarrassed, and a hint of red began to color his pale cheeks. Before I could answer, he went on. "Please don't think of me as forward, I would understand if you are busy, but..." This time I cut him off.

"Tomorrow, be here at nine. I really must run."

Before waiting for any more words to escape his beautiful mouth, I dashed away, my satchel thump-thumping against my leg as I ran. I did not look back. I was afraid that if I did, he wouldn't be there, and it would just be a dream.

It has been two weeks since Jack and I sat at Prodigy Coffee in the Village on a beautiful crisp Saturday morning. He loved the place as much as I did. It was airy yet cozy. As he sat there talking to me, I could see the back of him in a mirror on the wall, his dark hair slipping below his collared shirt. As we sat there with our cappuccinos that were lovingly emblazoned with a fall leaf, I waited for him to take the first sip. His awkward boyish charm as he moved his lips towards the cup, the same as when he'd moved them towards my hand, kissing it softly.

"I have walked by this place a thousand times," he said, a touch of foam on his top lip. "Had I known they had the best coffee in New York City, I would have ducked in on first visit to Greenwich."

In two hours and two cappuccinos and a ginger cookie later, I learned that Jack was twenty-eight years old and had moved from a small town in Montana with his sister Deirdre. She worked at a law firm in mid-town Manhattan, inches from where I work apparently. Deirdre is considered the success story of the family, Jack not so much. He sounded disappointed in himself. Me, I just got lost in those lovely eyes of his. He could have told me was a street sweeper for all I cared. There was something about him. His mannerisms, his awkwardness, the continual crossing and un-crossing of his legs, I found him a breath of fresh air. He was not your regular Joe.

He went on, telling me that Deirdre got a scholarship to NYU and had not wanted to move alone. Jack, being like glue to her, agreed that his coming with her made sense. They were only a year and a half apart in age and engrossed in each other's lives. Thoughts of my own brother David began to flood my brain. I smiled as he explained their relationship, trying to fight the tears that I could feel surfacing. He told me how they had stayed with his grandmother Sylvana until they became settled and found jobs. They moved out from their grandmother's after about a year in NY. Jack took a job at Raines Law Room but was quick to add it was not a law firm at all, but a speakeasy here in the Village where he tended bar. I nodded, telling him I knew exactly where it was. Me and my friends had deemed the third Sunday of every month 'Speakeasy Sunday', and would go to as many as we could fit in, before running out of money or passing out. I saw him wince again. He said he loved working there and of course the money was good. Mostly he talked about Deirdre, her boyfriend Esteban - 'Este'- and their dog Sidhartha.

He toiled with a napkin between sips of his coffee; wringing it like a dishtowel, then slowly uncoiling it. At one point he grabbed a straw on his way back from the bathroom and during the latter part of our conversation, put it in the right corner of his mouth, as though it were a cigarette. Yes, he was truly different, eccentric in a way, and I was entranced by him and his awkward beauty. The nervous crossing and uncrossing of his legs, the way he glanced at every person that stepped into the coffee shop, as though he were expecting to run into an old friend. The way he moved his hand as he spoke, as though he was conducting an invisible orchestra or writing on an invisible pad of paper, fascinated me. He seemed to be listening to me talk about my family and how I came to be in NY so intently, but he glanced at his watch.

Jack quickly announced he had to dash, said he wanted to hear more about it, and soon. He then grabbed my hand, gave it a quick peck and was gone. Had I said something wrong? I had made sure I let him have most of the conversation. It was listed as number three on Jackie Smith's 'Top Ten Ways To Impress On A First Date'. Let them speak a lot. Look interested and nod in agreement, flashing a smile and giving a sexy toss of the hair. Fuck it, I didn't need the list. If he liked me he liked me. Jenna the barista must have sensed something was up, coming over with another cappuccino, this one emblazoned with a heart.

"Potential beau, Stella?" She asked as she gave the table a quick wipe.

"I'll keep you posted, Jenna," I said, tracing the heart in the cappuccino with my finger and licking it off.

"He is very handsome. Seemed to be very into you, Stella. But why wouldn't he be? You're so goddamn beautiful."

I blushed as I thanked her and asked her for a to-go cup. As I poured my drink into the cup I saw the coiled napkin Jack had been playing with. I put my coat on, grabbed the napkin, pushed it into my pocket and headed out the door, thanking Jenna all the while.

I didn't hear from Jack for a week after that. Then he called, sounding almost frantic.

"Estelle, hi, it's me, Jack!"

"Is everything okay Jack, you sound out of breath."

"Yes, Stella. Elated, actually. Guess what? I got my grandmother's apartment. I inquired about it, as I know the landlord William and his wife Theodora. Theodora and Sylvana were very close friends. Anyway, they told me I could rent it, for the same price my grandmother paid! I move in the day after tomorrow......wait.....huh?" The 'huh' seemed to be directed at someone else, his voice sounding further away. "Sorry Estelle, I'll call you later. Gotta run."

Before I could answer and tell him how excited I was, he was gone. Was I excited? He would be in the same building as me, in fact just a few doors down. How would this affect our relationship? Wait. What relationship? We had only had coffee together. He hadn't even called me since, till now. But he must like me, he had called to tell me the good news.

Maybe he would be my neighbor and nothing more. My head was reeling. I obviously liked him or my heart wouldn't be dancing. Breathe, Stella, breathe.

Another week passed and no Jack. Had he moved in? Was he okay? If he had moved in, I hadn't seen glimpses of him at all. My friend Lissa's advice was to call him, that maybe he was waiting for me to make the next move. I told her I would give it a few more days; then I would call using the excuse that I was calling to inquire whether he had indeed moved in or not. As I climbed into bed, my column in tow, there was a soft rap at the door. Dang. I did a quick purvey of what I was wearing. Cotton drawstring pyjama bottoms with writing tablets all over them. A light gray tank with spaghetti straps, no bra. Nice. I hadn't slid my make-up off my face yet. I usually did that right after finishing my column and right before my nightly smoke so I knew my eyes would still look good. I pulled the ponytail out of my hair, letting it fall about my shoulders. I must have been taking too long, as there was another soft knock but a bit louder than the first. As I got nearer the door, I could hear him.

"Sorry Estelle, I should have called first. It's me, Jack." As I pulled the chain away from the door, he said in an apologetic tone, "If you prefer, I can just call you tomorrow. I wasn't thinking."

I was annoyed with him and his long lapses of non-communication. "Don't be silly Jack," I said as I opened the door. And there he stood, looking even more beautiful than the last time I had seen him. He ran his fingers through his hair, but I knew it was more of a nervous gesture than a vanity thing.

"Estelle, I'm sorry I didn't call earlier but Raines has kept me so busy I barely found time to move. I meant to call you earlier in the week but I...oh, nevermind. Would you like to come see my place?" He asked, nervously shifting from one leg to the other.

"Why of course Jack, I would love to. Come in for a sec, let me grab a sweatshirt." My heart was doing that dance again as he brushed past me and I closed the door. The Lagerfeld had gotten to me again and I wanted to take him there and then in the hallway. "Have a seat. Be right back." As I retrieved a sweatshirt from a drawer, he spoke out.

"Sorry Estelle, I just realized you need to be up early. I always think everyone is on my schedule. Well, I don't, but you know what I mean. I am such a night owl. I have the next couple of days off, so I can catch up on a bit of sleep and see Deidre. I was wondering if you would like to come over on Friday night. Dinner at my place?"

Shit. He did like me. As I pulled my sweatshirt over my head making my way towards him, I noticed he was leafing through last month's copy of the Concupiscent Concubine. Before he could get to my column, I was standing in front of him, trying to avert him from my magazine. I wanted to ease into this relationship slowly and I wasn't ready for him to read about a woman's orgasm according to me.

"I would love to have dinner with you. I will bring the wine. And please, call me Stella."

He put the magazine down, looking at me with those dark eyes. "You're really beautiful, Stella. Really, really beautiful."

My heart stopped, or so it felt. The sincerity, the way he said it, was in slow motion. I stared at him. It must have been awhile because he waved his hand in front of my eyes.

"Stella, blink. Earth to Stella!"

I laughed, embarrassed by his remark but equally sure of our mutual spark for each other. He stood up, grabbing my hand.

As we stepped into apartment 210, I felt a bit of sadness. Sad that someone had died here, but happy Sylvana had passed amongst her treasures and in her own bed, not lying in a sterile hospital room or an old folks' home. I thought it was what I wished for myself. I wondered if she was still here or if she had moved on. I had seen ghosts as a child, but as I got older was not able to anymore. That or they just were no longer appearing to me. It did not bother me much, the not seeing them part, until my brother died. I don't know how many times I willed him to come see me, calling his name over and over again, my eyes tightly closed, blocking out all other thoughts.

As we walked down the hallway and into the kitchen, I knew Sylvana was still here. I wondered if Jack felt her as well. Just like my column, I was not ready to approach the subject of spirits, past or present with Jack just yet. I was still at an early stage with him and thought it best to tread lightly. He must have sensed something with me.

"You don't like it? You're awfully quiet," he said.

"Oh no, no Jack, I love it!" I snapped out of my daze as I looked around the kitchen. I felt as though I had stepped into another era. The kitchen was cream and green with a chrome dinette set donned with a formica tabletop. Along an island counter were chrome and vinyl stools. It was clean and neat as a pin. The curtains on the kitchen windows were a green and cream floral print with pink thrown in. I loved it. I think my mouth was open as Jack led me into the dining room.

"Well, if you liked that, wait till you see this!"

The dining room walls were painted the most beautiful red and instead of a dining room table, there was the grandest black piano I had ever seen. It looked old but had been tenderly cared for.

"Oh Jack, it's incredible. Will you play for me?" I asked, my fingers on the keys.

"Actually, I don't play. It was my grandmother's. It is the one thing that would stay in the apartment, no matter who moved in. No one is really sure how they got it in here, so they are certainly not going to take it out. Do you play by chance?" He asked, with that hopeful tone in his voice.

"Sadly Jack, the same old story most of us share. I had piano lessons as a child, but hated them and my mother got tired of trying to coerce me out of the car. I regret that decision but don't we all. Oh well, it doesn't matter. This room is so beautiful Jack, really beautiful." I walked ahead of him now, stepping into the living room. The walls were charcoal and there was a red couch with a red leather chair and grey carpets. Red, brown and cream floral drapes hung from the windows. "It's so vintage, Jack. It is simply incredible. How did you do all this in such a short time?" I asked, fluffing a floral pillow on the couch.

"Well, actually the walls were already painted. A few months before my grandmother died, I stumbled upon a furniture shop in Williamsburg called The Fabulous 40s. The moment I walked in, I felt at home. An odd draw to the nostalgia of it all. The décor was simple, homey and peaceful. I told my grandmother about it and she said her place could use a makeover. She helped me purchase most of the items, drapes included, ensuring that eventually everything would go to me, when I had my own home. Deirdre helped me arrange all the new furniture and Esteban and I had it painted in a week. Voila."

We made our way down the hallway, taking a right into a bedroom. My mouth dropped open, again. Along two of the walls were built-in bookcases. At least eight shelves were stacked to the top of the ceiling with books. I had never seen this many books in someone's home before. Not ever.

"My God Jack, this is incredible. Have you read all these? Are they all yours?" I asked, making my way closer, taking in titles. I noticed the collection had been put into sections, like a bookstore. How clever. Someone had written 'Erotica' in the most beautiful calligraphy and taped it down to the back of the shelf, right above where the books sat. Of course I would stumble upon my favorite section first. As I glanced to my left, I saw 'Sci-Fi' and to my right, 'Horror'. My eyes reverted back to the 'Erotica' section. There was Erica Jong's 'Fear of Flying', 'The Story of O' by Pauline Reage, 'Les infortunes de la Belle au Bois Dormant' by A.N. Roquelaure. All works that put E.L. James to shame. If you want to read some knock your panties off submission and dominance, check out the 'Sleeping Beauty Trilogy', I would often tell my friends. Those books made me instantly wet. I wasn't surprised to see a huge section of Anais Nin, along with a selection of her lover Henry Miller's work - 'Sexus', 'Plexus' and 'Nexus'. I touched the spine of 'Sexus' running my fingers lightly up and down.

"You can borrow whatever you want Estelle," said Jack, his voice softly hitting the back of my neck as he stood behind me. I was so entranced with his collection I hadn't noticed him so close, his Lagerfeld strong in my nose again. God how I wanted him to take me right now, in front of the erotica section. I wanted him to pull my pants down in a frenzy, penetrating me from behind as I held on to the shelves in front of me, staring straight ahead at Portia Da Costa's book 'In Too Deep', his cock moving in and out of me, his hands, holding my waist, his moans filling my ears with the sweet sound of his pleasure. I smiled at my fantasy. Downright sinful and delicious, I thought, as he suddenly grabbed my hand.

"Are you ready for the icing on the cake?" he asked, leading me back down the hallway and into the kitchen. There, past the refrigerator, was a window. It was small and close to the floor. Bending down he pushed it open and climbed through. He still had my hand as I moved myself over the sill, my legs suddenly tangling, and I laughed as my body spilled out of the window. Jack was quick to grab my elbow, steering me to stand.

"Thank you Jack," I said, clearly embarrassed. The patio was awesome. He had chairs and pillows with a cute little bistro table.

"Yea, I really lucked out Stella. Only the corner units have the patio," Jack said, grabbing my hand to go back inside. I was curious then to what Jack was paying compared to me, but then not sure if I wanted to know. Rents were astronomical and I wasn't making enough writing a column, though I was ghost writing for a few authors. That wasn't a constant pay-check, more of a sporadic one. I was grateful for the waitressing gig, but the cash I had saved for my move to Brooklyn was beginning to run low. Thankfully my parents were still sending money, but I knew that would begin to get less and less as well.

"You're deep in thought," Jack said, touching my shoulder as we stood in the kitchen.

"Just taking it all in. This place is really beautiful and I think your grandmother would be pleased with what you have done with it." His hand moved from my shoulder to my chin. I closed my eyes at that moment, feeling his touch. It was then he kissed me. His lips were soft and full on mine. I kept my eyes closed, kissing him back. He spoke softly as he pulled away from me.

"She is, Stella. She is."

*   *   *

It was Thursday and Jack reminded me as I left his apartment last night to be at his place around seven-thirty on Friday.

"Oh yes," I replied, still in a fog as he shut the door, whispering goodnight to me. I stared at the number 210 for what seemed like an eternity. As I made my way down the hallway and into my apartment I could have sworn I heard a woman's voice whisper in my ear, 'be good to him, he's fragile'.

I barely made it through work the next day. Jack's kiss stayed with me throughout the night, braved my rush hour subway ride on the R train and was still with me after finishing my lunch of sashimi and sake.

That evening the beautiful girl I had previously seen going in and out of apartment 210 opened the door as I began a second series of five quick knocks.

"You must be the lovely Estelle that Jack has been gushing about! Hi, I'm Jack's sister, Deirdre." She put her hand out and I stupidly thought it was to shake mine but then realized she was grabbing the wine.

"I hope you like Shiraz," I said quickly, trying to cover up the awkwardness I felt.

"As I say to Esteban, if it's red it will eventually put me to bed, if it's white, I'll be up all night." She then tilted her head and laughed, her beautiful white teeth encased by red pouty lips. "In other words," she continued, "something in the white doesn't agree with me and I can't sleep a wink, so yes, red is wonderful!"

I liked her immediately. She was definitely the yin to Jack's yang. "Jack will be right in. He and Este are having a smoke on the patio. I just got off the phone with Paquito's. Hope you like Mexican food. They have a salsa verde and a ceviche that are to die for," she said, shutting the door behind me. I followed her into the kitchen as she still kept talking, her red dress swishing back and forth over her lovely ass as she walked. "Jack tells me you work at the Concupiscent Concubine. Holy high roller, I fucking love that magazine! I feel as though you are royalty in our firm. 'The Standing O'; brilliant Stella, or should I say, 'Fonda Cox.' Jesus, another good one! Did you come up with that name?" She asked, placing the wine on the counter and rummaging through a drawer, clearly looking for a corkscrew.

"Uh, yea, I was...." She cut me off.

"Brilliant, funny and wonderful. You really are a gifted writer. Did you know Jack dabbles in writing here and there?" She asked, finding the corkscrew and cutting the foil. "Mostly in his journals. He's kept one since he was like nine or something like that. He's written a lot of poetry, being published in an assortment of magazines and local papers back home. I know he has written a few short stories and says he is working on a novel. I haven't read anything, nor do I ask. He will show me when he is good and ready. Ask to see his poetry though. It is beautiful and powerful. Ah, he is so private. I shouldn't even be telling you all this. Don't mind me, I'm kind of a busybody when it comes to my broth…" Jack cut her off as he climbed through the window. Esteban was right behind him.

"What about your brother?" Jack said, coming up behind Deirdre and planting a kiss on her head. You could feel their love for each other. My arms ached to hold my brother once more. I felt the tears well up, knowing that would never happen again.

"Just talking about Stella's column and that you dabble in writing, dear brother," said Deirdre, pushing a large glass of wine into my hand.

"Jesus, Stella, where are my manners?" said Jack, quickly, turning from Deirdre to me. "You're here! And lovely as hell, I may add. I see you've met my sis. Esteban, meet the lovely Stella. Stella, Esteban." We reached for each other's hand. He was quite a bit taller than Jack, with sandy colored curly hair and a beard. He too was quite handsome. His voice was low and sweet as he shook my hand.

"I see Deirdre is making you feel at home," said Jack, looking at my wine glass.

"I am and by the way," said Deirdre, "I ordered from Paquito's already. They should be here in about forty-five minutes or so."

Still holding my hand, Esteban spoke. "Jack tells me you haven't lived in the building long. Where are you from?"

"Well, I was living with a few gals from Columbia in Chelsea but...."

Esteban cut me off. "No, I mean, originally. You just don't strike me as a native New Yorker." I wasn't sure how to take that. He must have picked up on that, quickly adding, "You just have that small town way about you, is all I meant. Refreshing. Not tainted and cynical like us natives. And, of course, no accent either."

Deirdre spoke up. "Well Este, you never struck me as a native and there is nothing tainted or cynical about you." She handed him a glass of wine as well, along with a quick peck on the lips. I hated telling people where I was from, it was easier to say Chicago, but I had a feeling I would be seeing much more of them.

"Woodstock, Illinois," I said, waiting for the usual barrage of questions or jokes. Jack spoke quickly, sounding excited.

"Woodstock? Really? That's where they filmed the movie 'Groundhog Day.' I fucking love that movie!"

"Wow Jack, I can't believe you know that," I said, completely surprised.

"Jack knows a lot of stuff," said Deirdre, sipping her wine.

"Nah, not true," chimed Jack. "The only reason I knew that is because I wanted to find out everything there was to know about Woodstock. When I googled it, Woodstock, Illinois popped up. Woodstock wasn't even held in fucking Woodstock! It was held on a dairy farm in Bethel, in the Catskills."

"Actually Jack, it was advertised from White Lake, Woodstock Ventures," said Esteban.

"Ah, I see," said Jack. "Well, did you know the Beatles were asked to perform but Lennon said only on the condition that Yoko Ono's 'Plastic Ono Band' played as well? Woodstock laughed and said no fucking way! Can you imagine the Beatles at Woodstock? She shit on everything. Always wondered what John saw in her. Ugh!"

I spoke up. "I read that she stalked him incessantly. Phone calls, letters, hanging out at their studio and later at his house. These days she would have been arrested. A real piece of work. Poor John. Married a stalker, killed by a stalker."

"I have heard that as well," said Deirdre. "About Yoko the stalker. But about playing at Woodstock, I think they didn't because John was stuck in Canada, having issues getting back into the United States."

"Hmmm, interesting," said Esteban, putting an arm around Deirdre's waist. They made such a cute couple. "Anyway, Stella, you're from Woodstock, Illinois. Please continue."

"Yes, let's all gather in the living room," said Deirdre, making a shooing motion to clear us out of the kitchen.

"Jack," I said, turning back towards the kitchen. "You didn't get any wine."

"No," Deirdre said quickly, "he doesn't drink."

I looked at Jack confused. "But you're a bartender. How can you not drink?" I asked, hoping I sounded more inquisitive than mocking.

"I had a bad experience with it. Just not my thing," he said, nonchalantly. I was sure something had happened, but I figured I would eventually find out. It's not that it was a big deal, but I liked to drink and hoped Jack wasn't uncomfortable with me, when I did so.

"Stella, I am around drinkers all the time. I don't judge nor does it bother me in the least." It was as if he had read my thoughts. "You do what makes you happy," he went on. "If you're happy all is well in my world." God, I couldn't believe he had just said that. He was wonderful.

"Stella, please give us your thoughts on growing up in a small town," said Deirdre, plopping herself on the floor between Esteban's legs, him seated on the couch. "As you know, Jack and I did as well, but I want your take on it." He immediately began to play with her hair. Jack came up behind me, playfully putting his arms about my waist. If felt right and comfortable.

"Yes, thoughts please pretty lady," said Jack, quietly in my ear. Before I could answer there was a buzz at the door.

Deirdre jumped up, cash in hand.

"Saucy salsa time," she said in a sing-song voice. I watched Jack's eyes as he watched her open the door, making sure it was indeed the delivery guy and not some deranged dude. I could see the closeness of her and Jack. She seemed to take care of him and vice-versa. I wondered again about Jack's bout with alcohol. What had happened? I debated asking him or just dropping it altogether. I didn't feel comfortable drinking without him and I knew I would need to get over that. Alcohol. Such a social thing, really. Deirdre had shooed us into the living room. Now Esteban, removing his green cardigan, was shooing us back into the kitchen.

"Your throne, Queen Stella," said Esteban, pulling out one of the lovely chrome chairs. He was as charming as he was handsome and I glanced back at Jack as I sat down. Though he was looking back at me, his lips curved in a smile, his eyes were a million miles away.

The night ended at about twelve-thirty. We had filled it with chips, salsa, tamales, three bottles of wine and a nasty game of charades. By the time Este and Deirdre finished kissing Jack and me goodbye, shutting the door, I realized I was quite buzzed. No, intoxicated. As Jack turned towards me after locking the door behind them, I kissed him. He kissed me back, hard and then picked me up, heading for the bedroom.

"I want to make love to you, Stella but since you are drunk, I don't want you to wake up with any regrets." I was taken aback by his words. What guy ever said that, knowing he might ruin his chance for a fuck? None, usually. We entered the dark room and he lay me gently down on the bed. He began kissing me again, his lips so soft on mine. His hand slowly unbuttoning my blouse, pulling my arms from the sleeves.

"Stella, I want you but I need you to sleep, for now."

"Yessssss, Jack," was about all I managed to get out, my speech sounding slurred. I felt so comfortable, though once I closed my eyes a bit of dizziness overtook me and I started to spin. I felt him turn my body slightly, his hand at my waist, unzipping my skirt. As he lowered it over my hips, past my thighs, I felt my pussy tingle a bit with a surge of wanting him inside of me. Maybe in a bit, I thought to myself as I closed my eyes, drifting away, the smell of his Lagerfeld cologne prevalent on the pillow.

* * *

Tap. Tap. Tap. Silence. Tap. Tap. Tap, tap, tap, tap, tap, tap ... .in rapid succession. The sound distant, but as I opened my eyes it seemed louder. I turned my head a bit momentarily forgetting my surroundings. Fuck, my head pounded. I knew instantly where I was and that I had drank too much. How long had I been asleep? I turned my head towards Jack's side of the bed, the smell of Lagerfeld on the pillow. It was still made. He had not even lain down with me? What the fuck? The 40s style clock ticked loudly, reading 3:04. Tap....tap...tap..tap,tap,tap,tap,tap,tap,tap,tap. Again in rapid succession. Jesus. I knew that sound anywhere. It was a typewriter. I shot up in bed, not believing what I was hearing. I had been through the entire apartment with Jack and had never noticed a typewriter. I did notice my clothes were gone and I was in just my bra and panties. I grabbed Jack's button down shirt, quickly putting it on. As I buttoned it up, getting up from the bed, I realized it was the same one he had worn last night. He had taken it off then. I knew we hadn't fucked, that I knew for sure.

"Jack?" I called out, afraid to leave the confines of the bedroom at that moment. "Jack?" I repeated, louder this time. No answer. Now I smelled cigarette smoke. Tap... tap..tap..tap..tap..tap,tap,tap,tap,tap,tap,tap,tap,tap. Clearly he was writing. As I made my way to the hallway, I could see the cigarette smoke thick in the air. "Jack? Are you okay? Jack?" Again no answer. As I rounded the corner and peered into the kitchen, there he was. He was seated at the chrome table, wearing a 'wife beater' t-shirt, a cigarette dangling out of his mouth. The typewriter he was pounding on looked very old but appeared to be well taken care of.

"Jack," I whispered quietly, not wanting to startle him. He never even flinched. It was as though he was in a trance. Tap. Tap. Tap. Tap. Tap. Tap. Tap....tap,tap,tap,tap,tap,tap,tap,tap,tap,tap,tap,tap,tap,tap,tap. He stopped, pulled the paper out with his left hand, ashed his cigarette, then laid the paper upside down on a stack of papers on his right. I stood there, completely mesmerized. It wasn't Jack. Well not like I had seen. His hair was askew, almost wild, in all different directions on his head. His legs were criss-crossed and he was seated a bit sideways. Though he seemed in a trance, a million miles away, he exuded a magnetism that I had never seen before. He had always seemed awkward before, nervous, fidgety. Not now. Now he appeared to be in his element. Completely at ease, a look of pleasure was drawn on his face. It was as though someone had commanded him to 'write' and he acquiesced. He picked up a pencil and notebook that were lying near the ashtray, the cigarette still burning. He re-crossed his legs and began scrawling quickly in the notebook, his dark hair brushing against the top of his brow as he wrote.

"Jack, Jack," I whispered again. Nothing. He never flinched. I watched him for another minute or so then turned, making my way down the hallway and into his room. I crawled back into his bed. I lay there, my head spinning. I didn't know what to think. Did Deirdre know about this? Should I say something to her? After a few minutes I got back up, took off Jack's shirt and began searching for my skirt and blouse. He had hung them up in the closet, taking care to button the blouse and zip up the skirt. I put my clothes on, being careful to hang up Jack's shirt in return. I made my way down the hallway, stopping in the kitchen to watch him. As he plugged away at the typewriter, still in his own world, I recalled an article I had read about a girl who sleepwalked and ate for hours late at night, not remembering anything in the morning. The empty wrappers and boxes were strewn about the kitchen floor, showing anyone the evidence of the previous night's debauchery. I labeled it 'Sleepwriting' then and there. It made me feel better though I was still concerned. It was possible. Anything was possible. I have a girlfriend who told me some of her best ideas come to her in the dead of night, as she lay fast asleep in her bed. I grabbed a pen out of my bag and scrawled a quick note on one of the papers next to Jack.

> *I had a great night, Jack. I woke with a terrible*
> *headache and didn't want to disturb you.*
> *We'll talk tomorrow.*
> *Love,*
> *Stella*

I put the note next to his coffee maker and crept out the door, the tapping now an incessant rapid fire. I made my way down the hallway and back to my apartment, hoping no one would glimpse me, my heels dangling from my left hand. Once inside, I grabbed a glass of water, still feeling a bit dizzy and dehydrated. I pissed, undressed and climbed into bed. As I lay there, going over the nights events, I couldn't get away from the image of Jack, 'wife beater' t-shirt over his lean chest, cigarette dangling, plugging away at that typewriter, a shock of dark hair hanging over his left eye. He looked so comfortable, eerily so. I closed my eyes and as I felt myself drift off, I swore I could still hear the tap,tap,tap,tap,tap,tap of the typewriter keys in the distance, dancing in the dark, led by the beautiful Jack, as conductor.

I didn't hear from Jack the following day or the next, nor the next for that matter. Fuck it. I was sick of staring at my phone. I shot him a quick text. Jack, hope all is well. Thank you again for the lovely evening. If you get a chance, could you shoot me over Deirdre's number, would love to catch her for a coffee one of these days. Talk soon. S. As I hit send, Fran, the new intern, popped her head over my cubicle.

"Estelle, there is a Deirdre in the lobby asking if you are available for a quick word."

I stared at her blankly for a moment, maybe too long as she asked me if I should send her away. "Uh, no," I said. "Tell her I will be right there. Thanks Fran."

Shit. I didn't know what to think. Not knowing what to think had become all too common since meeting Jack. Me thinks my thoughts I done forgots. I smiled. It was something my dad use to say when I asked 'but why?' every two seconds when I was three. I grabbed my purse and glanced at my phone. There was still no response from Jack. I slipped the phone into my bag and made my way to the lobby. As I passed by Fran's desk I asked her if she needed anything from Starbuck's.

She shook her head. "Thanks but my heart is still racing from the last cup."

I smiled and told her I'd be back in about a half hour or so. As I stepped through the glass lobby doors, Deirdre spotted me and quickly stood up from the chair she had been occupying.

"Estelle, hi. Sorry to bother you. I would have called, but I work so close and I wanted to see you. This place is beautiful. I've always wondered what it looked like inside. I've heard rumors. That only women work here. That you have man servants dressed scantily in the cafeteria, serving you grapes and wine as they massage you. I've also heard there is a curtain you can go behind if you want some 'afternoon delight.'

I began to laugh. "Someone asked me that before. Apparently one of our writers wrote an article about the place a year ago, 'The Perfect Workplace.' Some became confused about what was true and what she was dreaming of. Trust me, no scantily clad man servants are waiting to pleasure us in any way. Anyway, I just got done texting your brother for your phone number and here you are!"

"Speaking of my brother, have you talked to him?" Deirdre's light air had disappeared. "He usually gets back to me rather quickly when I call."

"No. I haven't heard from him. I need to tell you something that happened...." She cut me off.

"Wait, Stella. If you're going to tell me you slept with

my brother, fine. Great. But know this about him. He hasn't had a lot of girlfriends and he isn't like that. Don't think for one moment he is. I am not saying this because he is my brother. I am saying it because he is kind, thoughtful and caring. More than any man I have ever known. I knew he had met someone really special, because he doesn't go out a lot or see that many women. Of course, he could have his choice, they are always asking me about him. He turns heads, always has. I guess what I am trying to say, is that he by no means took advantage of you, or...."

This time I cut her off, mostly because I wasn't feeling comfortable about what she was revealing suddenly about Jack. After all, I had seen him only a couple of times. I had a feeling he wouldn't want her saying all this. He seemed too private for that. "Deirdre, no. This isn't about screwing or anything like that. I mean we would have, I certainly wanted to, but I was a bit intoxicated the other night and though I wanted him badly, he was a complete gentleman and put me to bed. In a caring and loving manner may I add! Anyway, I know Jack is different from most men. Most would have stuck it in me, no matter what my condition." As I finished this last sentence, a group of people got out of the elevator. I felt the need for some fresh air.

"Stella, are you okay? You look a little pale. Come on." Deirdre then grabbed my hand and steered me towards one of the brown leather couches. She sat me down and plopped herself closely next to me. I took a deep breath.

"Deirdre, it's probably no big deal but I haven't heard from Jack since our dinner together. Granted, I know it's only been about four days but, well, that night, I woke up around three a.m. Jack wasn't in the bed. I heard what sounded like a typewriter. And not one of those fancy electric IBM jobbies. More like an old-fashioned, one key at a time model."

Deirdre cut in. "Yes! Esteban mentioned it when he was moving Jack in. It was in my grandmother's bedroom closet, stuck behind a huge hat box. Anyway, I thought it was odd because I don't remember my grandmother using it nor had I even seen it. My grandfather either. My parents told me they had gotten everything out of Sylvana's apartment except for the furniture Jack purchased. Anyway, Esteban took it down from the shelf, and called for Jack to come and see it. Este said the moment Jack laid eyes on it, he was transfixed. Este said it was weird. He just couldn't stop staring at it."

I suddenly felt a shiver down my back.

"Stella! Are you okay?"

"Deirdre, Jack was sitting at the kitchen table, typing away on that old thing, like it was the newest invention. I called to him many times. Softly, loudly. Nothing. He never flinched, never looked up at all. It was though he was in a trance. I thought to myself, sleeptyping! Jack was sleeptyping!"

Deirdre seemed to be staring at me in disbelief. "Is that possible? No. It can't be," Deirdre said, answering her own question. My mind was racing now, concerned about Jack.

"I stood and watched him for a while. He never knew I was there. He was in his own world, focused only on his writing. Oh, and he was smoking, chain smoking. He stopped typing a couple of times, picked up a notebook, writing in that as well. I have heard you shouldn't wake someone that is sleepwalking, so I was afraid to touch him. I scrawled a note and left it next to him. He never looked up."

"Did you read anything he wrote?" Deirdre asked, her eyes as wide as her pretty mouth.

"I thought about it but then realized it was none of my business and that I was afraid of what he might do. Does that sound crazy? Deirdre, it was Jack but then not Jack. I mean, I haven't spent a lot of time with him, but he always seemed a bit nervous, fidgety, out of his element in some way. The Jack I saw seated at that typewriter was strong, sure and on a mission."

Deirdre grabbed my hand then, pulling me to my feet. She put her arm around my shoulder walking towards the elevator. I could feel the heat from her body, radiating outward, touching me. I could feel her love and concern for her brother. She stopped, turning to me.

"You did the right thing. Not waking him up. Weird. Jack only smokes outside. He is always adamant about that. This is all so bizarre. I am worried now. I've called him and he isn't returning my calls. It's not unusual for us to go without talking for a day or two, but he usually at least throws me a text. Look, I've got to get back to work Stella. I think he is at Raines tonight. I am going to call over there."

I fished my phone out of my purse, checking the screen. Nothing from Jack.

"Stella, don't worry. Sorry, easy for me to say but I am equally concerned. I am sure everything is fine. Jack may be a bit of a loner and an eccentric, but one thing he is not and that is foolish. I would call him brilliant, although at times it gets the best of him.

I will call you as soon as I get hold of him. I promise."

I gave her my number and watched her walk towards the elevator doors. I made my way back to my desk and spent the next couple of hours staring out the window at Manhattan. I was daydreaming. Thinking of all the things Deirdre had said about her brother. I wanted him even more. I couldn't shake the image of Jack, sitting in front of that typewriter, on a mission, his mission, whatever that may be. His cigarette smoke floating around him, as though it didn't want to leave his side, his space, or his aura. His legs, crossed over each other, swinging back and forth, back and forth, to music heard only within him. What struck me most was how contented, serene, soothed he had appeared. He had been in his element, buried deep in the vast expanse of his creative spirit. My buzzing cell brought me out of my thoughts. It was Deirdre.

"Stella. Hi. It's me. Now don't panic, but I need you to make your way home. Jack's okay, but I will explain more when you get here. In the meantime, I need you to stop at the store. Is that okay?"

I said sure, asking her what I should get.

"American Spirits, the dark blue. Couple bottles of Pellegrino. A couple of Glade candles, or whatever smells good to you. This is the weird one. Jack wants apple pie and ice cream." There was a long pause, by me. "Stella? Did you get that?" I replied I did and said goodbye, see you in a bit. What the fuck? The requested items would require at least two different stores. I felt the need to see Jack as soon as possible. I left the office, a brief wave to Fran and headed for the subway.

It seemed two hours had passed since riding the subway home, retrieving the needed items from a couple of stores, stopping at my apartment for a quick make-up and hair check before making my way to Jack's apartment. Deirdre answered the door, looking tired, disheveled but relieved. She wore a pair of grey sweat pants and a NYU sweatshirt. I could smell the stale cigarette smoke instantly. As I walked further into the apartment, the smoke hung in the kitchen like a low cloud haze, the light through the kitchen window displaying it proudly. Jazz music was playing. I wasn't sure who it was but I loved it. Deirdre must have read my mind.

"Miles Davis. Jack insists. Won't let me turn it off, or down."

"It's okay honey," I said, pulling the items from my grocery bag, immediately putting the ice cream in the freezer. "I like it and it's not that loud. Where is he?" I asked, rather timidly I'm sure.

She gave me a quick kiss on the cheek. "Thank you, for being you. You are amazing and if Jack pushes you away I will take you on myself!" I knew then we would be good friends.

"Thank you Deirdre. That means so much to me." As I said this, the thought of Jack pushing me away hurt me and I hoped and prayed she was joking. Making some sort of light out of this whole situation.

"He is sleeping but told me to send you in the moment you got here." I stopped, feeling as though it was a nurse talking to me and Jack was dying in the other room. My brother's death revisited me and I shut my eyes. Not now, David, not now. I need strength, not now. The little affirmation I would say to make myself not cry and lose it over my brother. God, how I missed him though. Watching Deirdre and Jack was wonderful, but oh so painful as well. Dedire pulled out a lighter and lit the candle I had brought.

"Please tell me how much this all cost, Stella," said Deirdre, putting down the lighter and going for her purse.

"Let's not worry about that right now. I want to see Jack."

I made my way down the hallway, reluctantly turning the corner to Jack's room. I felt I was dreaming and I would see my David lying in the bed, replacing Jack.

It was Jack though, sound asleep, one leg over the bedspread, the other tucked under the sheets. His head was turned away from me, his dark thick hair a shock against the white of the pillow. The typewriter was no longer in the kitchen. Jack had taken the chrome table from the kitchen placing it in front of the window. The typewriter sat proudly atop of it, a neatly stacked pile of papers, typewritten, sat to the right. On the left, at least a half dozen empty packs of American Spirits, the ashtray brimming over with cigarette butts. The windows were slightly open and I could hear faint sounds of traffic. I walked quietly towards the bed, sat on the edge and leaned my body towards the sleeping Jack.

"Jack, Jack," I said quietly, but this time I wasn't afraid of waking him. This time I longed to hold him close, my lips on his. I could smell his Lagerfeld again, mixed with cigarette smoke, the smell strong in his hair. "Jack." Before I could say another word, Deirdre was suddenly there, pulling me from the bed.

"Wait on waking him a minute. I want to show you something."

We walked together down the hallway and into the living room. She held a book in her hand, a small olive green book with gold lettering on the front that read 'my journal'. It looked old, just like everything else in the apartment. I looked at her intently, not saying anything.

"It was my grandmother's. Sylvana's. I found it a couple of years ago. I had borrowed a beautiful coat of hers for a party. It was in the pocket. Funny I hadn't noticed it until late into the evening. When I got home, I couldn't help myself. When I opened it, it opened at a page that had been earmarked. I read the entry, unable to pull myself away from it, it was so sad. I wanted to ask my grandmother about it, about what had happened to the couple, but she would have known I read her journal so I couldn't. I just couldn't. I put it back deep into the pocket feeling so guilty. There's more to tell but this first." Deirdre carefully opened the journal and I noticed as she did so, that her hands were slightly shaking. She read:

"Oct. 21, 1969. The evening started normally, well as normally as a night in the ER can. Lois and Diane with their usual gossip about their dating escapades and how much cock they sucked. Honestly, I think Lois is still in love with her x and it's her way of grieving. Then a very attractive man was brought in, his wife screaming at the top of her lungs to help him. I could see the sheer terror on her face and my heart went out to her. I rushed them in over everyone else. He was clearly in a bad state. He had blood around his mouth and down his shirt. A bad sign. His eyes, God his eyes were so beautiful. So dark and so full of fear. She had his coat in her arms. As I reached out to take it from her, to cover him with it he grabbed my arm and muttered to me, 'Save me, save me please, I beg you. I beg you! Save me'. It was horrible. For a moment, time seemed to stand still. I seemed to stand still. Unable to move. I don't know how long I stood there, staring at the scene around me. He was put into a wheelchair and whisked away with his screaming wife. His eyes. I will never forget them. Not soon after, it was the end of my shift. As I was exiting the hospital, I noticed his coat, the one his wife had been carrying. Had I not covered him with it? I was sure I had. But there it lay, on a chair. I picked it up and underneath it was a typewriter. I hadn't noticed it before. Then, there she was running towards me. She grabbed his coat. She told me she was sorry but he was so cold, shivering something awful. She kept apologizing saying she was waiting for blankets for him and that the coat would help. I looked at her and back at the typewriter. For a moment, she seemed consoled, like everything would be OK. She pointed to the typewriter, explaining how silly her husband was sometimes. Like he was going on vacation or something and was going to be in the hospital for a while. The poor woman was really talking gibberish. She told me her husband was writing a book and something good might come, so he needed his typewriter. She told him she would grab a pen and notebook, but he insisted on bringing the typewriter. So, here it is, she said. Could it be any more cumbersome? She asked me to keep an eye on it until they were discharged. I told her I was leaving and would be back tomorrow. She begged me to take it home with me. I told her I would put it in the nurse's closet and it would be safe until they were discharged or he needed it. When I got to work the next day I found out that he had died. I ran into the nurse's closet and noticed the typewriter, still there. She had left it. I think I will leave it and if she doesn't come for it, I will take it home."

Deirdre stopped reading and looked at me. "You're wondering what does this all mean? Well, it meant nothing to me at first. Then, when Esteban found the typewriter in the closet, I became curious. I kept some of my grandmother's clothes, the coat included. The journal was still in the pocket. I began to leaf through it and this fell out." Deirdre held a faded article in her hand. She handed it to me, her hand still shaking. "Jesus, Estelle, I've got to sit down."

I unfolded the article and began to read:

> Oct. 22, 1969 New York Times
> Jack Kerouac, the novelist who named the 'Beat
> Generation' and who exuberantly celebrated its
> rejection of middle class American conventions, died
> yesterday in a St. Petersburg, Florida hospital room
> from an internal hemorrhage - the result of chronic
> alcoholism. He was 47 years old. He was brought
> into the hospital by his wife, Stella.

I stopped, stunned. I stared at the last word, Stella. I felt dizzy. This wasn't possible. Deirdre ran into the kitchen, returning with a glass of water. She pushed me into the chair, my legs collapsing quickly into it.

"I know honey. It's hard to swallow, isn't it?"

"Deirdre, are there any more entries in the journal?" I asked, but not sure why. What difference did it make?

"No. The one I read to you was the last one. Maybe because she lost it, forgot it was in her coat pocket. It seems the last thing she did was add the newspaper clipping.

Anyway, it doesn't matter. My grandmother never spoke of it. She would have tried to return the typewriter, I am sure of it. Jack Kerouac. The typewriter belonged to Jack Kerouac."

"Deirdre, you don't know what happened after he died. How long the typewriter sat in the nurse's closet. Maybe Sylvana did in fact contact Stella. Maybe Stella told her to keep it, in her grief. Maybe she couldn't deal with it all. Maybe your grandmother wanted to protect them all somehow and didn't want anyone to know. You know how much that typewriter is worth? Jesus."

Deirdre grabbed my hand leading me down the hallway and into the sleeping Jack's bedroom. We stopped in front of the chrome table. Deirdre lifted the typewriter up with two hands and whispered.

"Look underneath." I ducked my head under her arm. Sure enough, 'property of Jack Kerouac' was scrawled on a piece of paper and taped to the bottom. "It's my grandmother's handwriting. I do know one thing about St.Petersburg. She hated it. She and my grandfather only lived there a year, before moving back to NY. I am surprised she never told anyone about this. Maybe she did. I need to call my mother. I...Estelle! Are you okay?"

I didn't feel so well. My head was reeling. The coincidences were unbelievable. Was she saying our Jack was 'the Jack?' Are we talking reincarnation?

I needed a cigarette. Deirdre followed me back into the kitchen, pouring herself a Pellegrino. I stepped through the open window and onto the porch, my hand shaking as I lit my cigarette. Jack Kerouac's wife was named Stella. I couldn't get the coincidence out of my head. I was somewhat familiar with Kerouac. I had read 'On The Road' and loved it. I knew he had been a tortured soul. I knew of his brilliance and the way he felt being pushed into the limelight. I knew of his drinking. My Jack didn't drink. He had a bad episode. Shit. Kerouac died of it. Was this my Jack's 'episode'? Breathe, breathe, breathe Stella. Breathe. I needed to be strong. I had fallen in love with him and I needed to be his strength.

I recalled a friend of mine, telling me his daughter, at the age of five, began to wake up at the same time every night, screaming. He had said the look on her face was pure terror and they couldn't wake her. This went on for a couple of weeks at the same time every night. They took her to a doctor. They did scans, tests, everything. The nightmares continued and the doctor recommended taking the child to a hypnotist. During that session they learned that their child and her mother from a previous life had died in a fire. An obvious past life. The doctor was able to help the child through the process and eventually she forgot. My head was reeling. Past life regression. I read an article some time ago, how a large number of philosophers, poets, writers and musicians believed in reincarnation. I needed to read that again. I snubbed my cigarette out and crawled back through the window. Deirdre was standing in the kitchen pouring bitters into a glass full of water.

"Is he awake?" I asked.

She ignored my question, like she didn't even hear me. "So many things make sense to me now, Stella." Deirdre turned to face me, her face flushed. "My grandmother's relationship with Jack, for one. She had insisted my mother name him Jack. She always coddled him, showered him with books, made sure he read. That grand book collection you saw? Most of those books were given to Jack by our grandmother. She encouraged him to read, to write, starting with the poetry. She begged for us to come to New York. It's where all the writers go, she would say. The alcohol thing with Jack is his doing. He never liked it as far back as I can remember. He was always the designated driver."

As Deirdre spoke I began to feel better about the situation. I began to see it as a gift Jack had been given. She went on.

"Who knows, maybe my grandmother was haunted by that. Maybe when she saw Jack as a baby, she saw the eyes of Kerouac, begging her to save him. Maybe this was her way. She couldn't save him then, so she was making it up to a baby. Her grandchild." Deidre's eyes almost begging mine to see what she was saying. "Stella, we cannot tell Jack about this. Please. Nothing about the journal." She then pulled off the taped 'property of Jack Kerouac' that was adhered to the bottom of the typewriter. "Nor this" and she crumpled the paper in her hand.

"I agree. He doesn't need to know. Our secret."

"What's your secret, ladies?" Jack appeared suddenly behind Deirdre. He looked chipper and well rested. He looked different. More confident? I felt relieved considering the last time I had seen him.

"Dammit Jack, you scared the shit out of me," cried Deirdre, turning and giving him a punch in the stomach.

"The secret of the O," I said, giving Deirdre a quick wink. "A woman's orgasm is all her own and something she usually doesn't share with other women."

"Speaking of sex, I had the most delicious dream of you, Stella," said Jack, coming up behind me and wrapping his arms about my waist, nestling his lips against my throat.

"My cue to leave," said Deirdre, putting her water glass down heavily on the counter. "Besides Este is getting restless, according to his last text. You're in good hands dear brother." She gave us both a peck on the cheek and grabbed her stuff. "Call me if you need anything. Let's get together for dinner again soon. That was a hoot." And with that and a wink, she was gone.

"Wow. Is it just me or did she seem embarrassed about the sex dream? She left in such a hurry," said Jack, still smiling. "I was mostly just fucking with her. It's not like I would actually tell her, Jesus, she's my sister." I started laughing.

"You seem well rested. Do you work tonight?" I asked hoping the answer was no.

I wanted him in the worse way, wondering if there really had been a sex dream.

"I do baby but not for a couple hours. Come with, I want to show you something." Jack grabbed my hand leading me down the hall and into his bedroom. He sat me on the edge of the bed and walked towards the chrome table. He picked up a stack of papers that were neatly placed near the typewriter. He handed them to me and lay down on the bed, enfolding his hands behind his head. I looked down at the first page.

The Return
a Novel by
Jack Leavenworth

I looked back at him. I felt trepidation, afraid to go on. I looked at him, his dark eyes laying into my own.

"It's far from done honey, but I want your opinion so far. And then I want you."

I turned back, moving the cover page to the bed and hungrily began to read...

I hope that it is true that a man can die and yet not only live in others, but give them life, and not only life, but that great consciousness of life — Jack Kerouac.

October Sky

poem

I am the tree in October.

My leaves, glorious, rich and green in the summer.

A year before, I stood in New York City, waiting
for him.

He never came.

I cried and lamented at the thought of not
holding him,

Of hearing his voice softly in my ears,

His lips, kissing mine.

Then, he came back, in April, his kisses hot
and passionate.

My leaves sprung forward, revitalised by him,
welcoming the Spring.

My love, my want of him, more desirous than before.

He gave me bits and pieces of himself over the
next few months.
He played with me, as always.
When would I learn he was a dead end,
Never intending to give anything of himself to me,
Really.
Not ever.
Now it is October again. I stand in New York,
My leaves have all turned golden and fallen.
There are but a few left, resplendent on various
branches.
I will see you when you get here, he said.
Days passed, I dropped a couple of leaves,
Dried and faded as they hit the dirty street below.
I will call you tomorrow, he said.
But, he didn't.
I am the tree, in October.
One leaf sits proud and golden on a top branch.
He walks under my tree.
I will not fall for you anymore, I say, as I dangle
high above him.
I am bright and golden in the cool October sun.
You are not great, I say to him. Look how small
you appear beneath me.

He ignores me, again, same as before.

As he departs, he provokes a gust of wind that
plays hard against me,

Moving me, shaking me to my roots.

But my stem holds strong, and I prevail, sitting high
In New York City.

For the Millionth Time

poem

I am not calling you
to
ask
for
help,
he says, his voice,
hopeless and sad.
Then why,
I ask,
Why? If not for help.
I am calling you
to tell you
this is
THE
END

FOR

ME.

I want to die, he says, his

voice quiet and

distant.

How much did you drink

this time?

I ask, afraid.

A lot, he says,

as though I better be fucking scared,

this time.

Different than all

the other times.

All the other

million times.

Because this time, he means business.

This time,

may be the last time.

The last time I

stay up with him for hours,

hoping and praying he keeps breathing.

The last time I

listen to him vomit.

The last time I

smell the stench of alcohol

leaking through his pores.

The last time I call his parents.

The last time I call his brother.

The last time I call his girlfriend,

crying and begging them

TO

COME

GET

HIM.

The last time

I feed him.

The last time I press a glass of water

to his lips,

begging him to drink.

The last time I try to

carry him to the car

because he can barely stand.

The last time I

check him into a hotel room,

because he can't stay at my place

any fucking more.

The last time I

watch him cry,

burying his head into my breast,

telling me he wished he were dead.

Me saying,

the caring brother,

the loving son.

He had it all,

Women at his feet.

The man my camera adored

time and time again.

I have gone through

EVERYONE

in my life,

he says.

My friends,

my lovers, past and present,

my brother,

my parents.

WHO THE FUCK IS LEFT?

I ask, crying on the phone,

for the millionth time.

You, he says,

YOU.

And I say,

stay where you are,

I will be right there,

FOR THE MILLIONTH TIME.

The Pasture/Europa
Part One

short story

'I do not want to be the leader. I refuse to be the leader.
I want to live darkly and richly in my femaleness. I
want a man lying over me, always over me, his will,
his pleasure, his desire, his life, his work, his sexuality,
the touchstone, the command, my pivot. I don't mind
working, holding my ground intellectually, artistically,
but, as a woman, oh, God, as a woman, I want to be
dominated. I don't mind being told to stand on my own
feet, not to cling, be all that I am capable of being, but
I am going to be pursued, fucked, possessed by the will of
*a male at his time, his bidding...' ~ **Anais Nin***

Violet – The year 2027

The ten men filed in, their faces downward, looking at the dirty stage floor. I have often wondered what is going through their tiny minds as they shuffle single-file toward the front of the stage and the bright lights.

Judgment day, of a sort, for them. Usually, they look defeated. Some stare straight ahead, motes of hope flickering across their otherwise hopeless faces. Despair and desperation are usually the main features of the day. I hate this part of my job the most. I want to choose all of them, knowing full well they all have hearts capable of being broken with the concomitant sadness filling their poor souls. Undoubtedly, all once had families or lovers who are now long gone, a faded disdainful memory.

Those who are chosen will be fed well and more. They will be allowed to exercise whenever they want, allowed to sleep instead of having to wake up at 6 a.m. roll call, allowed books to read, movies to watch, walks in the 'outer' areas. Alcohol and pot also within reach, in small doses of course. But their main purpose - the way they will win their small luxuries - is being chosen as an Arcturus. Those chosen will be allowed the privilege of making love with Ophelia, the most beautiful women in Europa.

My name is Violet, and I am part of the new world that is Europa. The year is 2027. There was an 'event' five years ago that wiped out most of civilization. I am not allowed to talk of the old world nor is anyone. It is strictly forbidden. We are not allowed to use words such as, 'I remember when', or, 'I miss', or 'I wish'. It doesn't help us to rebuild ourselves. It doesn't make us whole. It only brings frustration and sadness.

Many believe it was our own fear, anger, hate, prejudice, ignorance, and entitlement that caused the apocalyptic event in the first place. Many believe that men were the cause of our demise, men and all their egotistical rhetoric. Many changes have transpired in the new world. The most shocking change, no doubt, is Europa is run by women. Some say it's for the better, and who am I to argue?

I am 26. I had a brother, a mother, and a father. I was at work when the event happened and have not seen my family since. Such is the case of many of us. Rumors run riot. Most of what we know we hear from the 'vegas'. That is what we call the people wandering outside our perimeter. We have heard the whole western seaboard fell into the Pacific Ocean. We have heard the entire midsection of the United States was consumed by fires. We have heard there are groups of vegas who run in packs, some crazed and insane, and that there are also villages of vegas that have rebuilt and live such as we. All I know is that I lived in what once was New York in the borough SoHo. My memory of my before life is dim, as it is for most of us.

We have all been administered vaccines, a series of three shots given upon our arrival over a two week period, then an oral vaccine taken twice monthly for two years. A sort of memory blocker, which allows us to move forward and not be forever trapped in what once was. I have fragmented memories, bits and pieces, scattered here and there among my thoughts. Sometimes I can remember my mother singing in the morning, her melodious voice filling our quaint, blue and white kitchen. I have glimpsed my dad, staring at his iPad, wearing his favorite ratty t-shirt, and my brother, playing his guitar, singing a tune of Nirvana's from long ago. Not sure if these are dreams, visions, flashbacks, or clouded-up photographs in my mind.

I was told that, in the next couple of years, even these memories would be distant, few and far between, and eventually subsiding altogether. In the beginning, I used to cry a lot, lamenting, wishing I had died with most everyone else, but it was those memories that were killing me, and I was thankful to be given the vaccines, although they were mandatory.

Europa is split into many different lots. Calypso is where the pregnant women reside. Their caregivers and doulas, the Cassiopeia, adhere to their every whim. So far, there have been roughly two hundred successful births, thirty deaths, woman and child, and about eighteen stillborn. It is hard for us to acquire medicines, and what we do have is carefully rationed out. After a baby is breast-fed for six months, they are moved into Velocity. Here, they are nurtured, loved, played with, and allowed to be children until they are seven years of age. At eight, the child moves into Polaris.

This lot is the only area in which males and females are allowed to cohabitate. Here, they are educated and cared for by our most valued women, the Adharas. These women were once doctors, lawyers, teachers, and scientists. There are about fifty men, the Acrux, who are also educators but have been chosen wisely over a long period of time, as most men in Europa cannot be trusted. All men wear bracelets with their names and numbers, signifying from which lot they hail. There is a device installed which, upon activation, will paralyze them temporarily. Many men have managed to escape over the years. Given the type of creatures they are, that is to be expected. There is rumored to be a safe zone outside our walls called The Pasture. This pasture is said to be monitored by the Canadians, and, if you can successfully manage to get there in one piece, you have won your freedom. Everything is hearsay and gossip. Of course many are perfectly happy here. We all know most men are satisfied with being fed and fucked. Nothing more.

This is my second group of men today. It is springtime, and the warmer weather drives the vegas out of whatever dwellings they are currently in, be it in search of food, drugs, or some sort of communal living. Of course by now, most everything has been scavenged, but, every once in a while, we will get vegas coming in with stashes of alcohol, drugs, and candy, giving it all up just to have human contact again. We do have groups of men who go out, the Canes Venatici, or the Hunting Dogs, who are solely scavengers. It is amazing what they come back with, and it makes me wonder what may still be obtainable - treasures found next to a dead and decaying owner, somehow overlooked by a wandering vega.

As I look at the men before me, their heads bowed, I notice right away the black dreads of Number Five. I also notice the cleanliness of his clothes. His face, which holds a beard, as those of most vegas do, is clean, shorn, and not scraggly, the lines of it clearly manicured like a tended garden. His jeans, lightly discolored, have most certainly seen a recent washing, though he may have found a stash of clothes – though it was highly unlikely as they fit him like a glove, his body, muscular, sleek. Most vegas come in thin, disheveled, ill, or with open sores or infections. He eats well; no scars or visible wounds. I clear my throat and stand. All eyes turn towards me. Number Five's eyes stun me. His face excites me, thrills me really. His beauty is a melancholy song from years ago. His lips, full, enticing. I quickly look away and pretend to be writing on my clipboard. I gain composure and look at the ten men, going over them one by one. The majority are too short to be considered for Arcturus, except for Numbers One, Three, Five, and Eight. I clear my throat again. "Thank you. Numbers Five and Eight, please remain. The rest of you, please exit to your right."

The men not chosen look relieved, not knowing what the other two were being detained for, but, in their minds, it couldn't be good. The two men left standing are beautiful. In being chosen for Arcturus, that is a given. In addition to height, they must also possess bone structure, an adequate amount of hair, and beautiful eyes. No one past the age of forty-seven is even considered.

"Hello, gentlemen." I speak confidently, loudly, as I have been taught. "My name is Violet. You will be spending the next couple of hours with me. I am quite sure you are exhausted, hungry, and bewildered at what you have walked into. Every man, woman, and child who steps into Europa does so of his or her own free will. However, once inside, it is like the old song, Hotel California, - you can never leave. As you learn our rules, traditions, and way of life here in Europa, I believe you will find peace and a simpler way of living than the last five years have brought you."

I stop, noticing that Number Five is calmly crying. My thoughts turn to my father, and I have a glimpse of the only time I had seen him cry, at least what my memory allows me to see. It was when his mother died. I had not seen a man cry again until now. Until Number Five. I am struck by this. He quickly wipes his left cheek with his forearm, clearly embarrassed. As he drops his arm back to his side, I notice him touch the wetness of his sleeve with his other hand as if verifying the tears are indeed real. His hand lingers there for a moment, and he closes his eyes, takes a deep breath, his muscled chest moving slightly. I am taken aback with the pang of sadness I feel for him. As he opens his eyes, I speak, surprising myself at the melancholy quietness of my voice.

"Number Five, what is your name?" His large, brown eyes look directly into mine as he replies, "Luca, Ma'am." As he says this, I notice Number Eight shift from one leg to another, a clump of dirt falling off of his jeans and onto the dirty stage floor. As I look at him, I realize his appearance is also fairly clean, his hair maintained, his facial hair short, groomed.

"And your name, please?" I ask with a bit more authority than previously.

"Ezra, Miss."

"Now, if you follow me, we will continue the interview in a more personal fashion." With this, I open a door that reads Personnel Only. As I walk through and look back, I could have sworn I saw them engage in a glance and a slight movement of their lips as if exchanging words.

The sun is shining brightly as we enter Andromeda, the biggest lot in Europa. The majority of the men are housed here. They consist of builders, mechanics, cleaners, chefs, gardeners, and maintenance. We are shown into the interview room by Leah, one of the female guards. She gives me a quick nod as we enter. Luca stops suddenly, staring at the walls. They are covered with art. Paintings, charcoals, and drawings of everything imaginable, from portraits to landscapes, to long ago memories of a couch in a living room. I speak suddenly, quenching Luca's curiosity.

"You will find art in most rooms here in Europa. The pieces on display in Andromeda are all done by men. You see, we believe when you take away the things that don't matter in life like wealth, materialism, and power, it puts man on the same playing field so to speak. We re-teach men how to enjoy life, through music, art, and love."

Ezra suddenly turns on me, his eyes blazing. "You call imprisoning men against their will and spitting on us as though we are fucking dogs love?"

Luca suddenly reaches out, grabbing Ezra's arm." She is just doing what she is told, what she has been fed to believe."

Luca says this calmly, looking me squarely in the eyes, his words stinging me. We are taught never to show angst, always to speak positively, never to entice or anger the men. I turn away from Luca, hoping he can't read me, and face Ezra.

"Look, I know you are tired, hungry, and have a lot of questions. Everything will be answered for you soon enough. Please do not speak to me that way. I understand your anger, I..."

Ezra quickly cuts me off. "Fuck you. You don't know shit. Fuck off!"

Luca quickly grabs Ezra's shoulder. "Enough please, Ez, enough." Ezra bows his head, and his body seems to slump a bit. Luca speaks his voice soft and soothing. "Look, Violet...is that right, Violet?"

"Yes," I reply calmly.

Luca goes on, "It's been a long day; he didn't mean it. Cut us some slack here.

Why have you detained us? What happened to the men we came in with? What do you want from us? We have nothing. Please."

As the word "please" leaves his lips, I can't help but stare into his eyes, the sadness in them overwhelming. I am already breaking Rule Number One:

'Speak to them quickly with short bursts of eye contact.'

Fuck, I can't break away from those eyes, try as I may. Photographs begin flashing in my brain. My dad. My best friend Alex, her body lying on the concrete, blood running from her mouth. My mother, singing in the kitchen, then her voice suddenly wailing, screaming for me, her body, slumped in the kitchen, dead and bloated. My brother, Daniel, his Nirvana t-shirt pulled over his face, hiding his cold, deathly stare, his mouth open as if asking why. I begin to feel dizzy. I feel my eyes close, photographs flashing through my mind like one of those flip books, showing a fast-moving scene as you flip the pages quickly. I suddenly feel Luca near me, guiding my body into a chair, his breath on the back of my neck.

"You must sit. You look quite pale," he says quietly, still holding my elbow. Fuck, I have now broken Rule Number Two:

'Never show signs of weakness around a man.'

Is this a weakness? His voice, his touch, his eyes. Is this my weakness? When had I become so numb? Numb to the sensuality of a man. The feel of his arms, his lips, his body, tethered to mine. Somehow I had managed to bury it, and it had stayed there, lying dormant until now, until him, this man, Luca. If we wanted to lie with a man, to quench our thirst, we needed permission. The procedure is like going to the library to check out a book. You scour the shelves of Andromeda, and, when you find what you desire, you submit his name to the Hydrus, a group of women in charge of 'Sexual Release', and the man is brought to your room if and when available. I have only been with two men here in Europa. One, almost four years ago now, never lasted long enough to please me. The other, more recent, grunted like a dog in heat with each thrust, and I felt like a whore.

I found my own hand and vibrator more comforting, more pleasurable, but I missed the sensuality of a kiss, the closeness of an embrace. And now I find myself wanting this man, Luca, one who would possibly be chosen in the end as an Arcturus, granted he tested free of disease and his mind was sound. To me and most of the women in Europa, he would be unobtainable, except for Ophelia. Granted I am beautiful but was not chosen for Ophelia. We are not allowed to know of the requirements, for they admonish the judging and insecurities of ourselves. We live by the code of love and meliorism. Self-doubt and loathing of oneself is considered useless and time-consuming. Suddenly, my thoughts are disintegrated by a glass of water that is being pushed against my lips. The hand it hails from is Ezra's. His hand is strong, his fingers awkwardly long, like a pianist's, a glint of honey-colored hair against his sun-kissed skin. "Drink her down, all of it," he says as he tips the glass.

Luca was now seated next to me, staring, taking me in, his eyes on my breasts. Our eyes meet. The sadness is still there, but along with that is something else I had not seen earlier in his eyes. Lust.

Luca — the year 2022

I take the curve much too fast. As I gear down and brake lightly, the car shakes and spews out a low grunt. Look over at Ezra, hoping he hasn't opened his eyes. No, thankfully, he is still asleep, his hair hanging over his left eye.

I glance over to the screen on the dashboard, a map showing me every curve of the road. 4027 Ash Drive. Pocono Summit, PA, the address proudly displayed in its green hue at the top of the screen. We are only about two hours from our apartment in the Bronx, but the serenity and luster of this place deems us worlds away. We are headed to what Ez's girlfriend calls 'The Pocono Palace'. I have never been, neither has Ez for that matter. It is his girlfriend Lydia's parents' place. Her dad, C.V. Speros, the famous scientist, environmentalist, inventor. He has been building his fortress for what seems years. He had started our senior year of high school, and we are all twenty-four now. I have heard rumors of the home's indestructibility, withstanding hurricanes, tornadoes, nuclear bombs, and the dreaded zombie army. It has been compared to the Chateau d' Angers in France, but on steroids. Lydia's parents are attending a conference in Australia and will be joining us in a week.

Lydia and Ezra are having issues. They have been together since high school. They love each other and all that, but Ez wants to further his musical endeavors and believes Seattle will welcome him with open arms. Lydia wants to marry him and stay in Syracuse near her family.

A wrench has been thrown into the mix. Lydia is two months pregnant. Of course, Ez went off the deep end because she was supposed to be on the pill. I smell bullshit a fucking mile away. Ez told Lydia he wanted to get away for a while to collect his thoughts.

He and I were going to fly to San Francisco for a week or so, but Lydia wouldn't have it. With the Pocano Palace being completed a few months ago, Lydia begged her folks to let us stay here for our 'mancation'. I am surprised C.V. isn't going to be 'Johnny on the spot' to show us around. Instead, there will be a couple of his henchmen to greet us upon arrival. Lydia and her parents will helicopter in with true style, pomp, and circumstance bullshit.

Suddenly, my GPS comes alive. 'You have reached your destination…you have reached your destination….. you have reached your destination', the feminine electronic voice blaring at me. I look around and see nothing. No palace. However, the road goes no further. I must have taken a wrong turn. I put the car in reverse, and, as I turn to my right to back up, I see it, the numbers 4027 etched beautifully into the large, foreboding cedar tree. Odd. Ezra awakens, sensing the silence.

"Huh? Are we here?" He seems confused, a combination of being stoned and falling asleep, I assume.

"It appears, so, Ez, but I am perplexed. There is no driveway, no house, what the fuck?"

"Let's get out, Luca, take a look around."

As we step out into the fresh air and forest, I hear a faint alarm like a car alarm but so distant, and I can't tell what direction it is coming from. The air suddenly seems warmer. Odd, it is late October; the chill has been evident for some time. But it definitely feels suddenly warmer, and along with that warm air is a strong floral smell like a lilac, I think. I look at Ezra, his eyes huge. His mouth opens to speak to me, but nothing comes out. He drops to the ground as if in slow motion. As I begin to bend down towards him, blackness envelops me, and I feel myself fall as if shot by an invisible bullet.

Ezra

I open my eyes in the dimly lit room. I hear faint classical music. The temperature is perfect. I feel so peaceful. Where the fuck am I though? Luca. The last thing I remember, Luca's eyes as big as saucers. I slowly sit up, the bed I am laying on heated from within. As my eyes slowly take in my surroundings, I am aghast and in awe at the same time. The walls are rounded and appear to be a type of stone. There are pod-like bunks against the wall, maybe sixteen total, stacked perfectly and cozy-as-hell-looking. The room also has what looks like a bidet. It is made of the most beautiful green marble I think I have ever seen. The only reason I know it is a bidet and not the can is because of my ex. They had one in their sprawling Manhattan high-rise. I was quickly educated regarding such. 'The toilet is where you piss and take a dump. The bidet is where you wash your genitalia and asshole before and after sex'. Well, that is what she said anyway, and I am smart enough never to argue with someone I am currently fucking because I would like to continue with that until further notice. On another wall is one of the most beautifully set up in-home bars I have ever laid eyes on. The entire bar is covered with a glass that magnifies the bottles, readable from across a room. Comte de Lauvia 1960 Armagnac, Imperial Collection Faberge Egg Vodka, Bunnahabhain, Asombroso, Remy Martin 1965, Old Weller, Ketel One, Cragganmore, Watershed. It goes on and on. Holy mother of fuck, thousands of dollars' worth of the best of the best.

The wall opposite me looks to be a huge screen. I look down and realize I am not in a bed but in the most comfortable, soft leather recliner I have ever had the pleasure of dipping my ass in. I see there are two rows of the same recliners behind me. To my right is a console. I see two buttons, one red and one green. I am smart enough to know the meaning and press the green one. The console opens, and an automated voice comes on in surround sound, of course. "Welcome, Ezra. There are over 100,000 movie titles in alphabetical order. Scrolling slowly, beginning now."

As it moves down, one of my all-time favorites catches my eye. I see a small instruction that says 'Voice activate title of movie'. I speak loudly, clearly, and slowly. "Ferris Bueller's Day Off."

Sultry surround sound responds. "You have chosen Ferris Bueller's Day Off. If this is correct, say yes, or select another."

I speak quickly this time. "Yes."

The room darkens more, and the bar lights illuminate. The surround voice comes on again as I begin watching the trailer for 'Sharktopus Hits Manhattan'.

"Would you like a drink?"

"I thought you would never ask," I smugly reply.

"Please repeat," says surround.

"Yes. 42 Below, neat, thank you."

"Pouring 42 Below, neat, you're welcome."

I hear a swish sound, and to my right a quick shadow. Sultry surround comes on. "Welcome, Lydia." What the fuck? Lydia?

Suddenly, a hand on my cock and a quick kiss on my cheek.

"Your drink, Massa. Daddy has the bar down to a T, just hasn't figured out a delivery process yet. You were a sleepy boy. Luca is out playing with the security staff, think they are racing the ATVs."

"Baby, first of all, why are you here? How long was I asleep, and how the fuck did we get here? Last thing I remember was getting out of the car."

She continues to entice my cock with her fingers, her breast moving against my arm. I want to fuck her, but I am so comfortable, I don't want to move.

"Daddy told me they were going to drug you. I begged him not to. He trusts you, honey, but thought it best for security purposes."

"But I never saw anyone. How was it administered?"

She takes a quick breath, her nipple hardens against my skin. "The perimeter of the property has a security system that, when breached, releases a drug called Torpidity into the air. It has a faint floral smell."

Ah, yes, I recall the smell, the air warm. I hit the red button on the console. The screen goes black. Later, Ferris. I pull Lydia onto my lap; her arms instinctively go around my neck. I speak softly, the comfort of the chair still immobilizing me. "How long have I been asleep? When did you get here? I thought you were coming with your folks? I..."

Lydia cuts me off, silencing my mouth with hers. "Ssshhhh," she purrs, "pleasure me for a bit, and I shall answer all of your questions."

She picks up my drink, pressing it to my lips, the vodka instantly warming my insides as it goes down. Lydia then stands, her eyes never leaving mine. She unbuttons her blouse, and, with a quick movement, her breasts are unleashed, their fullness becoming more obvious with her pregnancy. Her stomach was beginning to round. Her sexiness overtook me as always, and I feel my cock pressing against my jeans, her dark eyes penetrating me in the dim room. She gets on her knees and unbuttons my Levi's, pulling them down far enough only to reveal my cock. She takes me into her mouth, her hand at the base, teasing my balls. My eyes close, the pleasure overtaking my body, my cock hard as hell, wanting to penetrate her.

The surround voice comes on. "May I get you anything else?"

I hear Lydia giggle.

"No, thank you, life is good," I reply.

"Yes, agreed," says surround.

Luca

The place was incredible. I had heard of similar structures being built all over the country, though I suspect not as elaborate as this. I was informed I had not been knocked out long. Ez, on the other hand, was sleeping like a baby. He had been working a lot as of late. Add some weed to that, and night, night. Lydia was already here, deciding not to fly in with her parents as they would not be coming as soon as expected. She wanted to show us around a bit and then let us go off on our own, deciding to dwell in another section of the house so we could have some man time. Lydia introduced me to Jeff, one of five security personnel.

"Luca, go with him, he can give you a more thorough tour of the place than I can. Besides, I'm feeling a bit nauseous. I may join Ezra and lie down for a bit."

God, she is beautiful. I find myself wanting her more and more. Heaven knows I would never act on that, but it was her face, her body, I envisioned every time I masturbated.

Though I love Ezra and he is my long-time friend, his mood swings and hot temper can wane on one sometimes. She deserves better. It doesn't help that I haven't had any action for a while.

Unlike most men, I need a connection. It's not just sex. Instant gratification, never to be seen or heard from again. I hate that shit. The closeness of mind is what turns me on most. The fucking is a bonus. Call me old-fashioned. Maybe because I was raised with three sisters, I have a better understanding of what treating a woman respectfully means. "Let's do this," Jeff says, touching my shoulder. "And, by the way," he adds, "everything you see here today stays with you, capisce?"

Lydia glides near me, her dark eyes dancing. "Luca is the most honest and trustworthy man ever. Our secrets are all safe with him. Now go; have fun. I'm going to see if I can rouse Ez. Jeff, after the tour, take Luca out on the ATVs. He likes fast, and these ain't yo' grandma's all terrain."

And, with that, she disappears around the corner, her lovely ass gloating as if teasing my eyes to follow her.

'Katabole'…the large, black words catch my eye. Jeff hands me a brochure on the Pocono Palace, which is actually referred to as Katabole. There is a brief description of the word underneath.

> 'Katabole'- a Greek word with two meanings; the
> first meaning foundation; the second referring to the

male sexual function, the casting of seed. Designer
~ Chrysanthos Vianni Speros

How appropriate. C.V. seemed to be the type of man that would remind those of his dick size on a regular basis and how his 'balls are bountiful'. I am sure he spewed his seed into the ground before laying the foundation. I read on as Jeff tinkers with an alarm on the fritz.

> *Built to withstand:*
> *-one megaton nuclear explosion from ten miles*
> *-electromagnetic pulse blast*
> *-distant asteroid or comet strikes*
> *-super volcano ash fallout*
> *-massive earthquakes in succession*
> *-external surface fires*
> *-deep freeze of climate, temporary ice age*
> *-pandemics and viral diseases*

As I said before, these shelters are popping up all over the place, but, as you can imagine, they're very private. Heaven forbid would you want to save as many people as possible; poverty, class, social status, and ethnicity being of no matter. These dwellings are only for the extremely wealthy. I think, honestly, I would rather die with the vast majority than live trapped underground with a bunch of pretentious motherfuckers with money stashed up their asses. I continue.

Amenities include:

~five year supply of medicines, food, and fuel

~on-site water distribution system, including two drilled wells with chlorination and water-softening system with 100,000 gallon, elevated water tank

~on-site power with solar energy-independent for long-term, off the grid living. 1,000 kw, emergency back-up power generator, switching to solar energy when exhausted

~underground sanitary sewer piping with wastewater treatment plant.

~Hydroponic Gardens, including fish tanks full of salmon

It goes on, but my eyes jump ahead. Full court basketball, workout room, and on-site masseuse. Mmm, now we're talking.

"Jeff, on-site masseuse?" I ask, handing back the brochure.

"Nah, only when C.V. is around. He calls her that, but we both knows that's his mistress. Wifey is okay with everything as long as he is shoving diamonds and Gucci bags up her pussy. She'll take that over his cock any day. Now, who the fuck said there is no happily ever after?" Jeff chuckles as he sets the brochure down, picking up a screwdriver and covering the panel of the alarm. "Good as new. Now, time for the tour. Get ready to have your tighty whities blown off! As Lydia would say, this ain't yo' granny's cabin!"

And, with that, Jeff pushes a button that says 'BG' in front of large, gray, elevator-looking doors.

"BG?" I ask as I gander down a stone corridor that is as sleek as it is long.

"Below ground," Jeff says as the large, gray doors open. An automated voice comes on, but from where I can't tell as it seems to be all around us.

"Welcome, Jeff and Luca, to the underground area of Katabole," she says in a rather seductive tone, reminding me of a recorded voice I had heard from an old James Bond movie.

"How the fuck does it know my name?" I ask quickly, suddenly looking for a brand or electronic device that may have been planted under my skin while I was out cold.

"Your retina was scanned when you were brought in. You will be greeted upon entering most levels of the home and in the movie area and all sleeping quarters. C.V. leaves no stone unturned."

As we descend, I notice Jeff bow his head a bit and push the black, tiny speaker deeper into his ear. "Sorry, could you repeat?" A concerned look comes over his face as he bows his head more, his skin becoming pale.

"Welcome to below ground of Katabole," says the automated voice as we step out of the elevator. Jeff pulls the tiny speaker from his ear, looking ashen and perplexed. I look at him as he seems to search for words, his mouth downward as though his pooch had perished.

"Sweet mother of Jesus. Seattle, L.A., and San Francisco have just been annihilated." As the words spill from him, he begins to weep. I can't even process what he has just said. He can't either; he starts jibbering about his family, his friends, most of his words lost between sobs as he searches desperately for his cell. I put my arms around him, telling him it will all be okay, knowing full well the world will never, ever be the same again.

Lydia

I climb on top of Ez, not wanting him to cum yet. When his cock is in my mouth, his moans are such that I know he can cum quickly this way but that he doesn't want to just yet. He wants to take care of me first, my pleasure his utmost importance. I push my panties down over my hips, my wetness all over them. For some reason, pregnancy has brought out a certain horniness flare, for I seem to want him all the time. I think of him inside of me endlessly, his arms gripping my shoulders as his cock moves hungrily within. I know his rhythm to a T. I know when he is close to his orgasm, his breathing will then slow, wanting to please me, to give me the multiples he knows I will have. I have never felt so loved, so cared for until Ez. It's not just the sex as my mother says. She thinks I am too young to differentiate between the two. Love and sex. That I need to date, to have other lovers, to experience the world and all the wonderful people in it.

Honestly, she is just upset that Ez is a musician, an occupation she feels is a waste of time. He will never be rich from that or support you, she says. How will he care for all of your babies? Sex only goes so far. Pull your head out. Marry a doctor. God knows with your face, you could land any man of your choosing. I know I turn heads, I know many men want me. But I have eyes for only one, Ezra. Call me a fool as my mother does. She doesn't know what love is. Money, materialism is her love it seems. She has no passion, no fire, no 'jutzpah,' as my giagia, Zebina, calls it. My giagia will never get over the fact that her son married a cold, heartless, uptight blonde. She says the gods had my back when they made me look just like my daddy. Maybe I am more like him than just what meets the eye. I go after what I want. Ez started this stupid talk of checking out the music scene in Seattle some time ago. He is in a band, The Defenders, playing a lot in Williamsburg to the rich, silver spoon-fed Brooklynites. Ez's beauty, his talent, his laid back ways make me think that Seattle would be a better fit for him. That's what scares me. He would fall in love with the city and the music scene there and never look back. I couldn't have that. So, yeah, maybe I trapped him.

Forgot to take the pill for a week or so. It's for his own good. When we marry, which we will now that I am pregnant, Daddy will take care of us, won't let us starve. Mom only wants Ez to get a high paying job so she doesn't have to share her money. Fuck her.

Suddenly, I hear Luca, his voice loud, almost screaming for us. Ez quickly pushes me off, buttoning up his 501s. I realize his voice is coming at us from the surround speakers.

"Ezra, Lydia, please come right away to the above ground kitchen area. This is an emergency." I have known Luca for years and have never once heard his voice quiver with the sound of fear. Ez and I share a glance and run for the door.

Luca

The following days, weeks, and months were full of heartache. We were glued to the television sets for six days until everything went out. Cell service was clogged, and we couldn't use the phones. Television broadcasting ceased. The West Coast suffered major earthquakes followed by a catastrophic tsunami. Jeff, who was hired from Microsoft to engineer the infrastructure of Katabole, hailed from Seattle. He left right away. We begged him not to go, but of course nothing could have stopped him from going to find his family, certainly not our pleas. We knew he was a dead man, but so did he. He told us not to leave. The house would take care of us for years. If the rest of the country was as riven with destruction as it appeared, we had a chance of surviving as long as we stayed put.

The news reports were not good. Most of the West Coast was gone. There were reports of pure mayhem and fires consuming most of the mid-west states. The military had taken over most major airports, putting high profile people on planes, trying to get them out of the U.S. It was not clear what had happened to the rest of the world if anything. But, needless to say, it was pure chaos. There was looting and murdering. Cars, buses, and trains were being hijacked, destination unknown, but thousands trying to save themselves and their families. There were reports of pilots being held at gunpoint to fly anything from light aircraft to jumbo jets. Needless to say, sky traffic was congested, and planes were going down everywhere. People were being told to go home and stay there, to wait for further instruction. The last communication the radio broadcasted for a month or so. Communication after that was spotty, and we weren't sure what information was truth or speculation.

The small staff at Katabole all fled, hoping to find loved ones and make it back to the fortress somehow. They took backpacks full of food, liquor, and first aid, loading their cars with gallon containers of water and blankets. We knew water would be the most precious of all commodities eventually. Lydia and Ezra wanted to stay to protect the baby at all costs. We all knew what our chances were once we left the confines of Katabole. So, we stayed. We were obsessed with our cells, constantly trying to contact anyone we could. We were never able to get through and were constantly on them, hoping for that long shot of actually contacting someone. After five months, we took hammers to them, freeing ourselves from the torture. We pretended we were the only people left on earth. We played every game possible. We watched movies, read books, sang, danced, laughed, and cried most days. We jumped rope, played make believe, did impressions of people, told jokes, played hopscotch, basketball, and tetherball, and worked out.

We also drank a lot. Ez more than I, but I certainly had my fair share. We smoked pot all the time. Lydia's maternal instincts kicked in, and she did everything she could to ensure the health of her baby. She had a drink here and there and got high on occasion, but mostly she slept. Ez and I worried about her depression as of late. She was clearly concerned about bringing the baby into an unknown world, and we knew she yearned for her parents, especially her mother. She had always been a daddy's girl, usually speaking ill of her mother, but she talked about her incessantly now. Lydia and Ez fought a lot, and I hated being caught in the middle of them. I tried to soothe Lydia by brushing her hair every day and giving her foot massages.

She grew more beautiful, her hair lustrous and her belly big and round. I wanted her more and more. Ez seemed to want her less and less. He began composing music and, many times would zone out, infuriating Lydia. We were always together it seemed, and, one night, as I brushed her hair, she kissed me. It started as a peck, a sort of 'thank you for being you' kiss, but I took more of her, planting my lips firmly onto hers. She kissed me back. And then I could feel my cock harden as she pushed her tongue deep into my mouth. God, her lips, her mouth was sweet and soft, and I craved to be inside of her. She pushed me away, laying herself onto the soft, leather couch. She began to undo the buttons of her blouse, her dark eyes staring into mine the entire time. Her breasts were so full, pushing out from underneath her too-small bra. I felt so sad for her at that moment. She had no one to share her pregnancy with. No friends, no mother, father, brother, sister, aunts, uncles, grandparents. She would get none of that. Instead, she was stuck with a man she loved but was not sure if he loved her back, and with me. I knew I couldn't give her what she wanted because I was not Ezra. But I could love her and be with her if she wanted if only for now, this moment. She unhooked her bra, still watching me.

She then pulled me towards her, placing my lips at her breasts. I suckled her, and she began to breathe heavily. I lightly bit her nipples, twirling my tongue around them, and she began a low moan. She took my hand and slid it over her pregnant belly and then between her legs.

"Two fingers, Luca, put two fingers inside of me," she said quietly, her mouth soft against my cheek.

Before I did, I lightly caressed her clit, saying, "Not yet, not just yet." She felt so warm, her skin so sweet. Then she sat up, covering her breasts, and began to cry.

"Luca, Luca, what will become of us? We can't stay here forever. I want to leave here. Please, Luca, I think I am slowly going mad." She buried her head deep into my chest, her weeping tearing at me. I wanted to get her drunk and make love to her so she would be at peace, her mind settled, her body pleasured if only for a few hours. I wanted her to forget her pain, her anguish. I feared both alcohol and sex could potentially harm her and the baby. I couldn't have her go off the deep end. She needed to stay sane and whole for the baby's health and her own. I hushed her, my hands running through her hair, my lips softly kissing her cheeks. She cried for a bit more and then fell asleep, her hand on my chest, her soft mouth against my neck. I slept as well.

I was awakened suddenly by Ezra shaking my foot. I must have been out deep. Lydia was no longer lying on me.

"Luca, wake the fuck up. There's people outside. Hurry. Come look." Ezra's tone was almost fearful.

"Where's Lydia?" I asked, suddenly alert as all hell.

"She's fine. She's in the pool. Leave her. Come on."

Outside. We hadn't been there yet. We had been in the house for six months now. We were told to stay inside, that if nuclear reactors burned or exploded, our air quality would be tainted . Upon departure, Jeff had told us the same thing. Don't be stupid, he said. Don't endanger yourselves or the baby. So we stayed inside, afraid of fallout or radiation of some kind. We had cameras that ran the outer perimeter of the home. We never saw anyone. Until now. We had been in lockdown since the event. Basically, the house was impenetrable. No one could get in, and we couldn't get out. Then what Ezra had said truly sunk in. There are people outside. Fuck. That meant air quality was safe, right? Or were they sick and had just not perished yet? The walking wounded. I thought of all the zombie movies that were made in the last ten years. Then I thought of the one that had truly scared the bejesus out of me. World War Z. The one with Brad Pitt. They were diseased. It seemed the most believable of all that I had seen.

"I know what you're thinking, Luca. They're not fucking zombies." As Ezra looked at me, he began to laugh. Then I started laughing. Then we started walking around, our arms in front of us. Our zombie impersonation. We had done it many times, but usually stoned. This time, we weren't stoned. Or drunk. Or loving life for that matter. We were stone cold scared out of our fucking minds. At what had gone on, what had transpired. We weren't watching the movie anymore. We were fucking living the dream, never able to wake up from it. We looked at the monitors. Sure enough, there they were. The first people I had seen in months. They were a motley crew. Seven of them. The youngest, probably thirteen. The oldest I guessed to be about sixty. They weren't scary to me, but those in between gave me the heebee jeebies. Five men and two women. The women looked like they could be sisters, their dark hair and eyes so similar. And they were holding hands as if one or the other would be transported suddenly via UFO. Their clothes torn, dirty. The three men in question I guessed to be from mid-thirties to late forties. They looked possessed in a way. In a way I didn't like. They would probably kill one another for a good night's sleep and a meal.

Normally, I would have given them the clothes off my back, the dinner on my plate, but I had three people who meant more than the fucking galaxy to me. Lydia, Ezra, and their unborn child. I would not and could not take that chance. They could have guns. One thing that C.V. hated more than anything was the right to bear arms. He didn't believe in it, that I knew. He spoke out against guns on a regular basis. He believed it to be one of the root of all U.S. evils. His favorite statistic: fifty-eight murders in a year by firearms in Britain, eight thousand seven hundred and seventy-five in the U.S. I had seen him on television, speaking his mind and arguing with the NRA on a regular basis. Though I felt for this group and wanted nothing more than to take them in, my survival instincts were high.

We watched them as they wandered around, banging on the doors and yelling, "Is anyone here?"

I thought of my own family. Were they dead? Sick? Part of the walking wounded? I pushed them out of my mind. Lydia, Ez, and I had all made that pact long ago. We wouldn't speak of our families and what may have transpired. There was nothing we could do for them. We knew what they would have wanted for us, and that would be to live, to persevere, so to speak. So that is what we were doing.

"Hey, guys." Lydia's voice broke our silence. "You two seem entranced. What is out there that has you so mesmerized?" She asked, coming up behind me. Before we had a chance to do anything, she saw them. Her cries were loud. "People! Oh, My God! People!!!" And she instinctively headed for the door.

Ezra

I reached out to grab Lydia, but, before I could, she had fallen to the floor. She screamed out for Luca and I to help them, to let them in. As I bent down to pick her up, I stepped into a puddle of water that had accumulated near her. What the fuck?

"Ezzzzz!" Lydia screamed, no longer concerned about the outsiders but holding her belly. "The baby. Ez, the baaaaaabyyyy. It's coming!"

Luca and I got her to the couch. We had watched a few movies where women gave birth, so we weren't totally unprepared, but I wasn't prepared now. I was scared shitless. Luca stepped into action, grabbing towels out of the closet. Lydia began to scream now, begging for her mother. Luca put her head on his lap, trying to calm her, stroking her hair and telling her to breathe. It wasn't helping much; she seemed panicked. I knew this wasn't good. I untied the knot she had made around the robe, exposing her round belly. Luca shoved a couple of pillows under her ass, her pelvis now high in the air. She opened her legs then, screaming in pain, and I saw the baby's head. It was though Luca had sensed my panic, my eyes wild with fear.

"Goddammit, Ez, help her!"

"Fuck! Luca, I see the baby's head! I don't know what to do!"

"Trade places with me, Ez, now! Calm her any way you can. Get her to start her breathing like we practiced."

I knelt next to Lydia, kissing her tear-stained face, her body now drenched with sweat. "Baby...calm...breathe, please, baby, calm down, please," I said. I knew she could sense my fear, my anxiety of this unknown.

"Ez, it hurts so bad, please, Ez, get the baby out!" She screamed, grabbing my arm so hard as though she could snap it.

Suddenly, Luca screamed. "Lydia! Look at me! You need to push, you need to fucking push!" As I moved her hair off of her forehead, I saw her bear down, her eyes shut tightly as she grimaced.

"Yes, yes," screamed Luca. "Good girl. Now stop. I need you to take a big breath in. Look at me, goddammit! Lydia, you can do this. Okay, ready? Push! Fucking Push!"

Again, Lydia bore down, her body tightening, her face clenched as she pushed. I heard a woosh sound, and I saw the baby, slick, in Luca's hands. Then I saw the blood. A lot of blood. Luca had left the room with the baby, and I was thankful when I heard her tiny cries.

"Lydia, we have a girl, a baby girl!" and as I looked down at her, I saw she wasn't moving. I began to scream.

Luca

Lydia was dead. We tried everything, everything. Ez couldn't and wouldn't accept it. He sat with her for hours on the couch with her lifeless head in his lap, stroking her hair. He wouldn't look at the baby. Every once in a while, I would see him put his lips to hers, pushing air into her mouth as though this would suddenly revive her. I saw him shake her, begging her to come back, to wake up. My heart was broken as well, but I had to take care of the baby. Ez was clearly not up for that job now if ever. I was thankful for the stashes of formula I had found, C.V. obviously preparing for his grandchild well in advance. Athena. I had named her Athena. Lydia had spoken about wanting to give the baby a Greek name. I had heard her list off a few names one night as I was brushing her hair, and Athena had stuck out. Ez still had not much to say about that or anything. He mostly grunted or cried and, on occasion, would sing, but usually something mournful. On the third day, I had had enough.

"Ez, I need to take Lydia now. Say goodbye to her."

As I picked up her body, Ez seemed almost relieved, his hands falling to his sides as if a weight was lifted, emotional and physical. He then looked at me and mouthed the words "Thank you."

"Ez, I need you to get up now. I need you to eat, to take a shower. Then I need you to go to Athena. Lydia needs you to go to Athena. Do you hear me, Ez?"

I didn't wait for a response as I placed Lydia's body in some sheets I had prepared to wrap her in. I had decided to keep her body in a freezer until we could bury her outside near the beautiful cedar tree with the house numbers etched into it. Outside. We still hadn't set foot outside. That surely would not happen anytime soon now that we had Athena. It was hard as hell taking care of a baby. I barely slept, and, if I did, it was always a light sleep, fearful of her crying and I not hearing her or it was full of horrific nightmares. Zombies broke through the barriers of Katabole, and we were all eaten. Packs of wild dogs came one night, jumping through all the windows in the house and tearing our bodies apart, limb by limb. Some nights, I lay in bed, crying, mourning the loss of Lydia and my family. I wanted to leave here as did Ezra. We agreed to wait until Athena was at least four. In the meantime, we would educate her as best we could. We would teach her how to be a survivor in a world that ate up and spat out the weak.

Ezra

Athena flourished, her beauty beyond comprehension. Thanks to Luca, she is funny, sweet, and smart as a whip. I spent months angry, sad, and depressed. I blamed myself for Lydia's death. I felt I had willed it somehow in some way. I knew I hadn't of course. I felt guilty because she had saved our lives. If not for her, we would not have come to Katabole in the first place. We most likely would be dead or wandering, fighting for food, water, and shelter. Luca and I discussed many times leaving the confines of the house. We knew we were meant to be here, we were spared. Lydia and her unborn child were also meant to be spared. Unfortunately, Lydia wouldn't be part of what we considered our 'new world', but Athena was, and we could not, would not do anything stupid that would leave her alone without her dads. Lydia would have begged us to keep her here as long as possible, and we knew it was the wisest of all decisions.

We had managed to locate and find the mechanism that released Torpidity. We realized it wasn't working when we had seen the people the day Athena came into the world. We were too afraid of going out and testing it on ourselves as we didn't want to take the chance of being attacked or jumped by wanderers. Though we had cameras and a security system that would warn us if someone was outside, we wanted to be outside ourselves, therefore, we relied on Torpidity. We were thankful the day a dog wandered onto the property. The alarm sounded and Luca dashed to turn it off, afraid of waking Athena. He spotted it in the courtyard, drinking out of the algae-infested pool, not maintained or used for years. Luca went out and trapped it with food, luring it into a small animal carrier.

He jumped on an ATV and dropped it at the perimeter, where we believed Torpidity to be released. He did this at the speed of light for fear of an attack. Once inside, we turned off the security system and switched on Torpidity. Sure enough, the dog was down within five seconds. Success! A whole new world had opened for us. We would be able to enjoy the outside again. We also began to prepare for our departure within the year. We needed to be with people again, in some sort of civilization if only for our own sanity. We wanted Athena to know a world with people, other than the two fathers she was raised by. Unfortunately, not even Luca and I would know what that world would be. The questions play in your mind over and over again. What is left of New York? What actually happened to the rest of the country? Did the West Coast indeed perish? How many died? What of our families, our friends? The questions never stopped. At times, I thought I would go crazy wondering what was or what is.

Luca

Our own messiah came on a hot day in July. We were outside, teaching Athena how to climb a tree. We knew Torpidity had been released into the air; we heard the faint alarm upon its discharge. Ez and I shared a glance, he nodding that I should go; he would stay with Athena.

"Daddy, I want to come," said Athena as I headed for the ATV.

"Not this time, baby. Stay with father. I will be right back." Athena looked so much like her mother, but she had a softness about her that Lydia had lacked. Athena was a gifted child. At the age of two, she had learned to play Ez's guitar. Shortly after that, the piano and then the violin. Ez and I held 'school' every day, teaching her from the books C.V. had stocked in the library. Everything imaginable. Moby Dick, Catcher In The Rye, Tom Sawyer, Moll Flanders, 1984, Wuthering Heights, to name a few. One of my favorites was Stephen King's Skeleton Crew, a collection of short stories. We watched tons of movies. We made a point to watch all apocalyptic movies, giving us all a taste of what the outside would or could be like. I Am Legend, The Road, Mad Max, and my favorite, The Book of Eli. Of course, we also watched comedies, musicals, and Athena's favorite, The Wizard of Oz. We tried to teach Athena not to be fearful and not to be afraid of the dark. Through all of the movies and books, Athena's vocabulary was incredible.

We read to her upon rising, in the late afternoons, and then at bedtime. Each night, she would say, "Goodnight Mommy, goodnight Father, goodnight Daddy. Kisses all around." I felt like the luckiest man on earth.

I went around the entire perimeter, confident that no one was here, but then I saw a boot lying behind our large, low bush blueberries. They were in season and abundant, and I badly wanted some, but I needed to move as quickly as possible since we had turned off Torpidity. I held an air horn in one hand, the blasting of it signaling Ez to turn on Torpidity at once if there was danger.

As I came around the bush, I saw it was a man, and it looked as though he was bleeding. He was of slight build and appeared to be Mexican. He had long dreads, blue jeans, boots. His clothes were filthy, and he had a nasty black eye. Clearly, though, he had won the fight. Though short, he had badass written all over him. Torpidity had a different effect on everyone, but I knew I was guaranteed two hours before he would begin to stir. As I bent over him, I found myself staring at him for long periods of time. He was the first human I had seen in years. To me, he was beautiful, and I eagerly anticipated his waking just so I could hear him speak, be it Spanish or not. I found it odd that he was alone. Where had he come from? We hadn't seen anyone for years. His shirt appeared to be once white but was now filthy and caked with dried blood.

I pulled his shirt back and noticed the wound right away. He had been bandaged quite well, but the wound had re-opened, the blood now beginning to run down his abdomen. Lifting weights most days had really paid off for me as I was able to get him into the ATV quite easily. I fished the walkie-talkie out of my back pocket.

"Ez."

"You okay?"

"Yes. Take Athena in. Put on a movie. I have a man here, and he's bleeding."

"What the fuck? He's alone?"

"Yes. He was eating blueberries. He is thin, so I am assuming he is hungry. Make a lot of quinoa, and get the medical equipment out. Oh, and pour some good tequila. We need to stitch him up. Turn on Torpidity in two seconds. Out."

Ezra

Arturo was sent to us, literally. One of the landscapers, José, a worker at Katabole, made it out and back to Mexico. He gathered his family, trying to return to the compound, where he knew they would be safe. They were jumped for their backpacks full of food, alcohol, and medicine. Arturo was a member of a group of Mexicans called the Empatías. They were traveling around the country, aiding everyone and anyone they could. Arturo had come upon José, bleeding and dying in the street with the rest of his family. Before he died, he gave Arturo two things, his boots and a map of where Katablole was located in the Pocanos. Arturo explained it took him almost two years to get here, living in safe houses along the way and usually only traveling at night. That was all the information he gave us. He didn't talk about his family, what happened to the rest of the Empatías, or the condition of the country. He said it best we "aprendera luchar y sobrevivir" (learn to fight and survive).

He told us of a commune in what once was Central Park, midtown Manhattan. A new city erected there, called

Europa. Luca and I looked at each other and smiled. We were both thinking the same thing. Possibly our families could have made it there! They could be alive! We hugged and cried. Athena joined us, jumping on our backs and covering us with kisses. We went to bed that night with a new kind of hope as we read Athena The Wizard of Oz. She called Oz 'our Europa'.

Luca

Arturo and Athena clicked pretty much from the get go. We weren't sure at first how she would react to him, never having had contact with another person before. But, when their eyes met, it was like an unspoken word of approval. His heart seemed to melt when she was near. Maybe he had had a daughter. If he had, he was silent about it, about everything in his past. He made it apparent that the past was the past and today was a new day. I loved his optimism, his outlook, his zest for life, be it bliss or bullshit. We had no idea what was out there. We had been safe in our haven for years. For whatever reason, he had decided not to share what had happened to our country. Instead, he said to us, "Pretend you are a baby, being born into the world. It is a new world, and you can never lament the old one, for it will kill you."

I knew he was right. I needed to be strong for Athena. He shared his wisdom with her. Many times, I came upon them often huddled together, as though he were the coach and she his player. He feeding her his strategy, his plan, Athena taking it all in, a knowledge sponge. Then, as if magically overnight, they became inseparable. She called him Papi. She looked for him in the mornings before breakfast. If he was asleep, she would wait till he got up to share her morning meal. I wasn't jealous. Neither was Ez. We loved him, too. We loved his heart, his wisdom, his love of life. He was always positive. He never showed a weakness or a glip. We admired his pursuit of happiness, his goal to be helpful and understood. He was much more powerful than we could ever be. Athena had the best of the best. Now, she had three men to love her, to nurture her, to make her strong, to breathe life into her.

One morning, Arturo called out, "Athena, come here. Look what I am about to do."

As she rushed to his side, he held a razor in his right hand. He had placed a mirror against the kitchen window.

"Papi, Papi, what are you doing?" a look of panic on her face as Arturo held a chunk of his dreads in one hand.

"Well, your daddy's dreads look wonderful as he has been able to wash and take care of them. Mine, not so much. There is dirt, sweat, and blood caked everywhere. He picked up a pair of scissors and handed them to Athena. "Baby, start cutting. In the olden days, little girls use to cut their dolls' hair. Pretend I am your giant doll, honey. Chop away!"

Athena gladly took on the job and began cutting at his hair but found it impossible as it was so coarse and thick.

"Papi, I am having problems. The scissors are too dull!"

"Well, then, I have no choice but to do this," said Arturo as he took the razor to a small section of his scalp. Athena watched in amazement as his smooth, brown skin begin to appear, the dreads slowly falling to the floor.

"Daddy, Father, come quick! Papi is shaving his head!"

Ezra

We began preparations to leave Katabole. Arturo had been with us close to a year now. Athena had just turned five. The past six months, Arturo had trained her in kung fu, karate, tae kwon do, and joint lock arts. I had never heard of the latter before. Arturo explained that a person learns how to push and manipulate an opponent's joints past their comfort level. It is most effective for a child to learn when up against someone larger. She was also taught Brazilian Jiu-Jitsu and Aikido. Her agility and strength were profound. I had never seen a child learn so quickly, her grace and speed quite remarkable. For fun, he threw in some break dancing, and, by the end of the week she was a natural. Two days before our departure, we took Lydia to the cedar tree and buried her near the base. Athena made a beautiful cross for her out of some twigs, binding it together with leather shoe laces. She adorned it with tiny blueberry leaves and baby's breath. It was quite remarkable. Arturo spoke in Spanish, reciting the Lord's Prayer. I sang one of Lydia's favorite songs, 'The Scientist' by Coldplay. I lost it as I sang Lydia's favorite line. Luca had to finish the song. Athena sang Paul McCartney's 'Let It Be.' As we walked away, the wind slightly stirred around us, and I could have sworn I heard Lydia's voice softly singing in the distance. I smiled.

I had somehow found my peace. Athena grabbed my hand at that moment and said, "Mommy will always be with us, father. Always."

I picked her up and held her tight and said, "Yes, baby. Always."

The Departure

Trepidation sat on all of us quite heavily, especially on Arturo. He had been out there, fighting the good fight, seeing first hand humanity at its finest. And its worst. Growing old in the confines of Katabole would have satisfied him just fine. His love for Athena is what propelled him forward. As dark or dreary as the world may be, it was her world and all she would know. It could be the bleakest of days for him, but he had to make it the brightest of bright for her. Her perspective on life thus far was simply through the turning of pages in a book and the watching of movies from the luxury of a soft, leather recliner. She had not yet felt what is was to be hungry, afraid, and helpless. He would try to look through her eyes, the eyes of a child. Full of wonderment, questions, and zest. He would be reborn through her. He knew Ezra and Luca would be devastated beyond comprehension at what they were about to see.

He knew that feeling when he had first witnessed the death and destruction. It had crippled him for some time. He knew though that, in their protection of Athena, they would not show their weakness, sadness, or fear. They would be men and do what men do best. Be courageous.

They gathered what they could from Katabole. They only took necessities in their backpacks. They walked through the fortress for what would most likely be the last time. They said goodbye to their luxuries, to their comforts of life.

"Daddy, Father, Papi, say goodbye to Kansas," said Athena, breaking our somber silence. We looked at her, questioning the word, 'Kansas'. Before we had a chance to ask her, she said, "On to Oz."

The end of part one, The Pasture / Europa

His Voice

poem

W_{ell,}
Hello
There.
His voice.
It owns me, fuels me, excites me, seduces me,
sends me.
It causes me to giggle like a schoolgirl,
To moan like a whore.
Each fucking syllable he speaks strums at my brain,
my heart, my sex.
His tone makes my fingers dance
Upon my clit, strumming it like a guitarist.
His voice pulls my hair strand by strand,
The pain so great and gratifying as he plucks
The follicles from my scalp.

My cunt, so wet and warm as his voice,
Soft, lulling, alluring, capturing.

My eyes closed, my body, lying upon my bed,
Arching as his voice figuratively stretches
Across me.
His voice captivating my senses, pulsing my
Awareness into a new form of ecstasy.
His voice is his hands, his mouth,
His fingers, probing my cunt,
Stroking my vaginal walls.
His voice then thrusts into me.
His cock.
His voice.
His cock.
Hard, erect, moving inside of me,
Driving deep into my womb.
His cock, his voice, fucking my mind,
Fucking my body.

His voice, making me cum again and again and again.
His cock, my pussy, his voice.
He says everything.
I listen. And hear.

Once

poem

I was inspired by you once.
Foolishly moved.
I was in awe of you once.
Foolishly moved.
Foolishly moved by your words,
Your actions, your gestures.
Foolishly moved by how you kissed me,
Your caresses, your fucking.
I was in love with you once.
A fool in love.
I was completely immersed in you once.
A fool in love.
A fool in love with a man who was
Searching

For something that doesn't exist.
A fool in love with a man
Who I let play me for years,
Holding me close, then pushing me away.
Once, I held you high.
Once, I couldn't resist.
Once, you caused my body to ache for you.
Once, your lips caused mine to burn.
Once, your voice sent me to outer limits.
Once.
Once.
Once.
I was inspired by you once.
Foolishly moved.

Click Clack

short story

Trace Urban was stuck. Fucking stuck. He had murdered his heroine, the beautiful, big-breasted seductress Antonie, a thousand times with the same dull kitchen knife her lover had pulled out of the drawer during an obviously heated argument. Some called what ailed Trace writer's block. God, how he loathed that term. He knew it was all bullshit. He knew there was no such thing. Then why, why was he in such a state? His wife, the erotic novelist, Addison Stern, was upstairs humming away on her laptop. He could hear her click-clacking on the keys every time he got up and walked to the window, taking his ear buds out, silencing the Nirvana that he incessantly played on his iPod. He did that a lot. Getting up. Walking to the window. As if the old hemlock he stared at was going to start spewing words from its trunk or swaying branches. Or the swing-set that sat vacated, its chains no longer clutched by the hands of a laughing child, would give him an insight into his next line of prose. He had been dry for a while. Addison was stealing his thunder; her runaway bestseller, 'Cum, Cum With Me', was getting rave reviews. Sure, he was happy for her. Who wouldn't be pleased for his spouse and/or fellow novelist.

He loved her after all and longed to see her content, happy and successful. She had already begun working on her second novel. He was shocked at how quickly she had completed her first. Six months! As a fellow writer - forget the marriage thing - this seemed ludicrous. She hadn't even been a writer when he met her. She worked at the Lancome Cosmetic counter at Nordstrom, obviously happy painting the faces of suburban, middle-aged housewives. At least, that's what she had expressed to him. Until that day. That day he saw her planted firmly in front of her laptop, coffee in hand. The words poured from her.

Click-clack. Click-clack.

He was dumbfounded.

He first laid eyes on Addison when she was in line at his book signing event at The Page Turner, a local bookstore he had frequented for years that adored him. He was only an hour into the signing of 'It's Complicated' and already jonesing for a quad Americano from Starbucks. As he closed his eyes briefly, shifting in his chair, there she was. Auburn hair, flawless ivory skin, green eyes, and breasts so wonderful he thought he heard himself gasp. She wore a light green dress, loosely tied at the waist with an orange scarf. Her hair, slightly curled, fell a tinge below her lovely bosom. He immediately started writing poetry to her in his head.

Not since Ms. Madden, the third grade school teacher whom he had a crush on, had he been so taken by a woman. He remembered his second week of pushing broom at Horace Mann Elementary, seeing Ms. Madden for the first time. She had called him into her classroom. Her blackboard was slipping on one side. He brushed her breast as he rushed to help her, giving him an instant erection. He knew after work he would go home and rub one out envisioning her writhing underneath him all the while. Same ol', same ol'.

"To Addison, my number one fan," burst from her full, cherry lip-sticked mouth. Her lashes long, fluttering as she spoke. He opened the book that he hadn't noticed she had already handed him and began to write. Had he even said anything back to her? He couldn't recall. He thought he had mumbled an OK, still mesmerized by her. He then closed the book, handing it back to her. She winked, whispered thank you, and walked away, her ass equally intoxicating. At precisely nine o'clock as the book store owner ushered him out turning the 'open' sign over to 'sorry we missed you', she was there.

She poured out of the shadows like one of the characters from his novel. She wore a long coat. Had she been wearing that before? No, he thought to himself, remembering the green dress. He hadn't seen her carrying a coat either. Before another thought entered his word-riddled brain, her mouth was on his. Her lips full, soft, and perfect.

Her tongue moving into his mouth, seeking his. Suddenly, shocking himself, he grabbed her hair, pulling her head back, and began ferociously licking her neck. Her moans low and soft as she opened her coat. She was naked, her breasts full, her nipples pink and so erect, his cock pushing against his pants, aching for her. Trace Urban never knew what hit him. They were married six months later.

Trace had always been single. He liked it that way. No one to muddy the waters of his ever-flowing mind. No time for partying, dating, bar hopping, and getting laid. After graduation from high school, he took a job as a custodian at the local elementary school just so he would have time to devote and focus on his one true love. Writing. He watched his high school friends date, go to college, get good jobs, and eventually marry. At twenty-five after numerous submissions and rejections, he got his big break.

His novel 'Games Of Mine' became an overnight success after its stellar review by the New York Times. He was in. Two years later came 'Bang Bang, Lights Out' and then 'The Triangle Letter' which became a blockbuster movie starring Johnny Depp two years later. He wrote another two novels, 'Mystery Loves Company' and 'It's Complicated,' both on the bestseller list for weeks.

That was a couple of years ago. He was forty-one now. He admired the writers that could pump out dozens and dozens of books at the blink of an eye. The likes of Louis L'Amour, Michael Crichton, Anne Rice, Roald Dahl, and his favorite, Stephen King. He often lay in bed at night, thinking of King closing his laptop and yelling to his wife, Tabitha, that he had just finished writing novel one hundred and one. Let's open a bottle of champagne and fuck all night, Tab dear! Yeah, he longed for that drive, that creative spirit that dwelled within King, prompting him to pump out novel after novel as though it were something he could do in his sleep. King was a God. And he, Trace, as usual, felt inadequate.

Click clack, click clack.

Addison. He was the writer, not she. It was, after all, his title, his description, his fate. He loved the attention, the spark he felt when asked if he was THE Trace Urban, award-winning crime author. His years of reclusion, drinking, and late night hunkering down over his laptop had been finally paying off. He had played the game, had earned it. What had Addison done to earn it? Nothing. Not a goddamn thing. Nope. Nada. He lay down on the blue velvet ottoman his mother had purchased after his first success. He closed his eyes, still hearing the click-clack, click-clack of Addison's fingernails on the keys.

*   *   *

He woke with a start. He had heard the creak of the swing-set. The chains needed oil, and he knew it every time the wind howled. The creaking would wake him. This time, there was no wind. He quickly got up and looked out the window. He closed his eyes, reopening them slowly, for he was sure he wasn't seeing what he was seeing. A man, a young man with dark hair and a beard, was sitting on the swing, his hands clutching the chains. Addison was atop of him, riding him, her dress hiked up around her thighs, her head tilted back, her beautiful breasts exposed to the bearded man, her eyes closed. Pleasure written across her face, her body.

He looked closer, his eyes still adjusting to the bright sun. She was riding him faster now, her breasts bouncing to the rhythm of their fucking. He knew that rhythm all too well. Soon, the bearded man would spew his seed into her but not before she orgasmed; he was sure she was almost there. He couldn't bear to see this. His heart seemed as though it were splitting open, the contents running down the front of his shirt. He stepped back, closed his eyes.

Click-clack, click-clack.

Addison's fingernails on the keys. The sound so loud. He heard her moan, the long, guttural sound of her cumming. Her screeching in the backyard as her lover's cock moved inside of her, pleasing her without end. He stepped back again, his hands over his ears, and fell back onto the blue ottoman. He sat there, desperately trying to block out his wife's moans.

Click-clack, click, clack.

He got up, not sure of how long he had sat there, his hands still covering his ears. Laughter. Addison's giggles mixing with the bearded man's low, deep chuckle. They were mocking him. Making fun of him. He was sure of it. He ran down the stairs, tripping over one of Addison's shoes at the bottom.

Click-clack, click-clack, click-clack.

They were both standing in the kitchen, drinking water from the same glass and laughing as they spilt it down their chins. They didn't even see him grab the knife, plunging it into the back of the bearded man. Addison's screams loud in his ears. So loud. What did you expect, Addison? Why would you defy me? I fucking write crime, you fucking bitch! The house was quiet. No laughing, no mocking him. No more click-clack, click-clack.

Trace Urban was un-stuck. The words flowed. Success. The big-breasted heroine was dead. She lay on the kitchen floor, her blood pooling around her. Now the only click-clack, click-clack came from Trace's own fingers, working feverishly late into the night, not noticing the blood of Addison hardening on his jeans.

My Comforter

poem

His voice makes me laugh.
No, like really, really laugh. Not just a
Chuckle, mind you.
But tears running down my cheeks kind of
laughter.
The kind of laughter that makes me forget
My anger
My loneliness
My anxiety
My exhaustion
My frustration
My sadness.
His voices, so different,
Each with their own personality

If that is possible.

But alas, it is.

The Puerto Rican

The Black

The Honky

The Mexican

The simple minded one who masturbates in public

The Italian

The black lady on welfare

The New Yorker

The guy from Connecticut.

There are more, believe you me.

They lurk, waiting to come out again

Whenever I am feeling

Not so me.

Homeless Baby

short story

I didn't start out that way. Homeless, I mean. Well, that is a weird statement, because no one starts out that way, homeless. I started in a warm place, a safe place, a comfortable place. Well, usually safe. A few things that came down the feeding tube, rushing into my veins were probably not the best things for me. Some made me feel weird. The alcohol made me giddy and smile. The cigarettes, lucid. The heroin, whoa!!! The best part was the food. The stuff that made me fat, nourished me. Well, it wasn't nourishing, or good for me really, but it was food. There were Funyons. And Cheetos. Stacks of Pringles. Raspberry and Apple Pop Tarts. An occasional microwaved burrito and a continual barrage of blue raspberry slurpee's from 7-Eleven. Those were wonderful, the sugar causing my feet to kick, my lips to smack.

I came early. I don't know if my mother even knew she was pregnant. She was on the streets, getting her fix every way and any way she could. An employee from Dick's Drive In found her body in the alley, behind the restaurant, near the bathrooms, when he was taking out the garbage. It wasn't so much the body that freaked him out. It was all the blood. Murder and mayhem ran across his mind. Could the killer still be lurking? Who could do this, near beloved Dick's to a young woman? The cops were called. An ambulance was behind them. The place was taped off. There was a huge crowd, gawking and gossiping, exchanging lewd comments or making up their own stories about how my mother was murdered and why. She was just a junkie on the street, they would say. Then they would walk away, still chewing on their Dick's deluxe with extra sauce, thinking... she won't be missed...life goes on....who the fuck cares... what a drain on society....good riddance...just taking out the trash. Perhaps they thought that because a needle was still sticking out of my mother's arm when the EMT's put her lifeless body on the gurney. So much blood.

The next day, the employees of Dick's would find out that she hadn't been murdered at all. She had died from an overdose of heroin. Then where the fuck did all the blood come from they wondered. Apparently as she lay dying, she gave birth at the same time to a baby girl. Now the question on everyone's mind was not what had happened to my mother, but what happened to the baby?

I was spirited away by Skiddish (Skid for short), Fang, Reba, Gordo, Little Prick and Jesus (pronounced

'Hey-Soos'). A mischief of rats. Now, before you go doubting the strength of rats, and how could they possibly lug, tote and/or cart off an infant, anything is possible. First of all, there is strength in numbers, and secondly, if your will is strong enough, well, it's that mind over matter thing. The rats were saving me from the system that I would most certainly go into following the death of my mother. They knew the system all too well. They had all hailed from it. Their stories, all similar to mine. They were the products of addicted parents, numerous abuses, both mentally and physically, and many foster homes. In and out, backwards and forwards, placed and misplaced over and over again as children. Somehow the system had failed each and every one of them. They became angry teenagers, eventually growing into bitter, abusive adults.

Let's start with Gordo. He earned his name by being the most ravenous and the largest of the rats. He had murdered two convenience store clerks during a robbery. There was Skid, who was nervous and easily spooked. He had killed a fellow classmate in seventh grade for his Air Jordans. There was Reba, the only female and a singer of country tunes. She stabbed her husband forty seven times when she found out he was boning her best friend. There was Little Prick, the arsonist, who had burned down his father's building for the insurance money. Five firefighters battling the blaze were trapped and died in the inferno. There was Fang, on account of one spikey tooth that curled down past his rat lip, looking like a talon about ready to pierce it's pray. He was a pedophile. He started out as a child playing doctor with the neighborhood kids. As a teenager he fondled and molested children at a camp he was a counselor at. When he was twenty-three, he raped, strangled and buried the bodies of two girl scouts out selling cookies on a Saturday afternoon. Last but not least was Jesus, a bad ass chicano that had murdered three border patrol officers because they had detained him too long for his liking, blessing them and reciting the Lord's prayer as he blew their brains out with his .22.

This gnarly group of vagabond misfit murderous rats were paying for their heinous acts. After their human bodies had died, their souls were sent back, as punishment for their crimes. They were to live their next life as they had lived their human lives, as rats, one of the lower forms on the planet. But they weren't lower, and they knew it. As best as a rat could know these things. They were good, sweet and kind. But no one ever hung with them long enough to see that. No one cared, no one listened, no one understood.

They had a chance to make things right, to do the right thing, and who was to say what was right or wrong in my case? Their particular act of toting me away was one of love, pure and simple. Well, not entirely. Okay, not at all. Well, not at first. They wanted another shot at life. They wanted the opportunity to come back in human form. They knew it had been done before. They had talked to plenty of humans. The ones that hung with them feeding them scraps from their back porches. Or those that sat on park benches, flinging seeds and bread from their palms, allowing them to scurry around their legs without flinching. They had said things like, once I was a rat just like you. Before that I was a human. A very bad one. I am on my third life now. Just trying to get it right, one life at a time. Yea, they said weird shit like that. Some of the 'bad apples' came back as parasites. Parasites in the form of lice, infusing blood from some disheveled dirty-haired child's scalp. Jumping from tot to tot, gulping the 'red juice'. Delectable it was. Then there were the roaches. The scurrying little bastards, eating their way across the shelves of America. Dining in and out of bags of garbage, boxes of cornflakes, fancy restaurants and dingy, poorly lit dives. Dick's Drive In on Capitol Hill was a popular hang-out for all the fuckers. The roaches, the parasites, the rats, the addicts and sadly, my mother.

Gordo was the first furry friend on the scene. His piercing rat whistle brought the rest of the rats soon after. It was Reba's idea to take me. She had been a mother herself, leaving a two-year-old behind after the slaughter of her husband. The guilt she felt for leaving her child, parentless, oddly enough lay heavily on her tiny brain. Acts of passion caused a relatively sane person to lose all self-control. That was her defense. So, this was her way of making it up, serving up her penance. She couldn't believe her luck. She took my birth as a sign. A chance to get it right. Her motives were selfish in nature. She was just looking out for herself. Don't we all? Humans and animals alike. Survival of the fittest.

Of course, the rest of the gang didn't argue with her. Reba could pretty much get what she wanted. She put out, after all. I never got the entire story of how they actually stole me away into the night. It had been shared between humans and animals alike many times, each time being exaggerated by the storyteller, loving the impact and bizarreness of it all, enjoying the look of pure doubt in the listener's eyes. Something about rolling me onto an empty garbage bag and pulling me through an alley on Capitol Hill, ending up in the back of a dilapidated, abandoned building where the group had built their nest. It was there, in that cold, dark, dreary, rat and cockroach ridden room that they cared for me. They fed me food they had chewed on, almost liquefying, and emptying from their mouths, like a mother bird does, into mine. Blankets were found. Baby clothes were snatched from strollers, or from the bags left outside of a Salvation Army after it had closed. They collected the tops from plastic bottles, leaving them outside to fill with the rain that seemed to fall incessantly, then carrying each lid back and forth, filling my tiny mouth with water.

When it was sunny, they took me to the window, my little body absorbing as much Vitamin D as it could. They cleaned me, on a regular basis, their tongues constantly licking, grooming. If you were to look closely at my skin, you would see tiny scratches all up and down from their claws 'petting me', 'loving me.' When I cried, they nestled their bodies against my cheek, my arms, soothing me with their fur. Reba would sing and it sounded like a high pitched hum. I would fall fast asleep. They all took turns caring for me, cleaning up the poo and piss. For the most part, they tolerated me. As best a rat can tolerate a baby. But not Little Prick. No. Little Prick fell in love. To most of the gang, especially to Reba, I was a chance. A chance to do the right thing, to care for something in their hope to come back again as humans. Little Prick had no ulterior motives for what he was doing. No personal gain. No selfishness. No narcissism.

When Little Prick looked into my eyes, he felt love. He was overwhelmed by it, actually. To Little Prick, I was helpless, homeless and a baby. He was smart enough to know I needed care, nurturing and love. When food was scarce, he made sure I got his share and more. There were many times he would lay in wait for the plump Gordo to fall asleep, then scurry around his nest, quickly gathering morsels that Gordo had stashed away for a late night rendezvous with hunger. Little Prick, smarter than shit, really. He had taken the most from his human life. An acute recollection, locked away in his brain. The rest of the rats could recall only bits and pieces of their lives as humans, mostly their crimes, watching their murderous acts over and over again on replay. It was part of their punishment. Little Prick on the other hand, could recall entire days, weeks, sometimes months of his previous life. He grew up much differently than the others.

He was raised over-indulged and silver spoon fed, in the frothy rich city called Mercer Island, a suburb of Seattle. While the other rats could argue that their childhoods, filled with poverty, abuse, foster homes and drugs had a hand in their demise, Little Prick would not hesitate to say that growing up on the other side of that coin had its downfall as well. There was that whole entitlement thing, for fuck's sake. It was great when he was a kid, but being a teenager on the 'island' with not much to do, had its fair share of ramifications. Kids with cash meant late night drives to Seattle, to get drunk, stoned, or coked up. Not much else to kill the lull. Of course, all the parents had the 'my kid wouldn't do that' attitude, material things being the bulk of mommy and daddies love. Little Prick didn't know his dad was knee deep in bogus investing of other people's money. He didn't know that his father was being audited by the IRS, or that his mother had been stashing money away in an off-shore account, planning to flee the marriage and hook up with her lover. Little Prick did know that he had been accepted into Yale and he couldn't wait to get the hell out of the Island.

He remembered the day his father had asked him to burn down one of their properties. He recalled his father's tired face, the look of desperation clearly written all over it. Son, we don't have as much in savings as I thought.

We need this insurance money. You want to drive a nice car to Yale, right? Little Prick had no idea what he was getting into when he told his father 'yes' on that fateful day. That people would lose their lives because of his and his father's greed. They never got away with it. His dad was sent to prison for thirty years. Little Prick, because he was a minor, got fifteen. He also remembered the day he was 'sprung'. The first clear day after ninety days of Seattle drizzle. He counted the steps that led him away from the prison. One, two, three, four, five. On the sixth step he fell dead, his heart deciding it was done beating.

As I lay sleeping, Little Prick nestled against my cheek. He told me in his little rat squeaks, that I was the first thing he had ever loved in his life. His human life, and now his rat life. I grew and flourished in that tiny room of an abandoned building in an alleyway on Capitol Hill, just a stone throw from my birthplace, good ol' Dick's Drive In. It was when I began to crawl that the rats called a meeting. Soon she will be walking, they squeaked. She will need to be outside. To run, jump and play, they exclaimed, their chattering sounding more like whistling. She will need to be with humans. We are too small to care for her. There is nothing else for us to do now.

They wouldn't be able to care for me anymore. The rats had already decided who those humans would be some time ago. The wisest of the wise, of all humans. Those closest to the dirt, the grit, the air, the sea and mountains. The only ones who knew the arrogance, selfishness, and stupidity of the white man. The ones that would surely know what to do with 'homeless baby.' The Indians. The Suquamish, to be exact. They could be found in the early mornings, gathering in Victor Steinbrueck Park, on the north end of Pike Place Market.

Most of them lived in Indianola, home to the Port Madison Reservation, just a short ferry ride from Seattle. What better place to hide and raise a baby, then on an Indian Reservation. Little Prick began to tear. His head hung. He asked to leave the group. To stay with me. He didn't want to live otherwise. The rats didn't see any harm in that.

Jesus and Fang took off to communicate with a murder of crows. They were the messengers to and for the Indians. In fact, the crows were the communicators between most of the city dwelling animals. They were the peacekeepers as well. As most humans see crows as a sign of death, or bad luck, this is in fact not true at all. The Indians saw the crow as highly intelligent, curious and simply misunderstood.

It was all arranged. A few days later, the twenty-three-year old daughter of Chief Running Reservoir, Lotus, got on a ferry from Indianola, an empty stroller in tow, headed for Seattle. It was a crisp but sunny day. It would be the first time I would be out, since my birth. The timing was good, for soon it would be November and the threat of snow and freezing temperatures would be inevitable. There would be no way for the rats to keep me warm much longer.

Lotus never made it to me in time. Had she, my human life would not have ended before it had barely begun. Instead, she along with many others would be kept back away from the burning building. There was so much smoke she couldn't even tell which building was on fire. The murder of crows that had gathered, and their incessant 'cawing' became jumbled words in Lotus's head. It was too hard for her to decipher anything with all the noise and commotion.

Reba, Gordo, Skiddish, Fang and Jesus all made it out. They tried to move me, but I was much bigger now, and they just didn't have enough time. They cried as they scurried out, sad and heartbroken, as much as a rat can be. Little Prick stayed with me, never even thinking for one moment of saving himself. You see, he believed this to be his destiny. His human life had ended as he knew it, the night the Seattle fire fighters had died in a blaze he had created. The fact that he would perish the same way was karma. That he knew. Now we are two souls together on the same playing field. We wait, for our next life, whatever that may be, be it human or animal form. We hope to be together, but it isn't for us to decide, one way or the other.

Be Patient

poem

*B*e patient,

He told me.

How do you tell a dying man,

I can't be patient, dammit! You're fucking dying!!

How do I say to him,

But, you don't have time. Patience takes time. You don't have,

T

I

M

E

That I knew, in my gut.

That I felt.

Make your way back to me,

I say to him.

Be patient, baby,

He says to me.

We will stay a weekend at Pensione Nichols,

In Pike Place Market,

I say to him.

We will watch the ferry boats come in with the dawn and

Go out with the dusk,

He says to me.

Yes, God yes, I want that,

I say to him.

He says to me,

I can't wait to see your brown eyes, again.

To run my fingers through your long brown hair, again.

To kiss your full lips, again.

Yes, God yes. I want that,

I say to him.

When, when, when will that be?

I ask him.

I don't know baby. The doctors tell me I am too weak to travel.

But, soon. Soon,

He says to me.

Honey, my eyebrows grew back in! Isn't that great?

My thoughts brighten when I hear him say this.

This to me seems like a good thing.

No, a fucking great thing.

But then he says,

I feel so sick, baby. Like really, so sick.

I forgot what it felt like to feel normal.

And I am so tired, baby. Exhausted. So sick.

My tears well up. I feel them run down my cheeks.

He mustn't hear me cry.

I must stay positive.

Then I say,

Whatever you need. Let me know. I will climb a mountain.

For you.

Let me know what is going on all the time.

He says to me,

Ok. I will. Just be patient, ok? I don't have all the answers.

But,

I will definitely keep you in the loop,

He assures me.

I say to him,

Of course, I'll be patient.

He died three days later.

Thursday's Child Has Far To Go

short story

I knew which suitcase was hers. It was a little pink jobby with a fluffy white lamb decoupaged on the front. I watched her get out of her car then opening the back door, her braids brushing against her cheek as she bent down towards the back seat to retrieve the suitcase. She had on a pink, green, and white plaid skirt, skimming just above her knees, and a white, cotton, short-sleeved blouse, buttoned all the way up. Her white anklets were folded in a neat cuff, made perfect no doubt by the hands of her caring mother. Saddle shoes. Braided, dirty blonde hair. Glasses which looked like small goggles, her eyesight obviously quite diminished.

She had a handful of zits, one looking recently popped, redness showing through the concealer she had tried to hide it with. She would never be or breathe in the same air as the 'EE's.' The name I had given to the popular girls. 'The EE's.' Upon seeing each other on arrival at school, or perhaps between classes, or at lunch hour, or maybe just for the fuck of it, they would grab each other, hug, jump up and down, and squeal what sounded like an endless spray of eeeeeeeeeeeeeeeeeeees! Yeah, just like that. 'The EE's.' They were the pretty girls, the popular girls. Their skin was perfect. Their hair was silky. Their breasts were bouncy. Clothed in the latest trends. No sister's or neighbor's hand-me-downs for them. NO WAY. They were the girls the boys masturbated to. They were the girls I wanted to be. And if I couldn't be them, I at least wanted them to like me.

She shut the car door and ran around the back of it to the driver's side. I saw her kiss the caring mother. A few brief words were exchanged. Inaudible, but I guessed them to be....Now, mind your manners. Be courteous, cautious, and caring! Did you remember to write your name in your bible? Yes! Yes! Okay, I will. Love you. Miss you already. Then caring mother drove away, yelling out the window, "I love you Stacy!!" Stacy watched her leave, the car tires kicking up a tremendous amount of dust on the gravel road. She looked a bit sad as she waved one hand in the air, the other holding tight to lamby suitcase. I wanted to talk to her, but I knew I wouldn't have time. I was waiting for Kristy, who was in the bushes off to the side of the road, no doubt finding a leaf to wipe with - or already had and was pulling up her panties. Her mother had driven us out to Lakeside Presbyterian Camp, and for the entire one hour drive Kristy had needed to take a piss.

"Why didn't you go at home?" her mother had snapped.

"I didn't have to go then!" Kristy snapped back.

The moment we exited the car, Kristy made a beeline for the bushes. Seconds later, Stacy and caring mother drove up. Now Stacy turned, standing there in the dust, looking like her dog had been put down. I could muster a "Hi" to her, but I didn't want to risk that. Kristi might see me talking to her, acknowledging her, which could spell double- doom for me. I couldn't take that chance. You see, Kristy was an 'EE', a popular girl. And she had asked me... me...to a weeklong summer camp.

I had never been to summer camp before. Summer camp was usually for the rich kids or the bratty ones whose parents wanted a week of relief from the long summer vacation. Kristy was the new girl, the shiny California girl who moved to our small town in early April. In two months, she had managed to catapult herself to the top tier of the popular chain. She had passed the likes of Shauna Greer, Nicole Roosevelt and Adina Adams. She was, at last check, the most popular girl in school and had first spoken to me during second period science class. It was to make a sassy remark in her California valley girl voice, dogging the teacher Mr. Dietrich's bad comb-over and mustard yellow plaid sweater. Of course, I nodded and laughed way more loudly than I should have. I didn't really hear the snide remark, for I was too clouded by the euphoric feeling of her even speaking to the likes of me. My fortune took an even bigger turn as the bell went off, class was dismissed, and Kristy, the shiny, new California girl, caught up to me, introducing herself as 'Kristy Compton from California'.

Yes, I know who you are, I thought to myself. I was rendered speechless, still grasping that her conversation was directed to me when she asked if I wanted to join her for lunch. This is a set up; don't do it, I said to myself. Her and her posse will pull a 'Carrie' on you, saturating you with pig's blood while the entire student body laughs hysterically. Sadly, that thought entered my head quickly but didn't exit quite as fast. I immediately looked around for the rest of her clan, perhaps lying in wait. She must have noticed my hesitation.

"It's ok if you can't, maybe some other..."

I quickly cut her off. "No, no! Sure, I'll join you. It sounds great."

Lunch went down smoothly. There was no pig's blood or a sign stuck to my back that said 'I'm farting'. We actually became pretty good friends, and, of course, I was instantly popular. I enjoyed hanging with the cool kids and having the best spot on the lawn, the best table in the cafeteria, and the cutest boys within reach. Things were good for a couple of months, then school let out in early June. I was actually grateful for the summer, not always having to worry from day to day whether I was 'in' or 'out'. After a month of summer vacation and not hearing from her, she called me on a Tuesday morning, wanting to know if I would be available to go to camp with her.

"Camp? Camp, what kind of camp?" I asked. I had never been to camp before. It sounded really cool. "Would there be parents there?"

"Yes," she said, "but not your own, so they are much nicer. Oh, and it's a church camp. Presbyterian."

" Oh no, Presbyterian? I can't go," I said, "I'm Catholic."

" Actually," she explained, "it really doesn't matter. You believe in Jesus, right?"

"Of course I believe in Jesus," I said.

He had been judging my every movement according to Sister Beatrice. I had been avoiding him lately at all costs. Since meeting Kristy, I had stolen eighteen packs of Juicy Fruit gum, three tubes of bubblegum-flavored Lip Smackers, two necklaces, four rings, and a pair of Ray Ban sunglasses. I had never stolen a thing in my entire life till Kristy showed up and I decided my being with the 'in crowd' was more important than one of the ten commandments, commanding me not to steal. Correction. Thou shalt not steal, to be exact.

Of course, none of the loot was for me. It was for Kristy and her posse. I guess I thought of it as more of giving than stealing since I didn't keep any of it. I tried justifying my actions any way I could, but I knew deep down inside wrong was wrong and this was fucked up.

I had also taken the Lord our God's name in vain a lot in front of Kristy and the posse, trying to look cool of course. In the Catholic religion, I knew I could go to confession, tell the priest behind the screen what I had done, say a couple of Hail Mary's, and all would be forgiven. However, I was pretty sure you could not be a repeat offender. That was just cheating the system, plain and simple. But this, this was different. Church camp. Basically a week of repentance! My prayers had been answered. This would be my time to do double repent duty for my various sins. I was certain that attending a few days of church camp would wipe my slate clean with the Lord our God. Sure of it.

"I'm in," I said, hanging up the phone.

Two days later, Kristy and her mom picked me up in their paneled station wagon. Kristi, looking all bright and shiny, her hair gleaming from her mayo treatment the night before, popping her juicy fruit gum as we pulled out of my driveway.

"Are you excited?" she asked, flipping herself over the front seat, one leg hitting her mother in the head as she landed on the seat next to me with a thud.

"Kristy Rose!" Screamed her mother, "I told you not to do that anymore!"

Kristy ignored her. "Mom, turn up the radio, it's Karen Carpenter. Don't you just love the Carpenters?" Kristy asked, grabbing my hand. She began to sing 'Ticket To Ride' loudly and out of tune as we made our way down the road and on to church camp.

"Now behave yourselves, and I will see you on Wednesday. Miss you already, honey o' mine," her mother called after us in her sweetest mother voice. 'Who was she kidding?' I thought, grabbing my suitcase as Kristy made a dash for the bushes. She looked happy as hell as she drove away, most likely looking forward to the peace and quiet that would ensue from having her only child gone for a few days.

It's all about timing, and, had the timing been different, things might have changed course, gone a different way, and Kristy may never have laid eyes on poor Stacy. But, sadly, she did, and as Stacy passed by us, looking already beaten, her eyes to the ground, Kristy smiled that witchy smile, her teeth pearly white as she nudged me and said,

"Oh, boy, this should be fun."

Camp was fun. Well, the first day anyway. Upon arrival, we were given a schedule and shown to our respective cabins. There were two cabins of ten girls, two cabins of ten guys, and about eight counselors. Our cabin mother/counselor led our group into Cabin A. Our luggage was individually gone through by her, making sure we hadn't smuggled in drugs or alcohol. All luggage was locked up, accessible to us in the evenings and mornings only. Supposedly, that rule kept us from hiding anything. The only thing we were allowed to carry on our person was our bibles.

Stacy was in our cabin. I noticed right off no one was talking to her. She had taken her bible out and was reading from it, lying on her bunk on her stomach. Big mistake. Come on, even I, never having been to church camp, knew that was not something you wanted anyone to see you do, especially if you wanted to be part of the 'cool kid' crowd. Sure-fire ways to look like a bible-thumping, loser dipshit. Pray in public. Make the sign of the cross in public. Sing religious hymns in public. The only thing I ever read that was worthy enough to warrant laying on one's stomach, on one's bed (in other words, this position means you are giving your reading material your utmost attention; it is that engrossing) was Penthouse magazine (not the pics, Forum only), Nancy Friday's My Mother, My Self, and French Vogue (for the sexy pics because I couldn't read French). So not only was she engrossed in the bible in public, but she was also reading aloud to herself. Huge mistake.

We all exchanged 'the glance'. Stacy had just won the role of top nerd, top dweeb, and was easy pickings. Was I a dweeb before the likes of Kristy saw something redeeming in me? Maybe I am still a dweeb and just too stupid to realize it (this thought had not entered my mind yet but would in a few days). I had empathy for Stacy. In fact, the old me would have befriended her, sitting side-by-side at lunch, eventually inviting her for sleepovers, commenting to her how much I loved her lamby suitcase and could the hands of caring mother make me one as well? But obviously, that isn't what happened, or you wouldn't be reading this story.

As I said, the first day of camp was fine. Well, fine until Stacy decided to read her bible in front of us, engrossed as hell. Now, I know you're thinking it's a goddamn church camp, you're supposed to do that.

Yes, but only when instructed to by an adult other than your parent.

Even sitting in Wednesday night CCD class when Sister Beatrice told us to take out our bibles and turn to page 321, I laid a smutty book between pages 321 and 322, never having really read one single page out of that dreadful book. Now, I did tell you I planned on doing some repentance, but that repentance in my eyes was just being at camp, pure and simple. Don't tell me you don't know someone who actually thinks their weekly stint to church on Sunday is their ticket into the pearly gates. Hey, I was just a kid, I didn't know any better.

Anyway, California Kristy decided it would be a hoot to make Stacy's stay at camp one of hell, and because I wanted to keep Kristy as a friend, reaping all the benefits that friendship brought me, I was not about to say This isn't right or Let's not do this. I had become a true piece of shit. It started by Kristy telling everyone in our cabin not to speak to Stacy. Then she hit cabin B. And moved onto the boys cabins, C and D. They would have burned themselves, shaved their heads, or some other crazy-ass shit, just hoping they might have a chance with her.

The silent treatment to some loser girl in cabin A, well, piece of cake. The silent treatment didn't seem to faze Stacy in the least bit. Sadly, that was probably a daily occurrence for her. No one sat with her during our first dinner. The counselors weren't stupid, they had seen it a million times. Our cabin mother came over, reading us the riot act, Stacy and her dinner tray in tow. Kristy smiled her amazing smile, saying it must have been an oversight. Of course, once Stacy sat down and the counselor walked away, the cold shoulder ensued.

On the second day as Stacy was showering, we removed her clothes and towel. She must have screamed for at least an hour before a counselor found her, cold and crying, sitting on the cold tiled shower floor next to the drain. There were a couple more heinous acts against Stacy that I won't go into because what it all comes down to is the suitcase, Stacy's lamby suitcase and the decision I had made regarding that suitcase. Kristy had seen where our cabin mother had hidden the key after locking our belongings away. She had a great idea and, because I still wanted to be her friend, I went along with her great idea.

We snuck away from a 'Kumbaya' sing-along, making our way back to our cabin. Kristy found the key hidden away under a pot of ivy by the front door. We entered the cabin, and as we walked across the creaky wooden floor, I wondered at what age Kirsty had become a bitch. As we stood in front of the locked cabinet, me slightly behind her, I could smell her hair. Expensive shampoo. Maybe that new one that came out, 'Gee, Your Hair Smells Terrific'. My mother wouldn't buy it. I use Prell. As she unlocked the padlock, she turned to me suddenly.

"You are sure it's the one with the lamb?"

"Of course I'm sure," I said, surprised she was doubting me. I saw her with it when caring mother dropped her off, I thought.

"Well, grab it then, hurry!" Kristy said, seeming annoyed with me. I am being used, and I am just too stupid to see it. I grabbed it quickly and, in doing so, the latch opened, spilling the contents on the dirty cabin floor. A toothbrush, toothpaste. Journal. Small photo album. Carmex. Two nightgowns, one yellow, one blue, with lace around the neck and the cuffs. Socks. Tennis shoes. A small make-up bag. Various shorts, skirts and shirts. Underwear, emblazoned with the days of the week. Kristy grabbed a pair. A dirty pair. Like, not just dirty, but crusty and yellowish dirty. She held them up, with the very tips of two fingers, as though they were highly diseased and already the cooties inside the crotch were doing a slow crawl up her arm. Kristy slightly turned them, the word Saturday written in cursive across the ass. It was only Friday. She had worn them out of turn. I began to think of the little poem my grandmother taught me years ago. Monday's child is fair of face. Tuesday's child is full of grace. Wednesday's child is full of woe, Thursday's child has far to go. I forgot the rest. I only remembered to Thursday, because I was born on one. Grammy, what does that mean, I have far to go? I didn't like that one. I wanted to be Monday's child.

"Oh, God," said Kristy, her face totally scrunched up, looking extremely unattractive for probably the first time in her life. "These are disgusting!" she said, pushing the lamby suitcase towards me with her foot. "Now hurry, put everything back in except the journal, and close it. HURRY!" She stood up as I gathered the contents, shoving them back in and snapping the latch shut.

Where was this going? What is she doing? At that moment, I wanted to run. At that moment I wanted to scream at her. I am not doing this Kirsty!

"Here, take the key, lock it up, hurry before we get caught." I tossed lamby suitcase into the pile, noticing mine was at the bottom. I closed the closet door, fiddling with the padlock.

"Why are you so slow?" Kristy screamed at me, eyes glaring. "Do you want us to get caught?"

Yeah, I want us to get caught. I want you to get caught. I want to see how you smile and lie your way out of this one with your beauty and charm.

"Of course I don't, but…"

Kristy came towards me, grabbing the padlock. "Hold these," she said, jutting Saturday's underwear in my face. "I have to do everything," she said, pushing the padlock into place and giving it a snap, the sound it made ensuring it was locked. This was a side I hadn't seen in her. Or had I every day since she had introduced herself? Once bad, always bad. Serial killers are born that way, don't you know. Evil to the core they are. Born that way! My grandfather had told me this when Son of Sam was on his rampage.

Kristy suddenly grabbed the soiled underwear from me and ran toward the door. I followed her as if I was still on a mission, a mission to please, a mission to be accepted, to be liked. How far will you go to destroy someone for someone else's approval? Will you sell your soul to the devil to be liked, accepted, one of the 'EEs'?

"Put the journal under your pillow!" Kristy screamed back at me, already out the door standing by the flagpole. What the fuck is she doing? "Go down the trail a ways; make sure no one is coming!" She said, her beautiful hair bouncing on her shoulders. She was hoisting the flag down, pulling the rope so quickly that it only took seconds and the flag was in her grasp. She removed it just as quickly, replacing it with Stacy's soiled Saturday underwear. A few quick tugs of the rope, and the undies were high above us, flying in front of our cabin, very visible. Inside out of course. My mouth flew open. It was at that moment - that too late moment - that I came to my senses.

Suddenly...ding, ding, ding. The bell signaling us all back to our cabins to wash up for dinner. Kristy suddenly ran past me, grabbing my hand.

"Quick, quick!"

We ran down to the middle of the trail and hid in the bushes. The scuttle of kids scurrying past us on the trail, their laughter and talking echoing in the forest. That's where I should be, with them, not here hiding. The mean girl. Isn't that what I hated about the 'EEs'? They were bitches, and now, I was one, too. I looked at Kristy, beautiful Kristy with the killer boobs, stunning smile, and hot body.

She looked back at me. "What? This will be great. Come on."

We stepped out onto the path, catching up with the rest of the kids. They had already gathered around Cabin A. I heard the laughter first, then I saw their faces. They were pointing and laughing. Laughing at the disgusting underwear that was fluttering in the wind. Kristy whispered in my ear, "Look at Stacy!" She pointed her out almost directly across from us. Stacy was laughing as well, but I could tell she was crying inside.

"Gross! I wonder whose underwear those are? Those puppies are fucking disgusting! Eeewwwww!"

Everyone was laughing. I laughed, too. I had to. I didn't want anyone to think they were mine. Watching Stacy's face was painful. Two counselors came in, breaking up the melee. They seemed very angry, demanding to know who had done something so mean, so horrible as they fumbled to hoist them back down the flagpole. One left, coming back a few seconds later wearing a pair of gardening gloves. He grabbed the underwear, asking the stupid questions.

"Who do these belong to?" and "Who did this?" A couple of the guys claimed them in a girl's voice. We all laughed even harder. The counselor then tossed them into the garbage, telling everyone to go wash up for dinner.

I am pretty sure everyone knew whose underwear they were. It was obvious. Kristy was still laughing as she turned to me.

"Wasn't that great? Did you see her face?"

"Yeah, you really got her good," I said, feeling like the lowest life form in the world. I slinked back into the cabin, retrieving Stacy's journal from under my pillow, hiding it under my shirt. I told Kristy I would catch up with her. Most everyone had cleared out of the cabin.

I opened the journal. 'Property of Stacy' was written in beautiful calligraphy inside the front cover most likely by the hands of caring mother. I laid it on Stacy's bunk then made my way to dinner.

Stacy never showed up for dinner. She wasn't at campfire sing-along either. In fact, as we all filed into Cabin A to get ready for bed, our cabin mother came in.

"Listen up everyone! Stacy has gone home, sudden case of the flu, or something. Is anyone else feeling ill?" No one said a word. She didn't have the flu. She went home because I, we, had made her life miserable. I looked over at her bed. Her journal and pillow were gone. I suddenly raised my hand.

"I'm not feeling well." I was lying, but I would take care of that next Sunday at confession. In fact, I would take care of a lot of shit next Sunday at confession. Father Ryan wouldn't know what had hit him.

"All right then. Go to the dining hall, and call your parents. See if they can come pick you up. It's late, so if they can't come until tomorrow, you can stay in the nurse's cabin tonight."

All I managed to say was "Okay" as I got up off my bunk where I had been sitting criss cross applesauce. I walked by Kristy without saying a word. My eyes said everything.

I didn't talk to Kristy the rest of the summer, nor did she talk to me. I started school in the fall as the same girl I was before she had looked my way, inviting me to join her posse. I lost my popularity. I was no longer one of the cool girls, one of the 'EEs'. I was back to staying home on the weekends, watching 'Mutual of Omaha's Wild Kingdom' on Saturday nights with my dad just like old times. I still think about Stacy a lot. I think about how badly I may have hurt her. I wondered if she ran into the arms of the caring mother, sobbing. Or was she too embarrassed to tell her mother, choosing instead to cry into her pillow?

Wherever you are, Stacy, I'm sorry.

Friends

poem

I have this friend.
This male friend.
You know, the one that
Holds you longer
When you hug?
The one that looks into
Your eyes when you talk.
The one that gets you
When you're down.
The one that tells you that
You are fucking amazing,
Beautiful, talented, artistic.
The one that tells you
All of his

Insecurities, his joys,

His loves, his breaks,

His weaknesses, his conquests,

Knowing full well I won't judge.

I tell him of my shortcomings,

My elation, my grief, my escapades,

My fucked up life,

Knowing he won't see me

In a different light.

He only sees me in one light.

His light.

We have known

Each other for years.

He is beautiful,

Charismatic, funny

Sensitive and creative.

I would do anything for him.

He says he would do anything for me.

Move mountains for me,

Walk miles for me.

Whatever you need, he says.

Whatever you need.

My friends say, can't you see

How he loves you?

That he loves you?
That he holds you
That certain way?
Ha...I say, nah, we are just friends.
Just friends, you see.
Only friends.
He doesn't love me like that.
I don't love him like that.
I have this friend,
This male friend.
You know, the one that
Holds you
When you hug?

Cancer

poem

The putrid toxicity
runs through his
sinewy beautiful body
unbeknownst to him.
It moves past
his golden, loving, beating heart
as we sit in a movie theatre,
holding hands and giggling
like school children.
It slides itself under crevices,
sneaking its venom into
his beautiful lungs,
dumping itself there,
deciding to take up permanent residence
as he anxiously asks me

how my day was,
a quick kiss on my lips.
It grows like a weed.
A sleazy rancid, foul, nidorous, contaminated thug weed,
as we sit on chairs
in front of a tattoo parlor,
watching the bustle
of a late Saturday night crowd
mingle on Capitol Hill.
He tells me how happy he is.
How we need to do this more often,
as he looks through the window
of the tattoo parlor
contemplating getting another one.
Never a sign.
Never a warning.
Never a hint.
Where is your red flag
you miserable piece of shit,
as you decide to take another victim?
Why must you hide?
Why must you cause so much damage
before you are ever found?
Show yourself you
pathetic

self-absorbed

selfish

hateful

sack of

pure evil.

He holds me tight as though I will dissipate.

He breathes in the smell

of my skin

my hair

as though it will be the last time.

Does he feel the impending doom somehow?

He sits next to me on the cold concrete patio,

moving his fingers between my toes

as I drink a glass of wine.

He talks about simple things.

Life according to him.

His love for everyone.

His devotion.

His love for me.

His caring for others

comes to him as easily

as another man breathes.

He would take a bullet for a stranger.

He has.

I feel his love for me

so strong

so powerful

so easy.

Not him.

Please, please

I beg you

not him.

Why him?

Why now?

You can't give me the most beautiful

and loving of men

only to take him away after three months.

What kind of sick twisted game

do you play you

incredibly vile, hateful demonic fuck?

After you were found,

after you gave up your game of hide and seek,

you made him suffer.

Why couldn't you just take him

like the thief that you are?

Quickly

quietly

calmly

serenely.

Instead you made him cry

wail

plead

beg

implore

pray

for his life.

You violent, obtrusive, ingrate prick.

Did you ever think for one moment

about his children, his family...me?

What this would do to us?

Did you ever think how cruel

it would be to make us watch you

drain the life out of this angelic

magnificent, beautiful man?

What do you get out of this

you

repulsive

vicious

immoral

noxious

element

of utter shit?

I know of the pain he felt.

He told me.

How taking a breath was nearly impossible.

He told me that too.

Imagine breathing through a straw,

he said to me.

Soon you would take his voice from me.

I could no longer hear him talk of

his love for life

his utter joy

his children

his family.

I couldn't hear

him laugh

breathe

just be him.

Then you took him.

You took

his skin

his muscles

his bones

his brain

his blood.

Fuck you, cancer.

Fuck you.

Lovely

poem

Being there. In his arms. In his presence.
Enfolded in his skin. His smell. His essence.
He intoxicates me.
The drunkest of the drunk.
His mouth, his saliva, his taste.
Upon me. His breath.
Sweet. His tongue. Savory.
Incredible. I want him to nurse me. I want to
suckle him.
Though he is a man. A woman cannot suckle a man.
Who says?
I lay at his bosom. At his chest. His arm, heavy,
enfolding me
Bringing me in, forcing me to be

Pressed up against him.

I can't move. I won't move. He is beyond brilliance.

His mouth, his touch, a million sparks emanating,

As I stare in wonderment at him.

For he is simple. He is but a man. Not young

anymore. Spent. His best years gone.

But in my eyes,

He is the lover of all lovers.

His embrace is like my first.

His kiss, the sweetest of sugars.

Nectar.

He is nectar.

His intoxicating sweetness drives itself deep, into me.

Into my belly, my breast, my sex, my core.

I want him,

Like I have never wanted a man.

Or anything.

Him, only him

Always him,

He is simply, purely, always.

LOVELY

Snapshot

short story

Jace Hadley snubbed out his cigarette in the week old paper coffee cup only to immediately light up another one. He had just opened up a new pack of American Spirits and knew he would smoke at least half the pack in the next hour and ten minutes, give or take. He had seen her go in and he would patiently wait for her to come out, like always. He wondered if they had started fucking yet. Sometimes he would open the car door, get out, walk across the street, hands buried in his jean pockets and take a peek in the side window of the weather worn 60's rambler. He didn't do that anymore. Too painful. He wondered how many times they did it. How many times she came. Did she sound different with him? That guy. He supposed so. She probably arched her back more, wrapping her legs voraciously around his waist, taking him deeply into her. He wasn't sure when it had started.

He had got an inkling of her differentness one Saturday morning over cereal and stale English muffins. She was seated at the table, not like a woman, but like a little girl, her feet joined together as she swung them underneath the stain soaked wood. He had never seen her do that before. Swing her legs like that. As though she held a secret or contained a happiness within herself that was all hers. She beamed, glowed. What? He asked her. What do you mean, what? She shot back. You look giddy. Downright exuberant. Dare I say, glowing? Please share, he said to her. Nah, nothing to share, it's just a good day. She said it dismissively, like she didn't want to engage in further conversation. She looked at him directly as she said this. But her eyes...her eyes were a million miles away. He drank his orange juice in silence. She averted his gaze after that. She picked up the bowl and drank the remaining milk. She got up to pour herself more coffee, and then disappeared to the outside porch swing, leaving him there to ponder her sudden secretive way.

About a week later, he crept into bed after a long night of work as he had done many times in their three years of marriage. He nestled his head on the pillow, then moved his pillow closer to hers. He smelled it. The scent of a man was in her hair. He quietly and slowly moved his face towards her neck and breathed her in. There. It was stronger there, on her skin. The cologne of a man had moved itself into her pores, basking in her soft, pale, beautiful skin. He got this sudden urge to command her to wake, to strip, to show him her nakedness. Would he find her cunt stained with semen, still wet from their lovemaking? Would he find her nipples taut, red and swollen, from being feasted upon? He also thought of brushing his cock against her ass, enticing her as he grew hard, wanting to take her. If she denied him, he knew this would answer his question. She loved sex, never turning him down, no, no, not once. Instead he lay there. Silent, lifeless, as though he was a wounded animal unable to lick at his own pain. The wound small, but soon it would gape, letting all sorts of shit in. Shit like, who, when, where - and the big fucking blazoned question, showing in red neon, WHY?

Many of the answers came. They came because he crept home early from work. An hour and a half early. His timing was exact. Perfect. Like it was meant to be. This was his destiny, and hers. Whether or not the results would be fair, right or make sense, was not for him to decide, certainly not her. Her car was pulling out of the driveway as he inched his way along the quiet, sleepy street. As he passed the Sorensen's tire swing and their 1965 orange Stang, he saw her car, the tail lights shining brightly like a beacon, as though beckoning him, summoning him, urging him on. He slowed as the silver Acura stopped opposite him in the middle of the street after exiting their driveway. Did she see him in her rear view mirror? He thought not as it sped forward, moving up the street. He instantly pushed his foot to the gas, quelling any notions he may have had of not doing this. He followed her. Something he had never done before, only seeing it in the movies. It never turned out well, in the movies. He instantly heard a voice in his head. What makes you think it is any different in real life, you fucking cock-smoking retard?

That was two months ago. He didn't know how often she would see him. That guy. He did know that if he left work early a couple times a week, and if he drove by the guy's house, he would see her car proudly parked in the driveway. He hadn't said anything to her. Not yet anyway. He hadn't let on that he knew. He still made love to her. He still called her, asking how her day was. He still made her breakfast on Saturday mornings, taking great care to make her omelette perfect, her oatmeal clump-free, her coffee strong, as she liked it. They still took walks around Greenlake. They still talked about having a baby. About his job, her job and upcoming vacations they wanted to take. He didn't care about any of this. Not really. He went through the motions, his heart having already bled out. He had cried more times than he cared to think about. Waking every morning was the most painful for him. The moment he opened his eyes, looking around the room, sometimes seeing her readying for work, he realized it was not a dream. Not a bad nightmare. It was his new reality. The question, over and over again, running through his mind. When had she stopped loving him?

He inhaled deeply, taking the smoke profoundly into his lungs, welcoming the calming effects the nicotine gave him. He smoked more than usual. Way more. He knew this would not kill him. No. Surely his broken heart would do the job of ending his life. Is that why men had heart attacks? He contemplated this as he looked at his watch. He still had roughly forty-five minutes. He glanced in the rear view mirror, looking at himself. His eyes so green. It was what first drew him to her, or so she said. She said a lot of things. He had tried to decipher and breakdown each day since they had married. Going through events, motions, arguments, sex, looking for 'that sign.' He had begun doing that most days. Certainly doing it the entire time he waited for her to come out. Smoking, drinking coffee, glancing at his watch thinking, pondering, at what moment had she deemed herself out? Tonight he felt restless. He glanced away from the mirror, looking around the car. Back at his watch. He had time. He started the car, lights off, and rolled away from the rambler, throwing his cigarette out his half open window.

He pulled into Slick City Carwash. A do-it-yourself jobbie. It was late and he had the place to himself. He drove into the middle stall. It had less graffiti so he reasoned it to do a better job cleaning his car. He called himself a dumbass for even thinking that as he fished quarters out of his jean pocket, dropping them into the machine. Clink. Clink. Clink. Clink. They made a hollow sound, as they hit the metal. Someone had obviously already cleaned the quarters out for the day. Another dumbass thought. He opted for the 'light wash, heavy soap, no wax' cycle. He pulled the sprayer out of the holder just as the water began to sputter through. Then within seconds the sprayer came alive, the water gushing through the hose and into the nozzle. He had to grip it tighter, it had a mind of its own.

He drove out of the middle stall, stopping his car near the vacuum. What the hell, he thought, as he glanced at his watch. The outside is clean. Might as well go all out. He got out of the car, fishing through his pocket for more quarters. He had only three nickels, four pennies and a dime. As he splayed the coins out in his hand, hoping one would magically appear to be a quarter instead of a nickel, he noticed they were all heads. No tails. What were the odds of that? He made his way to the bill changer, feeding a crumpled up one that had someone's phone number written across it with orange pen. Did people actually call those numbers?

Yea, hi. My name is Jace. I got your bill here. You know, the one you wrote your number on. Wanna meet for coffee at Denny's? I will tell you all my troubles. My wife is fucking some dude, for starters. He grimaced as he retrieved the coins from the metal pocket. One…Two…Three…Four. He scooped them up and made his way back to the car. He fed them into the quarter slot of the vacuum. Power. He started with the back seat. It wasn't that bad. A few tossed dirty napkins. About half a dozen of those green things from Starbuck's that you put in the opening of the lid to keep your drink warm. A few butts that didn't make it into the ashtray. Coins. A birthday card that he had purchased for his wife but forgot to give her. Hmm, maybe that was what had pushed her. Nah. No way.

He admitted to being not much of a romantic. She always laughed and said it didn't matter. But did it? Had his lack of showing her that he loved her outweighed his telling her? Actions speak louder than words, don't you know. He deposited the wayward coins into his front pocket. He put the card on the passenger seat. He glanced at his watch. He had about twenty minutes left. He did a quick sweep of the front seats, then coiled the still running hose onto the metal base of the vacuum. He got back into the car and as he put the key in the ignition he noticed something under the front passenger seat that he hadn't seen before. He grabbed it, feeling a twinge in his back. Shit. He hoped he hadn't pulled something. It was the Carpenters cd. The one his wife had purchased when they were still dating. It had their wedding song on it. She had asked about it numerous times, asking him to check his car for it. He told her he had, but he hadn't. It slipped his mind. He hadn't bothered. It's just a dumb old cd. As he stared at the brown cover, the Carpenters name in yellow, he began to cry. He started the car, heading back towards that guy's house.

He pulled in front of the house this time, not opting for his usual parking spot across the street and a couple doors down. He opened the cd case. There was a picture of the two of them, sitting in a field. A small snapshot, her smile hopeful, bright and beautiful. His eyes as green as leaves, she used to say. He retrieved the cd, pushing it into the slot. Their song came on. 'We've Only Just Begun'. He loved this song and began singing with Karen, her voice beyond rich and beautiful. He stopped and began to sob again. His grief and anguish cocooning him, wrapping him so tightly he couldn't breathe. The dark hole encompassing, penetrating and mutilating him.

Then, there she was, standing on the porch with him. That guy. His arms wrapped around her waist. They were kissing goodbye.

He opened the glove box, retrieving the cold metal. He put the gun in his mouth and pulled the trigger.

Saturday Knocks

poem

"We don't have many left," he told me.
"Don't have what many left?" I shot back.
"Saturdays. We don't have many left," he repeated.
I had never thought of this before.
He thinks of things like that sometimes.
No. A lot.
Things like Saturdays and love and age and youth.
I don't want him to be right, but sadly, he is.
It's the truth.
Fuck.
The reality of our predicament sets in.
But wait, I love him.
I want and desire him.
I want many, many Saturdays with him.

But every day, not just Saturdays,

will be a day I steal from the universe.

A day I will now cherish.

My youth I didn't cherish.

My age now sees my limit of Saturdays.

My limit of him.

But each day I am given with him,

I will live deeply, passionately, freely

And bask in the time we are allotted.

I never looked at Saturday this way before.

I never looked at things such as these before.

His mind opens mine like it has never been opened.

I want to live in his world,

And I want him to live in mine.

I want every day to be Saturday,

With him and me and us.

Crystal Blonde Persuasion

short story

She glanced at herself in her rear-view mirror.

"Shit. Shit," she muttered as she spied a couple of dark hairs on her chin she had forgotten to tweeze.

A downfall of being a brunette, albeit the only downfall she thought as she glanced at the blonde wig splayed out on the passenger seat.

In time, Crystal, in time. She took a deep breath then slowly let the air seep from her lungs in a meditative, tranquil sort of way. As she approached the red light and came to a stop, she took another turn at the mirror. Admiring her still youthful-looking face, she thought she had glimpsed some fear, some trepidation, in her eyes. Fear? Not Crystal. Maybe the weak Katherine, but not the headstrong, outspoken, fearless, whorish Crystal. All of these attributes would be her constant companions in the next couple of hours. That was usually about all the time she had, just a couple of hours. She traveled her usual route that led her away from her daughter's school, her neighborhood, her beloved Seattle where she could possibly run into a friend or admirer of her work and be recognized. Crystal would be able to play it off, laugh, and say, "I'm sorry; you must have mistaken me for someone else." Crystal was good at that, playing the liar, the cheat, the whore.

But Katherine, in her state, would or could possibly surface, her eyes, her sadness giving her away. Crystal couldn't take that chance. She headed across the 520 bridge to the despised Eastside. The 'fucking, horrid Eastside' where everyone was typical. Typically boring, typically dressed, typically predictable. The men she called 'The Hamsters', always on the wheel, day in and day out to afford their grotesquely large SUVs, to send their children to private schools, to vacation four or five times a year, to buy their wives whatever they so desired, hoping to get a fuck out of them by the end of the day. Yep, 'The Hamsters' were an easy target. Open their cage, drop a sunflower seed in, and they jumped off the wheel, glad for some attention.

She took the first exit off the bridge, hung a left, and drove into a deserted park and ride. It was always emptied out at this time, the bulk of the commuters having left for work between five and six am. She glanced at the car clock. Nine-thirty. Perfect. By the time she reached her destination, there would be a steady stream of men making their way to Starbucks to catch their first break of the day. Get them at their weakest, most vulnerable. The haze from their morning meetings, piles of e-mails, and boring chit-chat with co-workers would find them yearning for a caffeine or nicotine break. She killed the engine.

As she reached into the glove compartment for her little Ziploc bag of bobby pins, she again felt that unease slipping its way into her conscious. Dismiss it, she thought to herself, for if you don't you will mess this one up. It had happened before. She had encountered one who didn't want what she was offering, and her cover was almost blown.

She quickly but methodically began to wrap small sections of her thick, brown hair around her finger, tethering it down with a bobby pin to her scalp. As she swiftly worked her hair up around her head, she thought of her husband. His quietness of late and his abysmal tone. Things had been lost between them for some time. How long? She wasn't sure, but it had been awhile. The quietness in their home was eating her. She would watch him lying next to her in bed, eyes wide open.

"Talk to me, baby, please," she would beg him.

But he lay there still and unspeaking, staring at a spider on the wall, or perhaps he was dreaming of banging her in earlier, happier times.

At times, upon entering the house, she would find herself in her daughter's room, lying on her bed, staring at her Justin Timberlake poster. She would yearn for her to come home from school, filling the house with her laughter, her sarcasm, even the slamming of her door when she was angry or in need of privacy. Any emotion to fill the void of solace.

"Baby, please don't go to Rachel's house tonight. Weren't you just there last weekend for a sleepover?"

"Please, mom," she would beg. She used to want to spend every waking moment with her. When had she so relentlessly transitioned into a teenager? How had she missed that leap? She yearned for that toddler again, that baby, her baby, Daniela.

Stop it. Go away, Katherine. You are Crystal now. And with that thought, she picked up the blonde wig and carefully maneuvered it over her pin-curled head. She smoothed it down as best she could in the back and pulled the car visor down to expose the small mirror that lit up. She fished her eyeliner out of her purse and began to paint her eyes a bit more. She thought she looked a bit tired today. It's no wonder; Katherine had kept her up late, working on that sorry-ass novel she was writing. Katherine, her disheveled, long, dark hair, her thinning body, her sorrowful eyes, dripping tears down her face as she plugged away on that cute, old, vintage typewriter her husband had given to her as a gift upon publication of her first book. Crystal gazed upon Katherine's typed words.

I decided to wait for him in the garden. Surely, he would come to me there. It was one of his treasured places. Many times I saw him, sitting in the old Adirondack, his tan arms standing out against the white of the chair. His lovely eyes closed, his dark lashes caressing his skin. Yes, he would surely see me here, my lugubrious face, my head hung, my long, brown hair cascading around my despondent shoulders. He would know I had been weeping for him. Surely, he could hear my soft, shallow sobs. My sorrow, canvassing itself over my face, traveling down my throat into my heart, searing the pain into my pallid skin. I walk further into the garden, my soft nightgown caressing my thighs as I step deeper into the darkness, the abyss. The long grass licks and swallows my feet with its dewiness. I stop, standing still for a moment, my eyes peering into the desolate darkness, barely making out the tops of the trees.

Gibberish. Unreadable. Unprintable. She pictured Katherine's editor, Ryan, laughing and asking her if she was for real. With that thought, she fished Crystal's coral lipstick out of her purse. As she finished filling in the top lip of her pretty mouth, her thoughts sifted again to Daniela. She would be in health class right now. Would she be learning about how babies were made? Or perhaps how healthy masturbation was and not something to be ashamed of? Or maybe showing the class how to use a condom with a banana playing the part of the penis? She smiled, knowing the girls would be blushing and the boys wishing they were that big.

Stop it. Focus. As she flipped the visor back up, shutting the mirror away, she muttered, "Goodbye, Katherine; hello, Crystal." With that, she stepped out of the car and made her way to the bus stop. It would be here in just about two minutes. At this time of the day, there were only a handful of riders. It was a short jaunt to the strip mall, the godforsaken strip mall. She loathed them. Their stiffness and lack of décor and personality. Everyone looked the same. The skinny blondes in their yoga pants, their uniform of choice whether they worked out or not. The men in their pressed slacks and long-sleeved dress shirts. It was a place where one would not be noticed much, everyone was wrapped up in their tiny lives. Not like the city, with its dirtiness, its rawness, benevolent variety of spice. She loved the quaint and varied shops the city offered, the indie coffee houses and locally owned bookstores, with their slight, musty smell. She found a calmness in seeing the same homeless man claiming his same corner, or a musician treating her ears to his rendition of a Pearl Jam song, played mournfully on his violin.

On the Eastside, not much pleasure from anything except a cheerful greeting from the baristas at Starbucks. She loved Starbucks, though it was on every corner. It was locally owned, so that did score points for her. That and the fact that the original Starbucks in Pike Place used to be her stop every morning on her way to her breakfast shift at work. It's also where she met him. She was in line, waiting to order her quad Americano, with a shot of sugar-free vanilla with room for cream. She smelled him first, his scent filling her nose with an intoxicating pleasantness. A faded cologne, mixed with his own slight musky scent and a faint tinge of tobacco. She pictured a disheveled brunette with a leather satchel. Before she had a chance to turn around, he bumped her with that leather satchel she thought of, and as she turned to him, he began to apologize. His beauty astounded her. His graciousness swept her up, floated and caressed her.

"No worries," she replied as she turned back to the barista who was greeting her. She ordered her drink and paid for his as well. As she moved aside to fidget with something in her bag, she heard him talking to the barista.

"What? She bought my drink? Wow, how sweet of a gesture." He then turned to her, thanking her profusely, telling her that wasn't necessary.

"No problem," she said, "I just felt like it."

She grabbed her drink, not wanting to make any more of a deal out of it and sat down next to the fireplace. He sat across from her and pulled out a book. She noticed he was reading Henry Miller's Tropic Of Cancer. Damn, she thought, I am now his. She recalled her voracious appetite for everything Miller in her late teens. Maybe because most everything he wrote was banned in the U.S. for over thirty years, deemed obscene. Thus, her love affair for Miller began. She found his writing hard to digest, forcing her to read and re-read sentences to really grasp what he was saying. A man who had spoken of sex and his disdain or loathing for Americans so nonchalantly. Of shitting arpeggios or referring to a woman's cunt as a valise.

She dreamt of having coffee with Miller, talking candidly about her sexual desires. How she preferred her pussy to be hairless, or making love wearing a man's shirt because she didn't like the sound of two bodies slapping together. It wasn't sexy to her. How, at random times during the day, she would retreat to her bed, pleasuring herself because she was always insatiable when it came to orgasms and the pleasure she retrieved from them. She pictured Henry, sitting back in his chair, one hand placed casually over his cock, perhaps hiding the impending rising as she spoke of her desires so freely. His hand caressing his chin, nodding as he stared at her large breasts.

"Excuse me," he said, awakening her from her Henry spell. She opened her eyes suddenly, his face now inches from her own. "I didn't get your name." His brown eyes staring into her, looking, wanting to know her.

"Oh, yes, I am Katherine. My friends call me Kat," she said, extending her hand.

"Hello, Kat," his voice smooth, low. "My name is Edward. My friends call me Edward." He said this smiling, mocking her response in a cute way. He shook her hand. His skin, so soft yet his grasp firm, masculine.

"Pleasure." she said.

Edward. Her mind jolted suddenly as the bus doors opened, the driver looking impatient as though she were interrupting his own day-dreaming. She climbed up the steps and surveyed the seats. She could have sworn she had spied one of them. He sat, looking down at the Seattle Times. She recognized his hair, the way it fell and the bulkiness of his leather jacket, like it was almost too big for him, looking like an older brother's hand-me-down. She thought it had looked odd then, but not really thinking much of it until now.

She was sure she had seen it before. She sat down quickly near the front; he was located near the back, hoping he had not seen her. She quickly fished her Ray Bans out of her bag, hoping to appear a little more incognito. As they drove out of the park and ride, her thoughts again whiplashed, and she remembered back to the last time she was with Edward. He had taken her by surprise. She had just dropped Daniela off at school, and as she neared their home, his car sat in the driveway. As she came in, he had told her he had forgotten his cell. As he retrieved it from the kitchen counter, he turned around and gave her that sheepish grin of his.

"So baby, wanna?" he asked as he traced her mouth with his finger. Then, his lips, wet, warm, delicious on her, spurring her. His breath, so sweet… his mouth, moving over her lips, her throat… unbuttoning her shirt and sucking her nipple through her sheer bra. His tongue, twirling around her nipple, causing her to moan, her pussy to moisten. He bites down hard, her nipple reacting, springing forward, and with that, he unhooks her bra and immediately cups a breast into his hand.

"Baby…God," she breathes. He unbuttons his pants, pushing his boxers down. She quickly begins to dismiss her jeans, plopping her ass down on the cushy kitchen rug, freeing her legs from their denim confinement. He lay on top of her, pushing his erection into her as she wrapped her legs around his thighs. He began to slowly pump her, and she gasps, her breathing raspy as it mixed with her moans.

"Yes…my baby…" she says as he fucks her, her body arching with every movement he makes on her. Her pussy so wet with her desire for him. Her lust, wanting him to take her, faster, faster, fucking her like an intruder that had snuck up on her, taking her at his will. She had masturbated many times to him, he pretending to be a thief, sneaking a fuck from her, stolen during her pretend, deep sleep. She would grab his hand, covering her mouth with it to stifle her screams, fearful of the neighbors hearing her rapture.

"Quiet, bitch," he would whisper in her ear, knowing this thrilled her. Then he would stop, pull his cock out of her pussy, look into her eyes, and tell her how much he loved her, idolized her, and needed her. Then he would ask if he pleased her, if she wanted him.

"Oh, yes, yes, fucking yes," she would say, trying to move her body against his to take his sex back inside of her. He would tease her with it, moving his hips the other way, or he would grab his cock, rubbing the tip on her clit, between her labia, teasing her until she begged for him to enter her again.

As Katherine stared through the bus window, the tears moved out of her eyes, caressing her cheeks as they fell. She pulled out her tablet and began to write.

It is the animalistic simplicity of our act. The twining of our bodies enables our minds to intercept bold, warm, hazardous thoughts. Our kisses interjecting words we will never need to voice. The rawness of our sex devours and locks us into a dismal, distant interpretation. His thrusting locks my pain into a fucking tiny, dark, foreboding closet. His cock fills me with a solace of maniacal sorts, a meditative, insulting comfort. He encircles my clit, my breasts, my mouth, my skin, puncturing itself with his own guided and despotic repertoire of perfection.

Before she was able to continue writing, Crystal closed the tablet, stuffing Katherine's craziness into her purse. The bus jerked to a stop. As she rose, she saw leather jacket man move towards her, his head down in a defeated manner, slipping past her as she gathered her thoughts. As she stepped off of the bus, watching him walk ahead of her, she knew it was him. She was sure of it. He was an escapade from a few months ago, but she couldn't remember what Starbucks bathroom the tryst had been in. Had there been that many? Fuck, how long had she been at this? She started by telling Ryan she was doing research for her book. Was that a year ago? Fifteen months ago? Crystal might know. Katherine certainly didn't. What kind of research? Why does it involve Starbucks? Are you conducting interviews there? Crystal explained to Ryan that everything would make sense, soon.

It was him. She knew for sure. The same brown Oxford shoes. She had been sitting in Starbucks working on Katherine's boorish, pathetic, piece of shit novel, her blonde wig cascading around her face, when he had walked in. He had that boy-next-door look. She smiled when she saw his red tie. Men not wearing those much anymore unless they work in a bank or are going after a new job. He would be easy. He ordered his coffee, and she watched him grab a newspaper and sit near her. She needed to make eye contact. It was mandatory with all of them. It was a green light of sorts. She would know in that instant when eyes met whether or not it was a go-ahead. Locking eyes spoke volumes. He must have felt her staring at him, because he suddenly looked at her without provocation. She smiled at him, close-mouthed, and he returned the gesture.

She was fucking in. Now he just needed to go to the bathroom. Her cell rang. She looked down at it. Fuck. It was Ryan. She didn't answer, knowing it would be the same, old rhetoric. How is the book coming along, Kat? Got anything to send me? Want to meet for coffee? I haven't seen you in months. She would reply with the same old answers. Now is not a good time, Ryan, she would explain. Still going through a bit of a dry spell. Come on, Kat, he would say. Push through it, darling, give me something, hell anything. Yeah, yeah, she would say. She pushed Ryan back into her purse, promising to call him later to get him off her back. Suddenly, he stood up. He headed into the direction of the bathroom.

"Yes," she muttered, and with that, she grabbed her bag and traipsed after him. Before he had a chance to shut the door, she was in. She locked the door behind her.

He turned, stunned, and before he was able to speak, her lips were on his mouth, and she was removing his red tie.

"Not a word," she muttered to him, "Ssshhhh, just fuck me!" And with that, she unbuttoned her jeans, pushing them past her hips. Before she could even get them past her knees, he had turned her around, pushing her down over the sink, her ass exposed to him. She heard him unzip his pants and she felt his cock enter her with his animalistic grunts as he began to fuck her, his hands sunk firmly into her bare ass. His cock moving faster, his moans louder, as his orgasm began to build. She began to feel her own pleasure, her wetness coming as he pumped himself into her voraciously. Katherine began to form words and sentences in her mind, writing them down on her imaginary tablet as Crystal was being fucked from behind.

Sorrow shows itself, it is so ugly. Swollen eyes, bulging with tears that can't be turned off, forever roaming and running down my face. Ugly, sorrowful sorrow, its red, bloodshot eyes. But then those eyes look at me, their color is azure. So lovely as they penetrate my heart, my soul. Wait, whose eyes are those that lock me down? They are not his eyes, God, no, his eyes are sienna. Deep, thrusting, pulsating sienna. I wish I could pluck them, put them in a tiny box. Hold them, take them, quickly closing it again because they are staring, trying to fuck mine with their putrid sienna stare.

He finishes and pulls out of her. She is still staring at the floor, his brown Oxfords pervasive in her vision. He then moves in front of the urinal and proceeds to take a piss. He shakes it, pulls up his underwear then his pants, and zips himself up. He leaves the bathroom, not giving her a second look.

It was him. She thought it odd, seeing the same person at an entirely different location. She was always careful when mapping out what Starbucks and the proximity of each. One visit only then onto another. It was her rule. She saw him enter a UPS store. Good. She walked into the Starbucks. She ordered her Americano and looked as she waited for her drink. No sign of leather jacket man.

What would he say if he confronted her, anyway? Hey, aren't you the lady I fucked in the bathroom a few months ago? Oh, yeah, hey, hi, how are you? Loving our late Indian summer? Fuck. Awkward. She retrieved her drink and purveyed the room. No place to sit. Sometimes she tired of those seeming to sit forever in one spot, glued to their laptops. Were they really that busy, or were they just trying to look so? Lots of men today. A few possible candidates for an interlude, but she wanted to follow her routine and grab a chair somewhere. Finally, an old man seeming to finish his crossword puzzle was slowing getting up. She ran over, waiting for his departure. She sat down in the warm chair, as she looked around. Then that uneasy feeling came creeping itself under her skin again. She couldn't seem to shake it. She felt as though she was jinxing herself. The crossing of the black cat or walking under the ladder. All negative thoughts wreaking some sort of havoc on her psyche.

She began to sing Stevie Wonder's song 'Superstition' under her breath. There. She had officially psyched herself out. Abort. Katherine pulled out her tablet and began to write.

I miss them. A fucking huge, gaping hole sits openly. My bereavement, despair, emptiness, oozing out of it and saturating me. I weep for them, I weep for myself. I weep for my own pathetic inability to proceed forward with my life. My cowardliness to face my pain, to look at it in the gut and slam it into the fucking ground. The putrid, filthy dirt where they now lie, trapped, their bodies rotting together, swelling with the seeds of decay and smoldering death. The stench overwhelming, but it is their stench, and I would bask with them if I could. Oh, would I now! My begging turning to pleading as I lay over him, dying, his cock still inside of me, as our bodies rot into one. My eyes, hollowed out holes, my lips shriveling, my breasts sinking into my rib cage, my cunt dissipating into credulous, crumbling dead folds of long ago love-making. My uncultivable womb, effete, echoes of the beautiful child it held, now an ashen-colored tomb, looking something like a deserted hornets' nest. My crying turning itself, cartwheel upon cartwheel, into hollowed, penetrating, banshee wailing, waking up the bones of the other carcasses that are decaying, trapped in their tepid, tumultuous, burned-out graves.

I put down my tablet, grab my purse, and go into the bathroom. I stare at the pathetic woman in the mirror. Her blonde wig, her rouged face, and her coral lips. What happened to Katherine? The beautiful woman, mother, wife, lover, friend, writer? I miss her. What had I become? I pull off the wig and begin removing the bobby pins methodically; studying myself, searching for a spark of me that is still left. I wash my face, welcoming the cold water as it touches my skin. I remove the eye liner, the coral lipstick, the rouge from my cheeks. I am a shell, hollowed out and emptied by their leaving. When does the pain eradicate itself and give my body a chance to breathe? When will I feel my heart beat normally and not with angst against my chest? I look at my clean face, my dark hair. A glimmer of Katherine left. I see her, still wanting, needing, desiring a second chance.

I grab my bag and exit the bathroom. I walk out of Starbucks and make my way to the bus stop, the sun on my face. As I walk down the sidewalk, they come flooding back into my brain, my thoughts paralyzed by them. Fifteen years of memories chasing me, overtaking me, pulling at me. I begin to cry.

My baby, crying in the distance. Daniela. Daniela, where are you? The crying turning into wailing, piercing my ears. It is a thunderous, loud, evasive crying. Tumultuous, panicked fits of hysteria. "I am coming, baby! Hang on, mommy is coming." The field I am running in begins to broaden and lengthen with each step I take. The vastness in front of me is so overwhelming as her crying continues to pound my ears, the sobbing tearing at my heart. Where the fuck is she? She feels so close, but I don't see her tiny arms reaching, or her shock of dark hair, or her lovely, sienna eyes searching. "Baby, where are you? Where are you?" I trip, falling, losing control into the vastness of the field. It feels as though I fall forever, tumbling, rolling, sliding, the ground make-shifting into a hill, and as I roll down it, her cries begin to stifle, to soften. I am losing her. She is disappearing. No, wait, Daniela, wait. Mommy is coming. Then nothing, nothing. She is gone. Nothing.

I feel a weight suddenly lifted from me. I reach into my purse and grab my cell. I call Ryan. He doesn't pick up. I leave a message, the first in weeks.

"Hi, honey, it's Kat. Things will be okay. Don't worry; I am on my way home to work on my book. It will be better than my last. I can be in Seattle in half an hour if you want to meet for coffee first. Okay, well, give me a call, Ryan. I love you."

I hang up. I get on the bus, greeting the driver with an optimistic light. Even he seems in a better way than previously, although I am sure he doesn't recognize me. I look out the window as Katherine, thinking of the direction my book will go.

I step off of the bus and into the deserted park and ride where my car awaits. I open the car door, hearing the rustle of the wind. As I sit down and pull my seatbelt over my chest, I hear the sound of movement behind me. I see the color red flash in front of my eyes. What the fuck is going on?

Kat...Kat...It will be okay, Kat. I love you, honey. We love you.

Edward? Baby, is that you? Where are you?

We are here, Kat, Daniela and I. Join us. We have waited so long.

My throat, suddenly seized, held by a strip of red that I realize is a man's tie. I am confused as my body begins to fight for life. The abuse swirls my head as I feel blows to it, the pain beginning to sear through my eyes, my ears. My throat, aching, gasping for air. I realize someone was in my car, waiting for me like a fucking vulture. Why? I realize my pleading is inaudible. Why are you doing this? No response. Did I even hear my voice? The tie is so strong around my neck, and I feel my breath no longer coming. I panic more, my body writhing, willing itself to be free of my assailant. To no avail as I plead. No, please, no, I will do anything. Please let me go. These are all thoughts and nothing more. They go unnoticed. They drop, incoherent. My voice, no longer. My body fights, still strong, vital.

But then I see them. They are standing there, hand in hand. I see them, their iridescent skin, strikes of dark hair. I see them now, their sienna eyes, calling to me. Wait for me, my babies. I am coming. They stand there, their outstretched hands. I let go. My body stops fighting, euphoria sets in, and I feel myself floating toward them, their smiles spread widely across their faces. I am happy and elated as their hands touch my face, their kisses covering me. Together, again.

THE SEATTLE TIMES
October 23, 2013
(Seattle, WA) Longtime Seattle resident and best-selling author, Katherine Adams, was found slain in her car

at an Eastside park and ride on October 21st. Friends and family are shocked by this last turn of events in this beloved and well-known writer's life. In 2010, her husband of fifteen years, Edward Adams, and their 13 year-old daughter, Daniela Adams, were killed in a car crash after driving home from Katherine's book signing in the Ballard neighborhood. Her agent, Ryan Reynolds, spoke to police at great length, talking about her depression and her state of mind the last couple of years. Friends said she had become a bit of a recluse. The police are not releasing any more information at this time as the murder is still under investigation. Katherine is survived by a brother, Jason Cantrell, of Ventura, California and her mother, Sophia Cantrell, of British Columbia.

The Poet and the Girl

short story

I rap softly on the front door, having forgotten my key. Hopefully, someone in the back kitchen will hear me. No sign of Loretta yet but that is not surprising as she is always running late. I remind myself to tell her for the umpteenth time how lucky she is to have me as an employee, saving her ass on many occasions. Like when she is too hung over to get out of bed, or is in a tiff with an over-privileged, tight-assed bitch, whose martini was 'stirred' not 'shaken'.

I am actually a bit early for work as I like it to look just so before opening at eight pm. Seems late for a bar, but we are not an ordinary bar. I work at a writing bar. Well, the bar is called Scribble, but it's called The Writing Bar, by the locals because it's what we promote.

It was Loretta's brainchild about a year ago. When struggling with writer's block, she would slam a stiff one, and her pen would flourish. Loretta, being born into a family with butt-loads of money, asked her parents for a loan on her new venture. Her parents thought the idea brilliant, and hence Scribble was born. The entire perimeter of the bar is set up with counters, stools, pens, pencils, and loads of paper. You can bring your laptop, but we didn't install outlets on purpose, as we don't want you camping for hours on end. The inside of the perimeter is laid with comfy chairs and a few couches. There is a splattering of rugs laid about over the dark, mahogany floor. Beautiful, blue lights drop down from the ceiling, giving the place a graceful, elegant look. Sconces are lit brightly along the counters, so you don't have to strain to see what you are writing.

This is pretty much a singles' bar. We don't get a lot of couples. I think that's what makes us so cool. It's a place to come, have a Campari, and brainstorm any ideas you may have lurking. Most of our clientele are writers, but artists of all sorts smatter in. I am a painter, my apartment is full of my work, which drives my roommate to the brink. Thankfully, Loretta has let me put some of my art on the walls of the bathroom. Actually, it's a great idea as people are forced to look at it while they take a piss. I have sold a few pieces, and that in itself makes me happy. Rent is high in The Village, so every bit helps.

I love my job, and I love Loretta. She is quite beautiful. I don't currently have a boyfriend, but I do like men. I am cautious to a fault, as my heart was severely broken a year ago. Geoff was his name. He was a nude model in one of my painting classes. That should have been red flag number one. He loved to show off his erection, and I caught him one night in my bed, erecting his cock into my next door neighbor. Goodbye Geoff; hello, tear-stained face for a good two months. He told me he loved me, but don't they all before or after they fuck the living daylights out of you? Loretta was right there to pick up the pieces with her bottle of wine and her 'men are all rabid dogs' speech.

As I lay in her lap looking up at her lips moving with her consoling words, I pictured myself pushing her auburn hair back from her eyes and kissing her full on her lovely, rose-colored lips, their softness sparking me to part them with my tongue and explore the inner regions of her glorious, sensuous mouth. I then begin to softly caress her neck, moving her hair behind her back and unbuttoning her silk blouse, exposing the sheer, vanilla-colored, lace bra she wears so often. At times, when we are in the back kitchen where the lights are bright, I can usually see her hard, pretty, brown nipples pressed against her bra. I have envisioned suckling those nipples, listening to her soft moans of pleasure, my pussy beginning to soak as Loretta's purrs echo softly in my ears.

Loretta has a boyfriend. Thaddeus Cole. I call him Cad the Coal as I find him hard, dark, and cold and not in the good, vampire, sexy way either. He's just an asshole, leeching off Loretta because she has money. He must be simply divine in bed, because I see no other redeeming qualities in him.

I don't share my negative thoughts of Thad with Loretta. She seems so happy, and besides, love is blind. She would just say, "Oh, Scar, you will like him once you get to know him." Maybe so. Maybe I am jealous because he is dipping his cock into her lovely, soft, pink-colored cunt. I told you I like men. But girls like to fantasise too.

Anyway, back to Scribble. We serve a mélange of sandwiches, a few salads, some greasy fries, and of course, lots of alcohol. We are known for our vast array of bourbons, vodkas, scotches and our witty drink menu. We stop serving booze at two am and stay open till four, serving coffee and croissants. By this time, the writers have slumped in their seats, being replaced by the 'bars are closed time to sober up' crowd. We are usually packed till closing time, and quite often I have pulled paper out from under a snoozing scribbler. Cleaning and doing my books takes about an hour, so I usually don't put the key in my apartment lock till about five am.

I knock louder. Jesus, it's cold out here. As I shove my frozen, almost numb hand into a pocket, Luis the dishwasher appears at the window, smirking through the glass. He gloats as he opens the door.

"Forget your key, baby-doll?"

"No, fuck-chop, I'm just enjoying the deadly freeze taking place out here."

"Such an ugly mouth on such a beautiful girl."

"All the better to eat you with, my dear," I say with a smile.

"That's what he said," Luis quips.

"Touché, love, touché," I say as Luis locks the door behind me.

"By the way, Scarlett, you left the writings in a pile last night. I picked them up and stashed them in the back office."

"Oh, oops, thanks, Luis. I knew I forgot something last night. I bought a new canvas yesterday and was deep in thought about what to paint."

"Paint this," Luis says teasingly, pulling his shirt up and exposing his firm, honey-colored chest. I smile slyly.

"Ah, yes, it is quite amazing," I say, rolling my eyes as I give him a playful punch to the gut. "I will let you know when I have run out of ideas, and have to resort to the male physique."

As we walk toward the kitchen, Luis drapes an arm across my shoulders and whispers in my ear. "Always here for you, beautiful. Let me know when your bed gets cold, and I will rush over to help you heat it."

I quickly laugh, pushing his arm off of me, and I begin to sing Aerosmith's 'Dream On' in my best Steven Tyler scream. Luis laughs and disappears into the kitchen. As I step into the office, I spy the heap of writing left over from last night. Wow, didn't realize that much was collected. I must have been exhausted. Don't even remember gathering it. You see, when someone writes, they often leave it. Some of the servers get tired of going through it. I don't. I like to take that voyage into someone's mind for a bit. It's never an everyday conversation I would have with a stranger. It is a flow of thoughts, however sweet, fucked up, or irrational. It lets me into someone's dark closet for a brief interlude. Oh, sure, people have left everything you can imagine. A recipe for oatmeal cookies or killer pot brownies, a few revelations from the bible, a Dear John letter, a Dear Jane letter, a fuck you if you're reading this note, directions to an apartment for a good time, and an elaborate scheme on how to rob a bank and get away with it. I could go on and on; you get the idea.

Don't get me wrong. There has been some good shit out there. If we really like it, we frame it. Most of the walls are adorned with framed scribbles. This is why my paintings reside in the pisser. Of course, a true writing bar should showcase just that. Writing. The first Thursday of every month we host an art walk with a few other galleries and a smattering of wine bars. We try to keep it fresh and new, replacing the writing every couple of months or so. Folks enjoy reading it. We see it as art in just another form.

I peel off my heavy pea-coat and hang it with my hat on the hook on the back office door. Eventually, my shit will be buried under everyone else's as they are all later to arrive. There are four servers and two bartenders who work here, not counting Loretta. As I pick up the pile of writings, stuffing them into my backpack for the pleasure of reading later, the one on top drops to the floor. As I lean to pick it up, the penmanship of the author catches my eye. It is quite lovely to look at. I begin to read.

A Girl

She strikes me down.

Her beauty qualifies but doesn't limit me to any one
Fantasy.

But to many thoughts of prurience as her aphrodisiacal
Face shrouds me,

Conceals me,

Towers over me, manipulating and twisting my
circumstantial mind.

I could sleep in her beauty, laying my head between
the softness of her thighs,

turning it this way and that between her legs,

daring myself to involve my lips, my mouth, my tongue.

Ah, come closer, you sumptuous creature.

The Poet

I read it again, this time out loud. It's not outstanding, breathtaking, or amazing, but it does captivate me for some odd reason. Is it because it is written to 'The Girl'? Or because he calls himself 'The Poet'? Or is it the beauty of his penmanship that calls me? I begin searching the stack for more. Boom.

The Girl

I shall wrap you, enfold you, guide you
Inside of my virtuous flesh.
My pores crawling with ecstasy as you fire them
With your transfixing heat, skin, and bones.
I hear your blood running through your veins,
Touching your heart, streaming into your
Fingertips, toes, filling your loins
Expanding your sex, opening your vulva,
Hardening your clit, marking it firm and red
With its blood red desire.
I part your sweet thighs, your sex entrancing me,
The smell of you pungent and sweet like a fig.
Your clit, ripe, summons me. Like a ripe berry,
I want to suck it, tenderly, its juices filling my mouth,
As you cum underneath me, your moans singing in
my ears.
My cock, erect and ready.
How shall I take you?

The Poet

I am so transfixed by this, by him. I read the second one again. *How shall I take you?* Oh, God, that line is wonderful. I read it over. Many thoughts stir. How shall you take me? Take me hard, fast. Take me from behind, pulling my hair as you thrust your cock deep inside of me. Take me forcefully, pushing me down on the bed, dominating me, your body pressing me firmly, your hands trapping my shoulders, rendering me defenseless. I smile at these thoughts, these forbidden secret pleasures I have. I look through for another. Success.

The Girl- Too

You speak to me. I hear your voice, siren song from the bed.

The huskiness of it, the darkness, indulging my cock.

"Poet, poet," you call out.

"Write your prose on my belly, trace your verses on my back, athwart my ass.

My body, my skin, your tablet.

Flourish your words down my legs, between my thighs.

Mark your sentences on me, replacing your pen with your fingers.

Caress your words on my breasts, on my nipples, warranting them hard.

Dip your digit into my inkwell, my wet sex.

Write your letters on my vaginal walls, your lyrics,

your story, your want of me."

As I approach you, move nearer to you,

I see your shaven, velvety cunt.

Your fingers look to be inside of you, your back slightly,

arching as you pleasure yourself.

You abandon your fingers from your sex and slowly

push them into

your slightly parted, sensuous mouth.

You close your eyes, and as you taste yourself,

you move your hand over your breast.

My aching for you is beyond inconceivable.

The Poet

As I stare down at the paper, my face flushed, my heart racing from his words, my space is suddenly violated by the ridiculously-loud, gum-chewing Jasmine.

"Whatcha so mesmerized by, Scar?" She calls out in a sing-song sort of voice as she bursts through the door.

"Oh, hey, Jaz. Nothing. The usual writing," I say as I stuff the papers into my backpack.

"Hmm, you seemed pretty transfixed there. How 'bout a looksee?" Jaz glances, suddenly interested, toward my bag. I turn and look at her quickly, suddenly not wanting to share this with her or anyone else for that matter. I want him all to myself as though his words were written for me, my eyes, no one else's.

"Hey, you have never shown an interest in what was left before," I shoot back. "Why now? You always say they bore you to fucking tears."

"Yeah, I guess I do say that, don't I? So can I take the front section tonight? I need to get out of here early. Meeting Cisco for a movie at the Varsity."

Cisco is Jasmine's boy, Francisco. They have only been dating about a month or so, but according to Jaz, he has been the only one in her life to produce more than one orgasm out of her, so apparently, he is in her 'Oh, my God' category. Life according to Jaz.

"OH, MY GOD!...did you read the book *Catcher In The Rye?*"

"OH, MY GOD!...did you guys see the movie *Django Unchained?*"

"OH, MY GOD!...did you see the homeless guy on Bleeker and 4th on your way home from work last night?"

"OH, MY GOD!...I finally met a guy who brought me to orgasm, twice!!!"

So you get that picture.

"Yeah, sure, honey," I mutter, thoughts of The Poet and what he may look like perplexing my brain, sending it swimming with impure, lustful waves of sinful...my thoughts seized again by the gum chewer.

"Scar, you sure you're okay?"

"Totally fine, and I will let Loretta know to let you be first off tonight as soon as she gets here."

"Thanks, Scarlett; you rock." And with that, Jaz turns and heads out to the floor. My mind snaps back to The Poet.

Write your prose on my belly, trace your verses athwart my ass. Who the fuck says that? I grow more and more intrigued. My mind begins to wander as I don my apron and apply eyeliner using the full length mirror placed haphazardly on the back door. I dream I am lying on that bed The Poet refers to, my pussy exposed to his beautiful, dark eyes, the lust showing through them as he wets his lips. I see the hardness of his cock pushing through his jeans. My hand moves down to the softness between my legs, and as I begin to move my finger over my clit, he comes closer. He glides his hand through his hair as he stops at the foot of the bed. He grabs my legs and pulls me down toward him.

My hand stays over my sex as he looks at it wantonly. He suddenly drops to his knees, grabbing the tops of my thighs, pulling my body down closer to the foot of the bed. He parts my legs further and moves his mouth to my pussy. He slowly begins to tour my clit with his tongue, flicking it back and forth, my wetness beginning to seep from my sex.

My fantasy is suddenly jolted to a stop by Loretta, as she comes bursting through the door.

"Well, hello, pretty woman," she says in her sultry voice.

"Well, aren't you here early in all your glory?" I say.

"Yeah, Thad and I had an argument, and I stormed out, deciding to cool off here. Good a place as any, I s'pose."

As I turn towards her, I notice her eyes look a bit red and puffy. My anger pulses towards Thaddeus. "Are you okay, honey?" I ask, concerned. You look as though you have been crying."

She dabs a finger under her eye as though fixing or removing running eyeliner, replying, "I am fine, Scarlett. No problem. Nothing a shot of Campari can't take care of. We shall talk about it later. Right now, I just want to get the dining room ready. I have a feeling we are going to be packed tonight. There is a writer's group touring The Village, and I heard we are one of their stops." I love it when we are busy; my night goes by quickly.

"Are you sure you don't want to talk now? I am all ears."

"In the immortal words of Paul McCartney 'Let it be'"....and with that, she turns and walks out. She seems sincerely rattled this time around. I have seen her after many arguments with The Cad, but never has she looked so beaten and hung out to dry. I pray to God she doesn't go on one of her benders tonight. If she starts drinking this early in the evening, she won't stop, and by the end of the night, she will be passed out on one of our couches. God knows I have seen it before. She is her own worst enemy. Growing up in the environs of a rich household and helicopter parents wreaks multitudes of havoc on one's soul. It eats at you, bit by fucking bit, until you are muck on the floor.

Poet Man is pushed forward in my mind, and as I straighten and retie my apron, I smile about my fantasy and head out the door. The night turns out to be one big cluster fuck. Etta was right; not only were we busy, but we also had a line outside waiting to get in. That is a rarity here. Perhaps the beginning of what is yet to come, as our popularity grows among the villagers and tourists alike. The writing group was a party of 27, and we just couldn't fit them all in. They ended up coming and going over the course of the evening.

The pile of scribbles was fucking huge, and as I gathered them up, I saw my name. 'Oh my God'....Jaz's catch phrase popped in my head, and I smiled. Yes, there it was, that same beautiful writing, his penmanship like a work of art in itself, but in place of 'The Girl' was this, and it read...

> *My Scarlett*
>
> *Your exquisiteness is driving me into a certain*
> *kind of frenzied weakness. Those lips of yours,*
> *ah, those eyes, those perfect breasts, bring me*
> *into a depth of male surrender that has besieged*
> *my senses. My yearning apparent now, acutely*
> *arousing every fiber in my body. My knees quiver.*
> *My heart races. Scarlett. Oh, Scarlett. Put down*
> *this paper. Go to the window.*
>
> **The Poet**

I stop dead. My tiredness, my weariness is forgotten. I put the paper down and walk towards the window. A man is standing there, a beautiful man. His dark eyes penetrate through the nightfall. His smile is embraced by his dimples. His beauty astounds me. He has a paper pressed against the window. It reads simply.....

Your Poet

Put on Charlie Parker

short story

I don't know why she left. It could have been my lack of caring one fucking iota, how shitty the house had been looking as of late, the paint beginning to peel and the color to fade. Maybe it was the way I chewed my food, clicking my tongue in that irritating 'cow-like fashion' as she called it. Perhaps she was sick and tired of my farting in bed, stinking up her baby powder scented cotton sheets. Maybe it was because I didn't bring my smoked cigarette butts into the house and toss them into the trash as per her instruction; instead dropping them still lit onto the ground, smooshing them with the toe of my shoe into the dirt.

Maybe it was my empty beer cans littering the rooms that had TV sets, our bedroom included. Or perhaps it was my leaving the toilet seat in the upright position, the underside splashed with my urine and shit, staining the white. Or the cap left off the toothpaste, causing it to do a slow leak onto the tiled counter. Could be she grew leary of the same old way I banged her every two weeks, the ol'familiar position, timing it to almost four minutes, the blank look on my face as I pulled out, cumming all over her belly. Maybe she was sick of the boys coming over once a month, dirtying up the back porch with our poker chips, empty beer bottles and Dorito bags. The belching, farting and loud cursing causing her to jump in her car and flee to her sister Abby's house.

Abby, with her tidy, perfect home, perfect husband, his crisp white button-down shirt, khaki's and Ken-doll hair. I knew how it would play out. She would tell Abby what a dead beat I was, asking her why the fuck she stayed with a loser like me. After a few hours of bashing my character, she would climb back into her piece of shit Honda Civic and head home, her mascara stained on her face from her tears. Although this time, she didn't come home. I lay there till three am listening for her car. Then, I dragged my ass out of bed, grabbed a glass of water and called her numerous times. She didn't pick up, so I called her sister. No answer. Then I called Angelina again. After the fourth time she texted me. Not coming home. What did this mean, not coming home? Not tonight? Not this week? Not ever?

After the not coming home text came through, she texted that Abby would be by later to pick up her stuff. I wanted to cry. But I held back. Instead, I went outside and picked up every last cigarette butt out of the dirt, the moon lighting my way along with the neighbor's bright back porch light. After this rare act of craziness, I went back into the house and made a pot of coffee. As the water began to dribble through the filter, filling the kitchen with that wonderful smell of fresh brew, I stripped naked. I walked over to the sliding glass door, the darkness outside culminating with the kitchen light, casting a full reflection on my nude body. As I stood there, looking at whom and what I had become, it was then I felt the tears roll out of my eyes.

I sat down on the hardwood floor. I felt shame. Shame for letting her go. For not fighting for her. Not pounding on Abby's door, insisting Lina come home with me. It wasn't the first time she had left. She had walked out numerous times but she always came back after a couple of hours. I would grab her, hold her, tell her that I cared and that I would look for another job, a better job, so we could move out of Aberdeen and into Portland like she wanted.

We were high school sweethearts. Inseparable. We were the ones drooling over each other at the lunch table or making out in front of lockers in between classes. After graduation, we moved into the dorms at Evergreen State College near Olympia. I was on a scholarship. Then, about a year into school, Dad was killed in an accident at the local sawmill. My Mom begged me to come home, to help her take care of the house and finances. Me being the only child, well, I just couldn't say no. I moved back and got a job driving for UPS. Angelina, missing me terribly, left school.

Shortly after, with a few friends and Lina's sister Abby in tow, we got married at the Aberdeen Courthouse. Not long after that, Mom started drinking. She lost her job, usually too hung-over to get out of bed. A few months later, she ran off with Dad's best friend, Earl Kincaid. That was five years ago. Haven't seen or heard from her since.

That made two now; two women who had left me. What was I doing wrong? I let my Mom down and now Lina. When had I left the ball game? In the first innings? Coming home after Dad died was a mistake. Jesus. Get over it.

I still couldn't get up. I couldn't stop crying nor could I stop staring at my reflection, seeing only a small boy staring back at me, not a man. I sat there for an hour or so, contemplating my next move. I felt like the king on the chessboard. The rook, bishop and knight are all able to move about quite freely. The queen is able to move any number of vacant squares in any fucking direction; forward, backward, left, right, diagonally or in a straight line. The king can only move one square at a time. So goes my life.

My queen was passing me by, all over the board and I was just a spectator. I couldn't or didn't want to see what was happening. My Dad always told me, "Happy wife, happy life." Lina was clearly unhappy. It was my fault. It was then I got up off the floor, my bare ass sticking to it a bit. The floor was dirty. What the fuck did she do all day? Oh, right. She worked ten hour shifts waiting tables at Tony's Truck Stop. Yep, I had turned into a tool, a douchebag, a lazy ass, sorry son-of-a-bitch. She deserved better. I poured a cup of coffee and headed upstairs to take a shower. The hot water felt so good as it hit my back, I lathered my face and grabbed a razor. I thought of happier times with Lina, when we first got together. The kissing, her long hair touching my arms as I held her close, her sweet soft lips as she kissed my ear, my neck. The many times we languished in bed long after making love, the scent of spring coming in through the open windows.

As I eased the razor down the length of my cheek and onto my chin, I wondered where and when we had missed the turn. You know how you see the sign that says dead end but you go down the road anyway? When did it begin to unravel? When had our love got swept up and lost in the day to day mundane? When had that glint from her eyes and that glimmer from mine extinguished themselves?

As I stepped out of the shower and dried off, I looked at the fogged-up mirror hung over the sink. Lina used to sneak into the bathroom as I showered, drawing a heart on the foggy mirror with our initials inside. That ritual had stopped a few years back. Now I yearned for it again. I decided to 'brown bag' it and went down to the kitchen, the towel wrapped around my waist. I made a peanut butter and jelly sandwich. I even crunched up some Lay's potato chips, scattering them on the peanut butter side before placing the jam side over it. My Dad had shown me this trick when I was four. I smiled at the thought of him now, his strong hands lovingly cutting the sandwich in half. One for Papa, the other for my Mattie, he used to say.

I threw some extra chips in a baggie, grabbed an apple and headed for the door. Once in the front yard, I turned back towards the house. It appeared how I felt. In disrepair. Lonely and neglected. I got in my car, and as I was backing out of the driveway, Coldplay's song 'Yellow' came on the radio. It was Lina's favorite.

The day was long, as they all are. It seemed that as my route neared the last couple of hours of my day, the packages seemed to breed, looking as though I had barely made a dent in them. That feeling of being overwhelmed again swept over me. The anxiety, the panic creepy-crawling its way into my skin, causing my heart to race, my breathing to shallow, the weight heavy on my chest. I had gone into the hospital a few years ago with what I thought was a heart attack. They couldn't find anything. Months later, another one. Another ER visit. Again, they turned up nothing. My drinking became heavier as I tried to alleviate the panic I always felt was around the corner, waiting and watching to jump me like a thief, stealing my calm and replacing it with pandemonium.

Suddenly, my phone came alive and I pulled over quickly thinking it was Lina, coming to her senses. It wasn't. Well, it was, but not telling me she wanted to work it out but that she and her sister had abolished most traces of her presence in the house. She would be back tomorrow for the heavy stuff with a truck. She talked quickly and hung up. I never said a word. I got out, lit up a smoke and sat on the curb. I felt the tears coming, faster this time, spilling down my cheeks in a stream, the saltiness touching my lips. I must have been a sight. Mommy, mommy. I just saw the UPS man sitting by the side of the road smoking and crying!

Yup. Looking good Mattie. I climbed back into the truck, surprised to see only one package left. I must have been in a zombie state the last hour or so, not recalling delivering that quickly. About a mile later, I pulled up to 406 Ashley Court. It was an adorable white house with green trim. A beautiful wrap-around porch graced the front and underneath the window was an old style swing for two. Ah, it looked so comfortable right about now and would be perfect with an ice cold beer in hand. As I climbed up the front steps, the lilac bush on my right was one of the most beautiful I had ever seen. The scent so strong in the air. I stepped over to it, pushing my nose against the most purple of the bunch. It was one of my favorite fragrances, bringing back a flood of happy childhood memories.

It also reminded me of Lina and the lilac wristlet she wore to the prom. She loved them as much as I did. I was so entranced by the lilacs and the house I hadn't realized until now how heavy the box I was carrying was. I looked down at the name, knowing this was a 'no drop' but requiring a signature. Helena Young. I knocked quietly, afraid of spoiling the serenity of the place, the beautiful stillness that seemed to encase it. Nothing stirred, so I knocked louder. Still nothing.

As I peered in the window, an abundance of butterflies seemed to come out of nowhere, surrounding the box as if it held nectar inside and they were trying to get at it. There she was. Well, there was someone. She was seated at a cute vintage farm table, the lace tablecloth adorning it reminding me of my grandmother's. She was sipping coffee or perhaps tea, her legs crossed. She wore a long, summery-looking dress although it was early spring, the cold and damp still hanging in the air. I knocked in quick succession on the window and as she turned, her green eyes warmly greeted me as she motioned for me to come on in. I froze, instantly drawn to her. She then got up, seeing my lack of movement. She walked across the room, her dress embracing her body as she glided, her femininity in every move, her hair shimmering from the light that suddenly poured in from the windows.

"Well hello there," she said as she opened the wooden door, the hinges squeaking a bit. "My apologies, I didn't hear you. Were you out there long?"

"No, no, I lied. No worries." I put the box down as I brought out the pad on which she needed to sign.

"Actually, could you please bring it in and open it up for me? I would really appreciate it. If it is what I think it is, it is quiet heavy."

"I'm sorry ma'am, we are not allowed to do that, enter a home, you know, that sort"....she quickly cut me off.

"Oh yes, I understand that, but this is different. Please, I wouldn't say a word and you are done working for the day, right? Rules, schmules." God, her eyes were incredible and looked so much like Lina's. She held the door even wider for me, her smile as long as the day. She had a way about her. Intoxicating way. "Please," she said again. "Mum's the word."

"Okay, just this once," I said, still hesitant as I picked up the box and stepped over the threshold, feeling guilty and giddy at the same time. She led me across the hardwood floor and into the kitchen, stopping in front of the table.

"Here, put it here," she said, clearing the morning paper that was scattered about. As I set it down, she had opened a drawer, clearly searching for something. "I know I have scissors here somewhere."

"No need, I got this," I said, quickly retrieving a box cutter from back pocket. I slid the knife through the tape, suddenly anticipating the contents, her face equally enticed.

She came over and stood by me, her hands folded in front of her mouth as though she were praying but looking more like a child at Christmas than someone in church. It was a phonograph. The old-fashioned kind. I had seen them only in the movies. It was beautiful and looked to be made of mahogany wood.

"Oh Mateo, it's beautiful!" She blurted out as she touched the wood. "Plug it in, plug it in!" And as she pointed to the plug socket, she scurried out of the room. How did she know my name? As I knelt down to the outlet, I saw my nametag. Oh, right. I had forgotten about that. It was a new practice at UPS. Apparently, scads of women were wanting to know their driver's name and corporate got tired of fielding the calls, hence, nametags for all.

As I got the phonograph plugged in and pulled the plastic from the needle and turntable, she came running into the room with old albums. It had been a long time since I had seen someone so gleeful over something so simple. I felt a pang of jealousy, wishing for a moment to be her, to feel the happiness that seemed to derive from nowhere in particular, for it seemed to be a part of whom she was, what she was. She plopped down on the hardwood floor, hiking up her dress to the tops of her thighs that she might sit comfortably.

"Mateo, quick. Sit, sit. Look at all these wonderful albums. When was the last time you held these in your hands? Just look at the artwork on some of these," she said, scattering them in front of her.

Most I had never seen before but I had certainly listened to. Elton John's 'Captain Fantastic' was just that, the artwork amazing. There was 'Blue Train' by John Coltrane. Pink Floyd's 'Wish You Were Here', The Beatles, 'Abbey Road', the famous shot of them on the crosswalk. Nirvana's cover with the naked baby in the swimming pool. They were all wonderful to look at, to touch. My parent's left behind many albums, but I couldn't recall now where they were.

Sadly boxed and dusty, long forgotten, making way for the Sony Walkman and CD's.

"Ah, here we are," she cried out suddenly, jolting to her feet. "You will love this Mateo, I am sure of it," she said, sliding the album from the sleeve carefully, her fingers touching the sides as not to scratch her treasure. She lovingly placed the record on the turntable, laying the needle down as the album went round and round. I stared at the movement, so mesmerized. Then the music started. A piano at first and then the rich, sweet sound of a saxophone. My football coach had one. He would play it in his office in the afternoon after eating the ham and Swiss on rye his wife had made him. He was good, very talented but this, God, this was magical. I had never heard anything like it.

"Who is this?" I asked, looking up at her. She had her eyes closed and was rocking her head back and forth rhythmically as though she had heard it a million times, her body lightly swaying.

"Charlie Parker," she replied, her eyes still closed, not missing a beat. Then she grabbed my hands, pulling me up from the floor. "Dance with me," she said, wrapping my arms around her curvy waist. "Lover Man. This one is called 'Lover Man' and it is my favorite."

She put her head to my chest her eyes still closed. I could smell her hair, the scent of lilac emanating from it. The sax was so rich and dark, so sexy and alluring. It called to me, as if begging to be heard. I know what my father would say if he were here. Son, they don't make music like this anymore. Now it's all garbage. I would nod, not really paying him any mind. Sorry Dad. Wish you were here now, you would love this.

I don't know how long Helena and I danced in her kitchen, the sultry music subduing us, keeping us close. It seemed hours. It was something I had never done with Lina. Dancing close like this in the kitchen. My heart sank. I needed to leave. Helena must have felt my change.

"Mateo, I suppose you must go. I can't thank you enough for helping me with the record player. Sorry to have been so bold. I got caught up in the excitement and wanted someone to share this with. Here you are dancing with me in my kitchen and I haven't even introduced myself. Helena Young." Then she laughed. "Oh, you already knew that. The package and all. And you are Mateo......"

"Wyman. Mateo Wyman and I really should be going. You were the last house on my route and I need to get the truck back before they put an APB out on me."

She laughed, her white teeth flashing themselves from her pretty full lips. Lina. For a moment, she looked like Lina. I felt the tears welling up again. I made a bee-line for the door, hearing her close behind me, her dress making a swish, swishing sound. Lilac. The smell so strong now, filling my nostrils. As I opened the door I felt her grab my elbow. I turned toward her.

"You forgot this." She had the box cutter in her open hand offering it to me instead of handing it to me. It struck me as an odd gesture. Fuck. This whole day was odd. She stood still, as if she were a statue. I retrieved the box cutter from her open hand and turned away from her before the first tear felt its way down my cheek. The door was slightly open. Had she not closed it after letting me in? I heard her voice behind me, close but so far away.

"Thanks again Mateo. Oh, and remember, it was Charlie Parker. Charlie Parker that we danced to."

How did she know I was wondering that? Asking myself that very question. I yelled a thank you at her, not turning my head, but staring straight ahead, descending the stairs and moving past the lilac bush. I jumped in my truck releasing the box cutter from my hand into the passenger seat. But it wasn't a box cutter. It was a lilac I had been clutching.

I dropped the truck off, anxious to get into my own car and get home as soon as possible. My hope was that Lina was there. That she had changed her mind. I pulled up to the house. Sadly, the piece of shit Honda Civic wasn't there. In fact, as I walked in, I noticed most of Lina's stuff was gone. I ran up the stairs and into our bedroom. The only things in the closet were my clothes. No sign left of a woman ever gracing it. Her books gone. Her make-up vanished. I ached to see even a bottle of fingernail polish, a tampon wrapper or a dropped pair of panties. She had even taken Boo Boo monkey. A cute stuffed monkey wearing a pink shirt that said 'kiss my boo-boo' that I had given her when she got her tonsils out our freshman year of high school.

"Bye Boo Boo," I said aloud as I collapsed onto our bed. My head was reeling. My new reality was beginning to push its way into my brain. I closed my eyes. She was there. Not Lina. Helena was there. I saw her holding the box-cutter in her open hand, offering it to me, her green eyes shimmering in the sunlight, her head thrown back as she laughed. I took it from her. I was sure of it. I felt myself drifting off to sleep, the lilac smell strong again in the air.

Tuesday morning. Lina had been gone for four days now. I hadn't heard a word from her. All of her erased from our home. I called many times but she never picked up, never answered my texts either. It was my day off and I was headed to Home Depot to pick up some paint and a few workers. I had decided to get the house in order. I needed it to look beautiful in case Lina were to come home or drive by.

I took the long way, deciding at the last minute I would drive by Helena's house. Just for the hell of it, I told myself. Just because! As I got nearer, I saw something on the sidewalk in front of her house. It couldn't be. Not possible but yet, there she was, Helena, seated at an adorable table dressed with a blue and white checkered tablecloth. As I pulled up, she jumped from her chair.

"Would you like some lemonade?" she asked, so matter-of-factly. Like it was her regular job and she did it every day.

"Oh my God, Helena. What are you doing? Are you

nuts?" I instantly regretted saying this, her smile disappearing. "I mean, wow. A lemonade stand? Is it yours? Do you have a child?" I asked, so confused.

"Nope, just me. Haven't you ever had a lemonade stand Mateo?" she asked, picking up a cute plaid paper cup.

"Yea, sure, when I was little. I think everyone has as a kid."

"Well, tell me then, what did you like about it, why did you have one?" She asked, pouring me a cup from an old glass pitcher.

"I guess to make a couple dollars, so we could walk down to the neighborhood store and buy candy. But now that I think about it, the rush I got when someone pulled up was better than the money."

"Exactly. That zap of excitement you felt as you poured them a glass, so proud of yourself. That feeling far exceeded the quarter or two they gave you. The weirdest part about it, when I think about it now, we never washed our hands. They never questioned who made the cookies or the lemonade. It was an act of trust, of innocence. It made them happy because it made the child happy. They remember when they were children and the feeling they got when someone pulled up. Do you understand what I am trying to say?"

"I think so," I said. But really I began to think she was fucking crazy as shit. "I guess I just never put much thought into it. I still don't quite get it," I said, taking a sip. It was delicious. The tartness of the lemon being chased with sugar, tasting more fresh-squeezed than store bought.

"I just wanted to bring that feeling back again. From the setting up of the table to the making of my sign. And the best part of it is that all of my customers have been children. They don't question or think it odd that a grown woman is selling lemonade. They see the lemonade stand in all of its joy for what it is, simple as that. Here, sit down, you will see." And with that she steered my body into the chair, pushing me down into it. She plopped herself next to me on the green velvety grass, hiking up her same dress as yesterday around her thighs, her child-like ways all about her. Before I could refuse, to tell her I was on a mission to fix up my house and should be on my way, a boy and girl on twin Schwins pedaled up, the girl sporting blonde braids and a toothless grin, the boy wearing a Seahawks cap, his face scattered with freckles. The look on Helena's face made me forget the everyday mundane and for the first time in years I felt hope.

I don't know how long we sat at the stand handing out lemonade and chocolate chip cookies. Helena had to make several trips to the house for reserves. It seemed her supply was endless. The third trip out she brought a vase of lilacs with her which she placed on the rickety table next to the napkins.

"I can't believe I forgot these," she said, her reddish hair glistening in the sun. "A lemonade stand just isn't a real stand without flowers." I had heard that line before. Where?

In a movie? I couldn't recall. The moment she put them down, their fragrance hit me quickly and I thought of Lina.

"It will work out Mateo, if it's what you really want. Fight for her. Walk ten thousand miles for her, if she is what you really want." Before I had a chance to question her or how she knew about Lina, she had pressed her finger to my lips, shaking her head.

I stood up. She grabbed my hand, pulling herself up as well. I hadn't noticed until now the tops of her breasts, spilling a bit out of her bra. Instant erection. Great, this was all I needed.

"Look, Helena, thank you for today. It really was fun. And I don't know how you know what is going on with me, but…."

She quickly cut in. "It's apparent you are hurting so it was just a hunch. You'll figure it out."

It seemed before she had even finished saying that, her lips were on mine. Her tongue on mine, her sweetness was filling my mouth. I pulled her close, my arms around the small of her back. *I shouldn't be doing this. I need to stop myself.* But I couldn't. I wanted her. I wanted to be inside of her. Was she testing me? She just told me to fight for her. Fight for Lina. This wasn't fighting for her. Men are so weak. Why are we so weak? Why am I so weak? I pushed her away from me. The lilac smell again. So strong. She let me push her away and without saying a word, she grabbed my hand, leading me towards the house. I walked reluctantly behind her, her hand still in mine. We went into the house, through the living room and then down a hallway. A long hallway, photographs were covering the walls. It seemed like there were hundreds of them, one after another after another. Some present, but most of them from long ago, faded with age. I yearned to stop and look at them, feeling myself being pulled by the people in the photos. *They want me to see them. To acknowledge their existence, their having lived, loved, breathed.*

"Not now, Mateo," she said, her hand grasping mine tight, so tight. We turned and were suddenly in a room, stark white with only a bed in it and at the foot of the bed was an easel with what seemed an abundance of paints and brushes. So many colors and they appeared so vibrant. They were the only colors in the room. The sheets, pillows and comforter were all white. The windows were open, a slight breeze blowing the sheer white lace curtains. The simplicity of the room was intensely wonderful, uncluttered, pure. I was so entranced by the room I hadn't noticed that Helena had slipped out of her dress and I watched her eyes as it dropped to the floor. She was completely naked, her nipples hardened by the incoming breeze no doubt. Her hair, so golden, falling around her pale bare shoulders as she lay on the bed.

"Paint me, Mateo," she said as she moved onto her side, her head propped on her hand.

"I can't paint," I replied, shaking my head.

"Have you ever tried?" She asked, moving her hair

away from her face.

"No."

"Then how would you know, silly? Pick up a brush Mateo. Paint me. Put your heart, soul and passion into it. Do it as though you were making love to me. Take your time, make each stroke of relevance."

I smiled at myself for even picking up the brush, for dipping it into the paint because it was something I would never have attempted before. Before what? Before losing myself, the love of my life, my mother, my father? I had numbed myself. As I began to paint her, I was surprised at the ease I felt, the natural way I held the brush as though I had been a painter all my life. I began to make love to her through the brush, it guiding me and pulling me through the curves and contours of her nakedness. I was amazed at her ease about being exposed to me in such a way. I basked in her beauty, the sight of her. I didn't want to fuck her. I wanted to make love to her. To cherish her, drink her, pleasure her the way she deserved. Lina. Lina deserved that. I didn't deserve her. Had I ever? I felt my hand being guided, some other force contributing its part to the ease with which I was able to paint.

"You look so comfortable there, a true natural. Mateo, the painter of nudes," she said, then begin to laugh. With that laugh a gust of wind, carrying with it a strong scent of lilac, raised the curtain high. I felt so peaceful. Comforted somehow. I knew I shouldn't be here, with this woman. But it felt right, for now. I would figure it out later. As my brush made the tiny goose bumps around her areola I began to wonder who she was. What was her story?

"I am just a regular Joe, ok, Jane, like you. I was put into a situation many years ago that made me look at life differently," she said, sitting up in the bed, drawing her knees to her chest and wrapping her arms around her legs. There she went, reading my mind again. "I watched someone I love die slowly," she continued. "His commitment to live each day was much greater than his desire to try to prolong his life for a few more months. He denied the chemo and drugs that would certainly keep him in bed or puking in the toilet for hours on end. I was selfish. I wanted him to seek treatment but he wouldn't have any of it. He watched me cry, scream in anger and hate the world for a week without saying a thing. Then he sat me down in this very room. He asked if I was done. Had I gotten all the why's and how comes out of my system? He spoke to me calmly, grabbing my hands and putting them against his chest. He said, you have two choices, my love. Enjoy my last days with me or walk away, sparing yourself the sadness and grief. I don't want to be around that. I want to be around life, as much as I can take with me."

"I chose to stay with him. He lived sixty-three more days. Sixty-three, Mateo. I did more things that mattered in those sixty-three days than I had done in my entire lifetime. I am not talking about traveling or being extravagant. We did things he loved. Simple things. Things I had always taken for granted, I suppose. I made him tuna fish with relish sandwiches. I mowed the lawn every five days because he loved the smell of freshly cut grass. I read to him, poetry mostly. We engaged in hours of foreplay as he re-explored every inch of my body. The art of kissing, the sensuality of caressing. When we did make love it was either really slow or really fast. He went barefoot everywhere. People looked at him as though he was crazy. He wanted to feel the concrete, the dirt, the sand, with every footstep. We bought an old phonograph and lots of records. His favorite was Charlie Parker. Now you can see why. We played many albums, drank red wine and danced in the kitchen until he was out of breath and exhausted. Toward the end, it was even smaller things that delighted him. His first cup of coffee in the morning, eating Cheerios while reading the morning paper. He would stand in the rain until he was absolutely soaked and chilled to the bone just so he could come in and take a hot bath."

"He loved driving fast on the freeway, blaring Jethro Tull's 'Locomotive Breath' or Hearts 'Crazy On You'. Then, as he lay dying, he asked one thing of me. That I find the small things in life and enjoy them to the fullest. He wanted me to make a list and read it to him. A lemonade stand. The smell of a dark room. My hair played with. Lilacs. A porch swing. People watching at the mall. Breakfast in a cosy mom and pop diner. Blasting music when alone in the house. Painting in an all-white room. You get the picture Mateo. Once a week, I make sure I do one of those things. I bought a porch swing. A lilac bush."

"The phonograph we had I gave his sister because she had given it to him. I got a new one, as you know. All these things make me happy and life is short, Mateo. Do what makes you happy and you will find it draws people to you. And that in itself will make you happier. Go to Lina. Tell her you love her and you will change, if it's what you want."

I put the brush down. How did she know Lina's name?

She got up off the bed. I watched her pick her dress up of the floor, stepping into it and then pulling it up over her thighs, her ass, her breasts. She turned her back towards me, motioning for me to zip her up. I complied. I wanted to ask her how she knew about Lina but I was afraid. After she told me her story, there was a silence now that seemed appropriate.

She grabbed my hand again and led me down the hallway. The photographs were bigger than I had remembered. The people in them appearing 3-D. They were staring at me, their eyes shifting as I walked by. They were talking now, shouting things at me. I couldn't understand what they were saying. I tried to say Helena's name, but nothing came out. I stopped, pulling her hand towards me. She looked at me again, tears rolling down her cheeks. The hallway seemed longer and longer. Helena let go of my hand and she began to walk backwards, her eyes still on me, her tears coming faster out of her eyes, dripping down her cheeks. Jesus. What was happening? The lilac smell was so strong now. Stronger than ever. A woman in a photograph reached out, and began caressing my shoulder.

"Mateo. Are you okay? Mateo, wake-up."

I opened my eyes. It was Lina, holding a bouquet of lilacs. I was naked, laying on the kitchen floor. It had all been a dream.

*　　*　　*

It has been six months since Lina left and I fell asleep naked on the hardwood floor. Lina still gives me shit about that but I don't care. She came back. I started to tell her about the dream and Helena and how real it seemed but then I stopped myself, lying to her that I didn't remember anymore.

I wanted to keep it to myself. Like if I told it, it would be just a dream and nothing more. I would never tell Lina how much impact that dream had on me. How I felt that dream had changed my life. Maybe it was my Dad, giving me a message. I guess I like to think that. Either way, it changed things for us. We ended up fixing up the house and it sold within a month. Lina and I headed for Portland. We ended up buying a beautiful white house with a wrap-around porch, just like the one in my dream. If I told you a large lilac bush sat proudly in the front, you might think, how ironic, but it would be the truth. When moving things out of my parent's garage, I had indeed found a box of old albums. You might raise an eyebrow if I told you I had come across an album of Charlie Parker's that belonged to my Dad, 'Property of Paul' scrawled across the top. I even ordered a beautiful mahogany phonograph. Lina was bustling about in our kitchen the day it arrived. As I unpacked it and plugged it in, she ran to get the box of albums.

"Baby, what do you want to listen to?" She asked, looking at me with that old glimmer back in her eyes.

"Put on Charlie Parker."

Ruled Out

poem

Lies,

Lost,

Lust and grammar,

Loses itself amongst my tendrils.

Sifting across my mind,

In a pattern

Of nervous restlessness.

Bring it home!

Bring it on!

He calls to me.

Bring me to orgasm!

His begging turning to pleading,

Making him look like the ass of scoundrels,

Drooling alcohol down bearded faces,

Pouting, pathetic,

Lost in a depression of robotic ideals on
How to live life.
A...B...C...
It's not that easy,
To be brilliant.
Genius, emotionally charged on some
Tight apparatus that you've designed.
Tying and binding my hands and feet,
Laying me on your makeshift mattress,
Infested with roaches, even the flying kind.
Hoping to split me open with your idiotic ideas of
How I should be fucked, taken.
Your erection dwindling,
Withering,
As my pungent sex and incoherent prose
Pours from my vagina at an
Apocalyptic speed,
Torturing you as you pull your arm hairs out and
Clip your infected toenails,
Deciding to masturbate instead,
But not on the bed
Instead alongside the window sill,
Showing those uncaring twits your cock,
As the rain is spitting against the glass, you spit
your semen,

Your putrid hatred of your own demise.

Your crying and angst as you bury your head into

The orange musty shag carpet, screaming

Why me? Why now?

Why not, be it for the love of a woman, a woman

spreading her legs, wide,

Her naked pussy exposed to you,

The words, pouring out of her, grabbing to your skin

Like leeches,

Sucking up and out the vile liquid that flows

In your clogged up veins

Finding it hard to digest the shit that

Pours out of your incandescent skin.

Me, now screaming,

Why, why, who am I?

As I lift my benevolent body from the

Makeshift mattress

Screaming at you to immerse yourself in

Something worthy,

Leaving me with my thoughts and desires,

Which infinitely,

Rule you out.

The Pasture/Europa
Part Two

short story

Luca

I wasn't new to tragedy. The sadness in my eyes had been there since I was a ninth grader. Since the day my three sisters and mother had not come home from dress shopping, their car hit head on by a drunk driver. A week later I moved in with my best friend Ezra, his mother insistent on being my mother's replacement. My father was too saddened to argue, and truth be known, I couldn't stand to step back into my house, remnants of my mother and sisters embedded in everything. Ezra was an only child and it seemed I was just the addition their family needed, bringing a new dynamic, though somber and awkward at first. My own father had grown thin and sad, a shadow of the bigger than life individual he had always been. It seemed he was just going through the motions.

I think he was grateful, thankful really, that Ez's parents had stepped in, offering me a chance at a nurturing and happy home. Our freshmen year, Ezra and three other classmen formed a band called 'The Bronxmen', playing festivals, highschool dances and under 21 bars. Ezra had always played the part of the tortured artist, being somewhat moody and a bit of a loner, so I was happy that he had found his niche. He had also met the beautiful Lydia at a gig. Apparently it hadn't been the first time she had seen him. Her and her girlfriends had been groupies following 'The Bronxmen', her eyes on Ezra for quite some time. One night, with her girlfriends egging her on, Lydia marched up to Ez, telling him she thought he was one of the best guitarists ever, throwing him into the category of greatness with the likes of Jimi Hendrix.

They were inseparable from that moment on. I liked her from the get-go, but was always a bit put off by her rich girl attitude. Her father was well known, and like him, she usually went after what she wanted. They were good for a while, until Ez began talking of moving to Seattle. From then on, they were always a bit up and down. Me? Well, about a year before my dad died from a heart attack (I was convinced it was a broken heart, pure and simple) he had given me a Nikon, encouraging me to capture things I had always taken for granted. I knew he was simply having regrets for not taking enough photos of 'his girls', his own camera gathering dust on the bookshelf. So began my love for photography. After graduation, I enrolled at The International Center of Photography. It was great not having to worry about the money thing. Between both my parents life insurance policies and the settlement from the drunk driver's insurance, I was set for a long time. I moved back into my home, Ez in tow.

About a year after graduation, Lydia moved in with us, enrolling in classes at NYU. Ez's band broke up shortly after high school. About six months later, he formed a new band, The Defenders. Lydia booked most of their gigs for them. No one could say no to her. I wondered if it was her way of controlling Ez a bit, keeping him close to her at all times, as though he could be easily averted. She believed most musicians to be unfaithful, but I knew Ez would never have strayed, so smitten was he with her. I had never really been in love. I had a few dates, but somehow my family would come up, then my sisters, and I never knew if I was a sympathy fuck after that or if they really liked me. I guess I never really waited around to find out, instead finding excuses for not pursuing anything. In fact, I had begun to say I was adopted by Ez's parents, that I was the product of a druggie mother living on the streets of the Bronx.

Frankly I was sick of telling my story. Lying was much easier and less painful. I was honestly thinking of heading to Seattle with Ez and starting fresh, a place where no one knew me or my tragedy. Easy breezy. Then Lydia went and fucked up everything by getting pregnant. Shortly after, Ez wanted to get away, and.... well, here we are.

So though I didn't know what to expect as we left Katabole, our ATVs loaded with supplies, I felt as though

I could endure any sort of catastrophe that was to befall us, of the physical kind, that is. I had, however, taken Lydia's death very hard and I didn't know how much more my heart would endure. Undoubtedly, Athena was the greatest thing to happen to any of us. She had saved our lives. I certainly saw that, and whatever anger I held against Lydia for trapping Ezra, was gone. Far, far away. I was relieved to leave the confines of Katabole, it holding us prisoner for so long. We had drained everything we could out of that place, physically, mentally, emotionally. I was ready for the new world. Optimistic, really. I had to be. It wasn't about me. It was about Athena. This would be her world. I knew Arturo would take care of her as well, at all costs.

We were so fortunate to have him. Beyond lucky. So far, we had been dealt all the right cards. Then things got weird. We left Katabole, Ez and I on one ATV, Athena and Arturo on the other. Arturo, a bit ahead of us, had stopped his vehicle and appeared to be having problems. Ez and I got out to assist him and that was the last thing I remembered. I woke up, alone, on a cot in a concrete room equipped with only a bucket, which I assumed was my bathroom, and a small jug of water. A couple hours later, a woman came in with food.

"Where am I? Where is the little girl and the two men I came in with?"

"My name is Deena. You are in Europa. I am not sure where your friends are, but you will see them soon."

Violet

Most of the Vegas that entered the confines of Europa seemed relieved. Relief in knowing they would have food in their bellies, a warm place to lay their bodies, human contact, without the devilish acts of theft, rape or murder. It was a community, a town, a city. I don't know if it was the face of the future, but it was our future, the few thousand of us that had survived. It was possible there were other communities out there as well, but if so I hadn't heard.

Our sovereign, Agatha, educated us in all aspects of starting over. Look to your future as a clean canvas. Don't think about what 'I' will do today, but what can I do for someone else? We were taught the three H's. Help. Heal. Humanity. It was a tremendous struggle for the men. It was a tedious job, re-teaching them. The more 'simple' ones adapted well. The 'smarter' ones were taught to swallow their egos, fuck their machismo, quell their pride. In this process of rehabilitation, their balls had shriveled, like a dog with its tail between its legs. It was an adjustment, for all of us. The world as we knew it had changed, and thus, so did human nature. It was natural for the woman to nurture, to make things right, to balance the scales evenly. To be the ground breakers, the torch bearers, the path finders. Men had fucked us, literally and figuratively. They are not as intelligent as we once thought. Their brains are wired differently than the female brain. They have no reasoning abilities.

After further testing, they were found incapable of certain emotions. Compassion, acceptance, forgiveness, gratitude, hope, remorse, homesickness, interest, empathy and ecstasy. They were found to lack the euphoria of sex, feeling only a need to ejaculate, or get themselves off. In other words, men were found to be using only about 30 percent of their brains, while women a staggering 90 percent. I was reading from some of the literature that Agatha had written. I was being 'taught' to agree with it, but whether I did or not was another matter. There was something strangely different in these men.

I sputtered some of the water, as Ezra had tipped the glass too much and I tried to swallow all of it, as to avoid it dribbling down my chin, looking like a fool. Luca quickly wiped my mouth with his sleeve, as though I were a small child. The act was endearing, and I was taken back.

"Sorry," said Ezra.

"No problem." I said back. These men were 'clean' in every sense of the word, physically and mentally. I would label them 'BA', our word for 'before apocalypse'. Nothing about them screamed Vega. Not their appearance, nor their words.

"Thank you Ezra", I said as he put the glass down on the table, shifting in his chair. His anger seemed to subside for the moment, his act of feeding me water changing his demeanor. He spoke quietly this time, calmly.

"The little girl that came in with us…"

"And the Mexican," Luca said, cutting off Ezra.

"Yes, and the Mexican," Ezra continued. "Where are they? Please, she is my daughter. She must be frightened and scared to death. I beg you."

I had never seen such desperation in a man's eyes before. As I shared his angst, our eyes locking, I felt Luca touch my shoulder, causing a sudden pleasurable twinge down my back.

"Please Violet. She is just a little girl," Luca said, his hand still on my shoulder.

I stood suddenly, realizing I had put myself into a compromising situation. This was going against the guidelines. They think and act like animals. Sex and food foremost on their brains. They can and will seduce a woman when given the chance. They fight easily amongst each other. Arguments between them always result in physical damage inflicted on each other.

I spoke quickly, smoothing down a pretend wrinkle in my skirt. "How old is the child?"

Luca answered, still close to me. "She is five."

"She is an area we call Velocity, with other children. She will be well taken care of, I can assure you."

"She has NEVER been with other children," Ezra said loudly, his rage beginning to boil again. Luca then shot him a quick glance, as if telling him to stand down, but he clearly wasn't. "And the man that came in with us. I demand that we see him. He has done nothing wrong. NONE OF US HAVE, FOR THAT MATTER!!"

Ezra was standing now, headed for the door. Luca reached out to grab his arm. I spoke calmly, as instructed, realizing how irrational 'the man' could be, how unpredictable and quick to anger he was. I couldn't show anger back, or retaliate in any way, for it would further complicate the situation. It was our way of re-teaching 'the man' how to behave, the correct way.

"Ezra, you cannot help the child or the man you inquire of when you act like a heathen," I said, trying not to mock him. Then he did something I did not expect at all.

He began laughing.

"Heeeeeethennnn? Ha, ha, ha ha ha ha ha haha ... you're so fucking fucked in the head you sorry ass bitch!!! If you so much as look at those two wrong, I will slaughter you as you sleep!!"

This one would need a lot of rehabilitation, a lot of drugs to control him. Becoming an Arcturus would be out of the question until he was 'under control.'

"EZRA! Stop!" Luca said, turning Ezra's body around to face him. He grabbed him by the shoulders, pushing him back down into the chair. Luca had a way with him, instantly calming him. I wasn't surprised. He had that way with me as well, and he was a complete stranger. It was a good a time as any to ask them the questions that had been gnawing at me since they had arrived. Before I opened my mouth, Luca asked for a gallon of water, said they were both extremely dehydrated.

"I don't know about a gallon, but I will see what I can do," I said, walking towards the door. I spoke quietly to Leah, then turned and walked back, seating myself at the head of the table. Ezra was already seated at my right, and I motioned for Luca to join me at my left.

"Okay gentlemen. First question. I want to know where you have been the last five years. You appear to have stepped out of an entirely different world than the one the rest of us have been, shall I say, acclimated to. Where do you come from? Can you tell me why you were drugged when you arrived, and what that drug was, and who administered it?"

Luca spoke. "I will answer one question only. We come from 'Da Bronx'."

Ezra giggled a little, like a school girl. It appeared Ezra really only would be good at one thing and one thing only, and that was a breeder. I feared he could administer a lot of damage, turning many of the men against us, slowly and surely, if he were put into Andromeda. I wasn't sure how intelligent he was, so I was hoping there was an artist buried somewhere in that anger and frustration. Most of the men, upon removal of their narcissism, pride and inflated egos, appeared to have artistic talents beyond their knowledge. They need to be re-taught, re-wired.

"Okay, I said, "let's start there then. You're from the Bronx, perfect. As you know, most what was left of the United States was just a small chunk of the east coast. Many of the buildings were left standing, but sadly most of the population was not. As you may or may not know, a series of major earthquakes hit in succession after the major eruption of the super volcano in Yellowstone National Park. The west coast fell into the Pacific Ocean. The country was bathed and blanketed in ash, smothering all vegetation and killing most animals. It polluted the water supply leading to a nationwide food crisis. This was AFTER the catastrophic series of earthquakes that caused most of the entire Midwest to be consumed by fire. The volcanic ash went into the jet stream, killing thousands immediately."

I stopped, taking in their faces, then continued, "It is obvious by the open mouths and wide eyes that you knew none of this. I suspected this. You both are what we call 'BA' or 'clean'. I will ask you again, where have you been?"

Ezra spoke. "We were taken by a band of carnivorous Mexicans, kept chained and shackled, and used as sex slaves." Luca began to laugh. I looked at him, his eyes dancing, and couldn't help myself. I began to giggle.

Ezra spoke out, as though serious. "What? What is funny about this? Have you ever sucked Mexican cock? It is not pleasant!!"

Now I laughed outright, the burst surprising me. Luca joined in, laughing more. We stared at each other, laughing, as Ezra continued to whine. "Look, I don't know what you find so funny. We were brutalized by them, truly. We did manage to escape, by taking the little one hostage. Bring him in here, he may be able to answer all of your questions."

Luca stopped laughing. He grabbed my hand that was resting on the table. "Please, he said. Please, our friend, Arturo. We need to see him. He is like a brother to us." Luca's momentary laughter was replaced with sadness. I truly began to feel for them. "Fine. I will arrange for you to all be together for a couple of hours tomorrow. Answer one question for me. The drug you were given, that made you sleep. What is it called and where did you get it?"

Luca spoke calmly. "We met a small group on our journey. We had some alcohol that we traded them for what they told us were some cannabis pills. It was not, obviously. It was some sort of sedative."

I spoke, now angered. "Why in the hell would you give it to a small child?"

Luca and Ezra exchanged a quick glance, Luca continuing. "We believe she had taken one that Ezra had accidentally dropped. We looked for it, but couldn't find it."

The bullshit smell was really strong now. I didn't believe a word of it. They weren't going to tell me, and honestly, I didn't blame them. Why should they? They were protecting and loving each other.

"And what of the Mexican? Why didn't he take it as well? " I asked, just for the hell of it.

Ezra spoke this time. "One of us needed to keep watch, so to speak, and to be with Athena."

Maybe they were telling the truth. I wanted to believe them, to save them from further questioning. "Where did you meet Arturo?" I asked.

"Just on the road. He knew about this place, Europa, and led us here," said Ezra, his eyes on Luca's.

"Where have you been the last five years?" I asked this, rather indignantly this time. They had not 'weathered' the storm, like the rest of us. It didn't seem fair. Part of me was, dare I say, jealous?

Luca spoke, shifting in his chair. "We managed to get out of harm's way shortly after the event, being taken in by some strangers in an underground shelter they owned."

"Hmm, I said, tapping my pencil on the table. "Well, where are these strangers you speak of? Where is this underground shelter?" Silence. Neither of them said a word. I spoke, beginning to stand. "I know you're both lying and full of shit. Don't think I can't see through it. We are done here. In the meantime, Leah will escort you to an area called Orion, where you will be tested for disease and given complete physicals. I promise you will be able to meet with Arturo tomorrow."

"And the little girl, Athena?" Ezra asked, hopeful.

"Yes, I replied, motioning for Leah. Athena as well."

Arturo

We drove away, me and Athena in one ATV, Luca and Ezra in the other. Athena blew kisses towards Lydia's grave as we passed by. "Honey, we can stop if you want to," I said, slowing down the ATV.

"It's okay Papi. I said goodbye already, right here," Athena pointed to her heart, "and here." And she pointed to her head. She was an amazing child. I had never seen a child so brilliant, so well-spoken before. She kissed me on the cheek just then, as though she had read my mind. It was hard not to fall in love with her. She made it so easy.

I had been planning how I would get us all safely to Europa for some time. Jose, the gardener from Katabole, had told me of a stash of firearms some of the men had hidden away on the property, unbeknownst to Speros, who I was told had apparently despised weapons of any kind. It was simply ludicrous to think they would not be needed. Since I had been accustomed to the 'goings on' of the outside world, I wasn't about to leave without firing power. Not carrying weapons would be madness. We simply would not stand a chance. I had about ten 'pocket glocks' and enough rounds to kill a small army. We would certainly be killed on sight for our precious cargo. Just the ATVs alone were a gold mine.

The problem was Ezra and Luca would slow our progress considerably, just gawking at the new world. They weren't prepared to fight. They weren't prepared for what they were about to see, and I didn't have time for them to get prepared. The main reason, however, for doing what I was about to do, was for Athena. I didn't want her to witness anyone's blood, demise or death, especially if it were her own two fathers'. I didn't know what kind of havoc it could wreak on her psyche and I didn't want to find out. I had weighed the pros and cons, and had looked at the situation from every angle. This was the right decision.

I had already taken one of the ATVs out earlier, loaded with dehydrated food, medicine, water, guns, blankets and tools. I dug a hole and buried everything. That was a couple of weeks ago. I had also taken Torpidity, in vial form. It would be simple. Our journey from Katabole to Central Park, was roughly two hours and thirty minutes. I planned on a day, at the most, factoring in overgrown roads, and speed of the ATV, with four of us on one. Nightfall would not be my friend and Torpidity would most likely have worn off by then. Torpidity, in vial form, when inhaled with cotton, was guaranteed to put someone out for at least ten hours. Plenty of time. I made the move. I had already pre-soaked three squares of cotton with the drug, marking Athena's with an X, as it contained a lot less. Athena would be first, since I didn't want her to think I was hurting her dads. She was already leaning against my shoulder. I pulled the cotton out of the plastic bag, maneuvering the ATV with one hand. I quickly put it up against her nose. She was out. I was a bit ahead of Luca and Ezra. I stopped the ATV, jumping out and bending down to the back tire, pretending something was wrong. Ezra jumped out first, as I had hoped. He would be easier to carry than Luca. As Ezra bent down next to me, I called out to Luca. "Will you grab those pliers out of the back, in the grey toolbox?"

"Sure," said Luca turning back towards the ATV.

I pushed the cotton against Ezra's nose. He fell over immediately. I quickly ran behind Luca as he fumbled through the tool box, pushing the saturated cotton to his face. As he slowly slumped, I pushed his body into the bed of the ATV. I was thankful these were the Mercedes of ATVs, very roomy and powerful. I had never seen anything like them. Custom made especially for Speros was my guess. He thought of everything, down to the last detail. I wondered how he had met his demise. Block. Stop. I can't think about that. My thoughts would turn towards my own family and I would not allow that. Athena, Luca and Ez are my family now. I was assigned to them, and they to me, for whatever reason.

I covered Luca with a blanket, then went back for Ezra, putting his body into a sitting position against the tire as he would be easier to pick up that way. I flung him over my shoulder, like a sack of flour, stumbling the couple of steps to the back of the ATV, nestling him in next to Luca. I then retrieved Athena, placing her between her fathers. With the three of them in the back, I didn't have much room for supplies. I expected this. If Europa turned out to be non-existent, I would simply make it back to the stash of supplies that I had buried half way between Katabole and Central Park. We could hide there for a few days if we needed to. It wasn't a perfect plan, but it was Plan B, and one ALWAYS needed a plan B, should plan A fail miserably. I started the ATV up, my precious cargo out cold, and made my way out of The Pocano Mountains, towards Central Park.

Violet

Her breathing slows down…it is her plateau time…he knows her rhythm, the time frame….as long as she keeps her eyes closed, her body adrift, she will go to that place, that far away lovely place that she holds dear, where there is everything good, and nothing bad, where her body and soul meet, together. Her oneness, as she opens herself, her mind, her senses, and it overtakes her, as long as her breathing remains shallow, he knows he has time.

He picks up the chair, carefully, with her still on it, and takes her into the living room, placing the chair on the berber carpet. He pulls her legs and ass down, away from the chair, laying her carefully onto the carpet, her hands still bound to the chair. He then pulls the chair even farther from her, arms now outstretched, belonging to the chair, her body splayed out. He looks at her in the dimly lit room, her breasts hard and red from his biting and nipping at them.

Her body, moving up and down, slowly, with each shallow breath. Her sex, hairless, vulnerable, waiting. He unbuttons his jeans, pushing them down past his knees, his cock erect as he picks her legs up and thrusts himself deep into her. She gasps, and then her body slowly reacts as he begins to fuck her. She wraps her legs around his ass. He loves the sound of her wetness, the slick sound it makes, as he moves in and out of her, slowly at first, and then faster, his pace quickens, her moans louder, her shoulders beginning to feel a slight burn against the carpet with each thrust, though the pain is delicious. Her hair splayed around her, her nipples erect. He is so turned on by her he takes her harder, more forcefully, and she screams out.

He takes a finger, gliding it up her ass, beginning to fuck her with it, his body in rhythm with the thrusting of his cock. The combination sends her closer to the edge, and her orgasm builds, builds, her breath quickens, faster, as her climax begins to mount. He pulls out of her, his finger as well.

He lays her body down, then lies on top of her, untying her hands. She is grateful for the release and begins to hold him close to her, softly kissing his face, his goatee scratching her lips. She loves the feel. He lays next to her, kissing her softly, her hair, her neck. She takes his cock in her hand, touching and caressing the tip. She climbs on top of him and sits up. The glint in his eye, she knows all too well. She kisses him, her tongue swirling with his, she feels his hands on her ass, drawing her closer. She stops and moves towards his chest, licking him slowly, her mouth on his nipple. She takes it into her mouth, swirling her tongue around it, slightly biting him. She hears his soft moans, and begins to feel her climax, again building, the pleasure in his voice propelling her body into ecstasy.

She guides his cock into her, taking him in fully, her cries of pleasure filling the room as he fills her to the top. Her mouth still suckling his nipple, she fucks him, her hard nipples moving back and forth across his skin.

His moans build her climax, faster, faster, as her moans fill her own ears, her sounds delighting her. Her orgasm releases then, rushing through her body. She feels him getting close, knowing when he is almost there. She moves off of him, lying herself on the floor. He climbs on top of her. She guides his cock into her again, loving the instant pleasure of his momentary entry. "Fuck me, fuck me!" She screams out.

There is a knock at the door. I put the book down. I was just getting to the good part. I glide across my studio apartment, my robe sash trailing behind me. The knocking is persistent.

"This better be good!" I call out, half joking, half serious.

I open the door to my good friend Genevieve, her beauty always catching me off guard. She kisses me on the cheek, a common greeting among most the women in Europa. Genevieve is the most recent addition to Ophelia and the most anxious to be impregnated.

"Vi, Vi," she says, pushing past me, headed for the kitchen. "Got any alcohol? I am dyyyyying for a drink!"

"Well hello to you too," I say, shutting the door. "You're not supposed to be drinking when you're ovulating."

"What a pile of shit," she says, opening cupboards. "I can understand when you're pregnant, but..."

I cut in. "Bottom left, next to the sink." She pulls out my stash of Absinthe, giving me a grimace.

"EW! This is all you got?"

"Well, since no one likes the stuff, I can get two bottles instead of the one bottle allocation. Ha! Why are you really here, honey, I am sure there is a lot of illegal alcohol floating amongst the rest of the Ophelia's. Not that I don't enjoy socializing with the 'higher-ups', but I was just getting horny and thinking of paying an emergency visit to the Hydrus!"

"Speaking of sex," says Genevieve, opening the bottle anyway and taking a swig, "I heard you interviewed two astoundingly handsome men today for my fucking pleasure. Ha,ha,ha...did you like my pun?"

"Yea, you're a riot. Wow, news travels fast."

"Well, it's been awhile since we've had some good fresh meat in. I think all the girls are getting wet just thinking about it. I heard one of them is mulatto. That's the one I am interested in. Some dark AND white meat...mmmmmm.... and I am sure he is well hung!"

I knew she was talking of Luca. "Genevieve, they haven't even been tested yet, keep your panties on!" I said, grabbing the bottle of Absinthye and taking an even bigger swig. I had never ever been interested in any of the men that came in. Until now. I felt compelled to protect him. The thought of him pleasuring the Ophelias and impregnating them with his seed simply turned my stomach. Genevieve grabbed the bottle from me, taking another swig. "Easy honey, easy. If you smell like alcohol they will kill you!"

"Ha, ha," she said, taking another swig. "Calm down babe. Now tell me all about them. Rumors are flying.

Something about they've been hidden away from the event somehow? Avoided the Apocalypse all together? How is that possible?"

"They said they were in some sort of underground shelter," I said, grabbing the Absinthe back, putting the cap on and spiriting it away into the cupboard.

"And you believe them?"

Protect him. Protect them! "Yes. I do. Besides, where else could they have been? Taken by space aliens and hidden away on Jupiter, only to return now that the air is clean and vegetation is growing again?"

"Well, ANYTHING is possible, Vi. Speaking of sex, gotten any lately? You seem a little pent up."

"As a matter of fact, I was just reading some erotica before you disturbed me. Now, if you don't mind, I would like to go back to my bed, and my book!"

"Sure. Hey, would you like to have tea tomorrow in The Commons? I heard some new blends came in the other day. I have been dying to try something new. Earl Grey and English Breakfast get old after a while."

"Sure. Let me check my schedule. I had promised Luca and Ezra a meeting with their daughter and Arturo.

"Okay, and if you find out any more about that lovely pair of men, do share."

"You'll be the first to know," I said, giving her a quick kiss and ushering her out. I made my way back to my room, dropping my robe at the foot of my bed and climbing back in. I didn't pick up the book, instead I had a fantasy that Luca and I were making love, his kisses warm and soft on my neck and breasts. I drifted off, the liquor warming my insides.

Arturo

In just the short time I had spent in Katabole, I was surprised how much had changed since I had been a 'wanderer'. Oddly enough, I didn't run into anyone. I was now regretting putting Ez, Luca and Athena to sleep, wishing now we could experience this together, but I had no way of knowing. Most of the road was overgrown and slow going at first. I was surprised by the number of animals I saw. We certainly wouldn't starve to death. I was thankful again for the guns, as that would be the only way to hunt, or at least the only way I knew. I had buried most of the supplies to make way for Athena, Luca and Ez in the back. I had made it out of the Pocano's and found what was left of Interstate 80. It was cracked and quite overgrown, but I made up for lost time getting out of the mountains.

Most structures I saw were either collapsed or overgrown. No sign of human life anywhere. Was Europa enough of a city that most survivors had ended up there? It appeared so. I began to feel a sort of euphoria, hopeful and excited to be around people again. I remained optimistic until I passed what appeared to be a mass grave. Then my thoughts soured and I thought of the woman, Jelena, whom

I had met when I was on the streets traveling with the Empinatas. She was from Bosnia and had fled her country in the early 90s. She had explained how her family had been broken apart, some choosing to stay, unable to make the journey to America due to personal, income or health issues.

She also spoke of Europa and seemed hopeful of getting there. Like many she had asked if we, The Empinatas, were sent by the military. This still makes me laugh. Yes, right you are!! The most powerful country in the world has resorted to asking a band of nomadic renegade Mexicans to save its sorry ass. Hahahahahaha. Where was our military? Deeply embedded in other countries, not able to get back to the United States to take care of their own. It wasn't their fault. It was the fault of the American government. I recalled that startling statistic...the American military was in 130 countries with 900 bases around the world. I remember Luca stating that all of the trillions of dollars this country had spent sticking their noses in everyone else's business, could have been used in saving and preventing their own country from crumbling, millions dead, the complete and utter downfall of the U.S.

I am sure a lot of countries felt the Americans got what they deserved. As in all countries, the innocent pay for the sins of the leaders. Ezra felt the American people had been fooled, tricked and brainwashed for years, relying on a government that never once had their best interests at hand. Now I stared at the downfall of one of the greatest cities in the world, a casualty of a government and country that had failed it miserably.

I made my way to the George Washington Bridge. It stood in all its glory, but empty of movement, making it look all the more ominous. There were abandoned cars littered at the entrances to the bridge, their rusted out interiors open and exposed. It was an odd and beautiful sight, and I wished desperately for a camera. I made my way through the maze of cars, hoping and praying that someone would rise from one of them. Hell, at this point I was even hoping for a ghost.

I made my way over the bridge, the water below littered with debris. The city, though desolate and abandoned, was beautiful. Grasses, shrubs, ivy and trees had planted themselves on streets, in buildings, anything that was abandoned. Most brick had long ago crumbled and fallen to the ground. All structures were a canvas for graffiti, proudly displayed. Art prevailed, in its own right. I thought of the prehistoric etchings marked on caves and rocks. Even in our demise, mankind was still etching, marking his territory, that he had lived, had been here. It was eerily quiet, and I somewhat expected to be pounced on by an animal at any moment.

I made my way through the streets of New York but it was difficult. Some streets were impassable, many of the cars bunched together. I had assumed many had been used for hiding, sleeping and taking a dump in. There was no sign of life, except for an occasional cat. I did see a few birds, mostly pigeons, and took that as a good sign. The streets were mostly cracked, broken, the potholes immense. The ivy was beautiful, overtaking pretty much everything in its path.

I stopped, studying my map again. Central Park running north and south from 110th to 59th. Shit. It was bigger than I had thought. I turned the corner, and there she was. Most of the park perimeter, for as far as I could see, was constructed of a brick wall at least 12 feet high. The street around the fortress itself was clean, no cars or litter. I could feel my heart beginning to beat faster, the thought of being with people again beginning to overwhelm me.

I stopped, lifting the blanket off of Luca, Ez and Athena. I wondered how much longer they would be out. As I stared down at them, I got another idea. A better idea. I backed the ATV up about thirty feet. I pulled Ezra out, lying him gently in the street. Then Luca. I got back in, starting the engine. I had passed a small warehouse full of old signs. I decided to hide the ATV in there. I left the supplies, hid the keys away from the ATV, and picked up the sleeping Athena. I walked the couple of blocks to where I had left Luca and Ezra. I sat down, Athena in my lap, contemplating my next move. I must have fallen asleep. I began to dream. I opened my eyes, quickly realizing I hadn't been dreaming of being surrounded by beautiful women. I truly was. I got to my feet, quickly, rather embarrassed.

"My friends and I, we have been on the road for quite some time. We are in search of a place called Europa. My name is Arturo. This is Ezra, Luca, and their daughter Athena," I said pointing to my sleeping friends. Oh my god, I am actually talking to people, and they aren't trying to bash my head in. Had things changed that much?

Suddenly, in the distance I heard the soft hum of ATVs. Oh god, they found ours. Shit. The tallest one spoke.

"My name is Claire. We are part of Europa." She looked at the three other women standing near her as she said this. They didn't notice or utter a word. They were too busy staring at the sleeping Luca, Athena and Ezra.

Before another word could be spoken, three ATVs came roaring at us from around the corner, all occupied by women. I surely then thought I had died and gone to heaven, although now I wondered where the men were. Not that women weren't capable, but I found it odd. Maybe roles had been reversed in Europa. I smiled to myself at this thought. The American term 'house husband' came to mind. I pictured a burly man doing the dishes, his feet newly pedicured.

The ATVs pulled up near us, a short blond haired woman jumping off one of them. "Everything is clear. We need to hurry though. We saw a couple of tigers nearby," she said, picking up the sleeping Athena.

"No, what are you doing?" I said, grabbing at the blonde's arm. She didn't flinch, continuing to pick up Athena.

"You were looking for Europa, right?" said Claire, calmly.

"Well yes, but…"

Claire suddenly cut me off. "Well, first of all, we are all from Europa, and second of all, you need to help us get your friends into the ATVs before the tigers decide you're going to be their next meal. Trust me, they are hungry as fuck."

Two other women were lifting Ezra, a third was beginning to lift Luca, yelling my way. "Don't just stand there!"

I dashed over, picking up his shoulders as she lifted his legs. Tigers? Shit. I hadn't seen any wild animals before. Had they been hunted from the zoos and eaten long ago? Claire spoke again, not as calm this time. "Get the Cannes Vieti out here at once and find those tigers."

After the stern brunette and I had deposited Luca in the back, she jumped on another ATV with two other women and they sped off. They really seemed to know their shit. I couldn't wait to see the men of Europa. I rode with Claire, Athena in my arms. "You must be hungry," she said, looking at me, almost studying me. She kept staring at Athena as well. I drew her closer to me, as if someone might steal the sleeping child at any moment. I noticed the other women that were hauling Luca and Ezra kept staring at them as well. Okay, what gives? Were there no men in Europa? What the fuck? Then I realized something that had not even crossed my mind. We looked too fucking good. Too clean, too kept.

Shit. They would want to know where we had been. How we had eaten. No marks on our skin, save for my knife wounds that were not visible. We looked well fed, groomed, healthy and fit. They wouldn't believe we had been out in the world, just getting by day to day. Hell they would have a lot of questions that I was not prepared to answer. They could never know about Katabole. They would raid it and take it over for sure. Whether or not we ever made it back there, it was still our home, Athena's birthplace, and I wouldn't let anyone desecrate it. Especially not these fucking bitches. I started getting a sinking feeling in the pit of my stomach. Something was not right here. Fuck.

We pulled into a monstrous structure located on the south end of Central Park. It was full of men. I started to breathe a little easier. They were working on ATVs and a few large trucks. They were solemn and quiet as they pulled Ezra and Luca from the back of the ATVs, transporting them into wheelchairs. I looked at them concernedly and as they did so, Claire assuring me my comrades would be taken care of until they 'came to'.

I realized then how exhausted I was, hoping that there would be a place I could rest. A woman approached me, her dark hair striking against the whiteness of her skin.

"I will take her now," she said, referring to Athena, still fast asleep in my arms. She undoubtedly picked up on my reluctance, as I slowly turned my body away from her. "No. She will wake up scared and confused, not knowing where she is," I replied. She spoke so calmly, quietly, her manner quelling my fears. She took Athena out of my arms. "She will be fine. You need to rest, get some nourishment. I will come for you as soon as she wakes, I promise." I nodded in agreement, looking around again. Something felt strange to me, not right. As I felt that sinking feeling again, there was a sharp prick on the back of my right shoulder. Before I had realized what was going on, two men were on either side of me, and then my world went black.

Ezra

I woke up in a small concrete cell, equipped with water and a bucket. I assumed we had arrived in Europa, though if this was their way of welcoming us it was very unfriendly. The last thing I recall was Arturo putting something against my nose. I had recognized the odor immediately, the lilac floral smell of Torpidity. But why? I trusted Arturo, but I was angered. Why would he do something like this? Knowing Arturo and the kind of heart he possessed, I could only conclude that he had done it not out of maliciousness, but out of love. To protect us somehow. Maybe he thought it easier to travel. Were there things he didn't want us to see? Something he hadn't told us? Evils? I doubted it, but my mind jumped to many different reasons.

Either way, it had been a long journey from the Pocanos and I had to give him credit for getting us here, evading the potential hazards that am I sure were lurking around most corners. Now I found myself wanting out. Wanting out of this fucked up place called Europa. I had seen a lot of women here, but very few men. It seemed as though the women were in charge. I never felt welcomed, only tolerated. I wondered what had happened to the men we had been on stage with. A couple of them seemed ill. We had been questioned at length by several women, Violet included. They seemed more concerned about where we had come from, how had we evaded the Apocalypse and where the drug Torpidity had come from, then making us feel part of a new city, a new life. Though I had been reunited with Luca, knowing he was okay, I had yet to find out about Athena and Arturo's whereabouts.

I had been told they were safe, but I felt I was being lied to, and was being treated like a dog in the street, by the women I had met so far. Clearly, they did not like men, did not trust us. It seemed power had changed hands. How had they accomplished this? Not that I believed women weren't capable of controlling men, fuck no. They were very capable. Lydia had controlled me, using her pregnancy to change the course of my life. Although had she not, most likely I wouldn't be here, nor would Luca, and certainly not Athena. I couldn't begin to imagine a life without Athena. She filled a void in me that I didn't realize I possessed.

The few men I had come in contact with seemed different, although I was never with them long enough to figure out what that difference was, being moved quickly from one area to the next. Violet had promised me and Luca we would be reunited with Arturo and Athena. I prayed this was true and not a ploy to get me to spill information. I liked Violet. She was different from the other women I had met so far. She had a softness about her. I felt guilty for having been a bit of an ass to her. I could tell Luca was attracted to her. I noticed right away the way he looked at her. He had only looked at one other woman that way. Lydia. I knew he loved Lydia; hell, who didn't. I had hoped and prayed many times he would find someone. I was glad he had envisioned coming to Seattle with me. It would have been a cleansing of a sort for him. I loved Lydia, but I guess just not enough. Not enough to want to stay in New York. I felt the tears welling up inside. I began to cry. I longed for my parents, wondering what had happened to them. My friends, bandmates. Everyone gone. I still held out hope of finding someone in Europa. Someone that had survived. I needed to walk through this place. I needed like hell to get out of this fucking cell.

Just as I stood up, Violet was there, unlocking the door. "Ezra, I am so sorry to put you in isolation like this, but it is for the health of everyone else. We just had to make sure you are not sick or carrying a disease. You're fine, as well as Luca, Arturo and Athena."

I decided to take a different approach, hoping I could get what I wanted. "I understand Violet. They are not your rules. You are just doing what you are told. I am sorry for being an asshole to you earlier. Understand that I am a bit out of sorts right now, being separated from my daughter. She must be scared, sad and upset. She has not had much contact with anyone." I looked at her then, my eyes still wet from my tears.

"That's why I'm here," she said, "I promised you would see them today, and you will."

Violet

Ezra's demeanor had changed a lot. I had heard him softly crying as I made my way to his cell. My heart went out to him. I found myself thinking more and more about my brother, my mom and dad. Though we are given shots to diminish our memories, I had skipped the last few. I was getting severe headaches following the mandatory vaccinations. I had signed off that I had received the shots knowing full well that lying and deceit was punishable. I knew I was taking a great risk, but the headaches had subsided and I was thankful to be pain free. I wondered how long I could get away with this. I knew I could lose my position within Europa.

Because I was a Zeta, one group down from Scorpius status, I didn't require a witness when the shot was administered. I was surprised at how quickly my memory was beginning to surface. With those memories, came a flood of emotions. I had forgotten what it felt like to feel empathy or sadness, love or anger. I had felt more of a numbness before that I hadn't realized was gone, until now. I felt an incredible longing. I felt like the old me, and I liked it. I also welcomed the pain, the sadness that came from missing my friends and family. I felt alive, for the first time in a long time. I had frequent thoughts of Luca. His face, his eyes, his lips, his voice, his touch. He had stirred something in me that had been buried by the drugs for some time.

"Violet, are you okay?" Ezra's voice cut into my thoughts. I hadn't even noticed he had grabbed my arm.

"Sorry, yes. Arturo and Luca are waiting for us. While you are 'catching up' with them, I will get Athena."

No sooner had I finished this sentence than I was in the arms of Ezra. The last person to hug me this tightly was my dad, proud when I showed him my first pay-check. I can't believe I remembered that! It came to me so quickly! I hugged him back, not wanting to let go.

This is so against the rules. Men don't have emotions like this, remember? Don't let them weaken you, coerce you, or manipulate you. This is how they take advantage of a woman. Their intent is solely selfish. They are deceitful.

No. They are not like that. Lies are being fed to us. Lies. No men in my life had been like that. None that I knew . Women on the other hand, women could be callous, back-stabbing bitches. Agatha and the rest of the Scorpius had been pushing this down the throats of the females of Europa for some time now.

Why hadn't I seen this before? THE VACCINES!! I have been given them as far back as I can remember. But for how long? Years? I couldn't even remember how I had got here. Did I have friends here? Was our past erased somehow?

"You're shaking....can you hear me? VIOLET! VIOLET!" Ezra had grabbed my face and was staring into my eyes, shaking my shoulders. "VIOLET!"

I opened my mouth, afraid nothing would come out. You know that dream you have, and something is coming at you, and you scream, but nothing comes out? There is no one to help you, no one can hear you. "Ezra?" I heard my voice. It was soft, but it was there.

"Violet, what is wrong? I have been speaking to you for some time now, and you were a million miles away. Are you okay? You're really freaking me out."

I couldn't believe what I was about to say. "Listen to me. Arturo and Luca are waiting for us. I will not have time to explain what is going on. Please trust me. Things are not right here. Things are not how they seem. I think they are drugging us. All of us! The men are robotic, their eyes glazed. They are not right. I didn't see it before, I don't know why. It doesn't matter, I see it now. We need to get out of here. I will bring you to where Luca and Arturo are. You will not say anything to them about what I have just told you, understand? The room where they are waiting is bugged. Not a word! I will go and get Athena. When I come back to the room, I will motion for you to follow me. Understood?"

I couldn't believe what I was saying. I couldn't believe what was coming out of my mouth. Ezra's eyes were like saucers as he spoke. "I knew something was wrong with this place! I knew it. Oh god. Oh my god. Fuck everything to hell right now. I wanted to see if I have family or friends here."

"No! You would not be allowed to do that. They will soon put a bracelet on you, branding you, so to speak. It will be hard for you to leave with that bracelet on. You will be electrocuted. Soon after the bracelet is put on, they will give you shots, drugs. Supposedly these erase your memories, but I think they do much more than that. Some have escaped over the years, it is rumored there is a place called The Pasture. I will explain more later. We need to leave now."

Luca

In the last forty eight hours I had been tested, probed, prodded and questioned over and over again. It was obvious women were in charge of Europa. I hadn't laid an eye on any men here yet, save for the ones in the garage and those we had been 'on stage' with. Most the women I had met so far were heartless and cold. There was something different about Violet though. She was transparent, unlike the others. She was struggling, I could tell. But with what? Her place in this fucked up city called Europa? There was more to her than just her beauty. She held a unique quality. Just different.

The thought of her, her dark eyes as I laid her on the bed, unbuttoning her blouse, her black hair in my hand as I pulled it slightly, kissing her soft golden brown skin... the thought of her made me hard. The thought of how her voice might sound as I pushed myself into her. Would she cry out, clutching my shoulder, or would it be a long smoldering moan? Not many women had 'stirred' me over the years. But she did. Oh god, her beautiful full lips. I envisioned them on my mouth, my neck, my cock. It was instant with her. A thirst. I had not touched a woman since Lydia. Was I just hungry to fuck? Yea, of course. But with her, I wanted more, desired more.

I closed my eyes. I hated this place. Loathed it. What had happened to the men? Had they killed them? What were they planning on doing with us? Whatever it was, I had a feeling we wouldn't see Athena anymore. They would take her from us. The thought of this paralyzed me, sickened me.

Just then, a tall blonde woman with a ponytail appeared outside my cell. "Hi. My name is Chanel and I will be escorting you to see your comrades."

She unlocked the door not waiting for me to answer, instead motioning for me to come with her. Violet had kept her promise. Oh thank god. We strode quietly through a narrow corridor, her behind me. Did she have a gun on me, instructed to shoot if I fled or turned on her?

"Take a right," she said, her voice flat, monotone. She suddenly reminded me of a movie I had seen years and years ago with Nicole Kidman. Stepford Wives. Fuck. That was it! The women were robotic, as if they were brainwashed, or drugged. But not Violet. No, not Violet. Her eyes. Her eyes had soul, depth, love.

"Right here," she said, opening the door for me. The room was similar to the one Ez and I had been in with Violet. There was a vast array of art on the walls, and I assumed it was done by the men as well. The invisible men I had yet to see. This place was beginning to freak me the fuck out. Chanel sat me down in a chair, then turned, leaving the room. "It won't be too much longer," she said shutting and locking the door behind her. I could see her blonde ponytail bobbing through the window as she walked away.

I began to look at the art. There were a lot of flowers. I found that odd. I had been in a few drawing classes. No men drew or painted flowers, not of their own free will, anyway. Picasso and Van Gogh were the exception, but hadn't they both been deemed crazy? Buildings, trees, cars or a woman's form was more the norm. There was a pitcher of water and a glass on the table. I wanted so badly to drink that water, but I didn't. I didn't trust them. As I stared at the water, the door opened, and in stepped Arturo, looking tired and confused. I got up from the table so quickly that I hadn't realized I had knocked over the pitcher of water, the contents spilling off of the table and hitting the floor in a whooshing sound. We held each other tight, like long lost brothers, our sadness and disappointment at Europa, our so called 'new world', evident even without words.

Violet

As I unlocked and opened the door, Ezra almost knocked me down getting into the room. Luca and Arturo were hugging and when they saw us, not only did they grab Ezra in an embrace, but me as well. Luca thanked me, giving me a light peck on the cheek. He looked at me then, longer than he should have. I knew that look. I took him in equally as fully, my want of him apparent in my eyes, I was sure of it. Arturo grabbed my hand then, holding it between both of his, thanking me over and over again in Spanish. I hadn't met him until now, and I liked him instantly. His face was beautiful, his cheekbones high, his smile contagious. I felt a deep love and care for each other among these men. I knew then, felt it in my gut, that I was making the right decision.

I gave Ezra's arm a squeeze, signaling that I was leaving to get Athena. I put my finger against my lips, reminding him to be quiet, that the place was bugged. He nodded.

I needed to move quickly, knowing that in less than an hour, the garage would be unattended while the Canes Venatici, our 'hunting dogs', were out. I normally walked from area to area, but today, I flagged down one of the gardeners on an ATV.

"I need to get to Velocity as quickly as possible," I said, jumping in. He looked at me and nodded. He looked so sad, so complacent. They all looked like this, did they not? Why hadn't I noticed this? I wondered where his family was, what his story was. I could feel the anger beginning to surface in me. What was really going on here? Not only were the men in Europa being controlled, but so were the women. All of the women? Some of the women? I was so confused. So much I couldn't remember. So much they had taken away from me, from all of us. This wasn't living. This was a dictatorship.

I looked at the gardener again, wishing for a normal conversation, an interaction. He had been taught not to speak until spoken to. He had been taught to bow down, that he was lesser of a person than the female. He was but a dog in the street, and the woman was his master. He would be told when to eat, when to sleep, what to think, when to fuck, when to speak. What if my brother and father had survived? They would be treated the same. Would I let this happen? No. Unless I was unable to think and feel for myself. Unless my mind had been taken away from me. We stopped in front of Velocity.

"Please, wait here. I will just be a moment," I said, touching his arm. He was taken back for a moment, at this gesture, as he flinched slightly. He looked me in the eye then, as if asking why, what have I done? The sadness in those eyes would further haunt me.

"What is your name?" I asked, my hand still touching his arm. He turned his body toward me, as if I was radiating heat and he was chilly, wanting to get warm.

"My name is Seth." I could tell he wanted to say more, but he didn't dare.

"Nice to meet you Seth. I will be right back," I said, quickly jumping from the ATV and into Velocity.

Ezra

When our huddle broke up, Arturo was the first to speak. "Please forgive me for.."

I cut him off quickly, by squeezing his arm hard. I mouthed the words, 'this room is bugged'. Luca still looked at me, questioning what I just mouthed, but Arturo got it, and whispered quietly in Luca's ear. I laughed out loud. Why didn't I think of that? I blurted out quickly how much I missed them both, then whispered in Arturo's ear "we are getting out of here. Violet will be here soon with Athena." Then I whispered the same thing in Luca's ear. We all looked at each other then, wanting to say so much, knowing we could not. "I can't get that song out of my head," Arturo said. We both looked at him, wondering what he was up to. "You know that song we sang on the road. Ninety nine bottles of beer on the wall."

On cue, Luca and I began to sing. As we did, Arturo began to whisper in my ear. "I have a plan. I hid the ATV. We can make it back to Katabole if we have to." I nodded, continuing to sing. He then whispered what I assumed was the same thing in Luca's ear. Luca nodded as well. Then I joined in. As we got to eighty five bottles of beer on the wall, Violet walked in with Athena in her arms.

"Papi, daddy, father!" she screamed out, and we all

rushed to her, kissing her, touching her, and were surprised to see how she clung to Violet, as if they had always been together.

Violet

I fell in love with her right away. The moment I spotted the big saucers for eyes she had. She was the most beautiful child I had ever seen. When I told her I was taking her to see her daddy, she asked me which one.

"I have three. Papi, daddy and father," she announced proudly, as though she was certainly the luckiest child on the earth. "Is your daddy here too?" she asked, her big brown eyes peering deep into mine.

"No, sadly my daddy is in heaven," I said, feeling my heart become suddenly heavy.

She touched my cheek. "My mommy is there as well. It's okay if you want to cry. I didn't know my mommy, she died when I was born. Sometimes father would pretend to be mommy. He would let me put make-up on him, and he made his voice high."

She began to giggle. Her laugh was contagious and I laughed with her. She was incredible. I took her hand, and we walked outside, to where Seth was waiting. We got into the ATV and I held her in my lap. As we made our way back, I chose my words wisely, whispering in her ear. "Athena, as soon as you are with your fathers again, we are going to go on a little adventure, okay? I need you to be very quiet, and not ask any questions until I tell you it is okay. Do you understand?"

She whispered back into my ear. "Are we in danger?" Her question took me by surprise. Before I had a chance to answer her, she whispered, "I know all about dangers. I know all about not telling anyone where I have come from, how I got here, what I know. My Papi taught me a lot of things, things that would protect me, keep me safe. I was taught not to trust anyone, until they have been cleared by daddy, father or Papi."

I couldn't believe what she was saying, and she was so matter-of-fact about it. We pulled into the garage and it was empty, just as I had suspected. The Canes Venatici were out, and I knew my time was limited. As Athena and I got out, Seth remained in the ATV, looking at me.

"Sorry, that will be all Seth, you may leave."

He got out, leaving the key in the ATV as I had hoped. As he trudged away, I grabbed it out of the ignition.

"Why is he so sad?" Athena asked, grabbing my hand again. "He didn't even talk to me, didn't even look at me." Seth's disposition seemed to really bother Athena.

"No honey," I said, picking her up then. "It's not you. He is sick."

"Well, if he is sick, my daddy says to take care of anyone who may be sick, sad or dying." I held her closer to me, for fear she would disappear into thin air somehow. She seemed too good to be true, and I was falling in love.

"Well, your daddy would be right Athena. We will take care of him later. First, we need to take care of ourselves, to make sure we are able to take care of others. Okay honey, we are almost there. I need you to play the quiet game we talked about."

"Deal," she said, and made the long ago motion of pretending to lock her lips, throwing away a pretend key. I can't believe I remembered that and I smiled as I opened the door. Arturo, Ezra and Luca were in some sort of huddle.

Arturo

It was a short reunion, as Violet motioned for us to follow her quickly. No one said a word as we made our way through the corridor unnoticed, opening the last door on the left that I recognized right away as the one that led to the garage. The place was empty.

As if reading my thoughts, Violet spoke. "The Canes Venatici, our 'hunting dogs and scavengers' are out right now. We need to move quickly, as they could be back at any moment."

Ezra took Athena from her as she climbed into the driver's seat of the ATV, pulling the key from her pants pocket. We all jumped on, Luca sitting up front with Violet. They exchanged a look that I noticed right away. Now I knew why she was doing what she was doing. She wanted him. But from what I could tell, it was reciprocated.

"Will they come looking for us?" I asked Violet, as we turned the corner.

"I don't know. Let's pretend yes," she said, seeming to be sure of where she was headed.

Luca, Ez and Athena were quiet, mesmerized by the overgrown decaying city that was once New York.

"Turn right up here, mid-way on the right side of the street."

"Arturo, I don't think we should stop. What is it?" Violet asked.

"Hang on," I said, jumping out of the back of the ATV. I ran inside the warehouse, unearthing the ATV I had hidden a couple days ago. Ez jumped out as well, grabbing Athena. As I got it started, pulling out of the warehouse, Ez and Athena climbed in next to me. We were off, Violet leading the way. We seemed to be heading East.

No sooner had I thought it, than Ezra said, "We are heading East, perhaps to get on state Route 22."

"Where does that go?" I asked.

"Well, it's a two lane rural road, passing mostly through villages. It makes the most sense, but hell, I don't know anything anymore. I had high hopes for Europa, and look how that turned out," said Ezra, holding Athena tighter as we were hitting rough road.

"Daddy, why are we leaving? I liked that place daddy. So many children to play with."

"I know honey, I know you enjoyed the children, and you need to be with children, to grow with those your own age. The problem with that place is that I wouldn't be able to be your daddy there. No Papi, no father. We wouldn't be together in Europa." As Ezra said this, he kissed her softly on the cheek.

"Well, I don't want to live my life without my daddy, my Papi or my father. Do those children not have daddies?"

"I don't know exactly how it works there honey, but no, I don't think they do. Violet will be able to explain it better honey." Ezra looked at me then, I could see a look of uncertainty in his eyes. I nodded slightly to him, indicating that to be the perfect answer.

"Athena," I said putting my hand on her leg. "I would be sad, the saddest man in the world, if I couldn't be near you or see you anymore." Athena popped her head up suddenly from Ez's chest, where she had been laying.

"When I was with Violet, a man gave us a ride. He was so sad, Papi. Do you think that is why? Because he can't be with his children?"

I nodded. "Yes baby, maybe so."

She laid her head back down, obviously thinking about this. I felt sadness then. Sadness for giving her a taste of this place, which she seemed to like and enjoy, then taking it away from her. Would she be better off there? No. It wasn't a life. Her life was with us, period, whatever that was. Now we had added to the family. We had Violet. Athena had Violet. But, most importantly, Luca had Violet, and that made me happy.

Seth, Route 22 and The Pasture

We had made it to the outskirts of the city, finding route 22. Luca and Ezra had toyed with the idea of going by their house in the Bronx, but then decided against it. They decided against it for many reasons. Perhaps it would prove to be too painful. All of the buildings, ghosts of their former selves. When looking at a structure, you couldn't help feeling sad. You couldn't help picturing those that occupied it. Their laughter, conversations, joy, sadness and anger, forever etched into the walls. You could picture the children in the empty playgrounds and schoolyards, playing tag, tetherball, hopscotch, or on their cells, showing their friends their pictures on tumblr or a recent tweet. It was gone, all of it. But, we still held the most important thing of all. We still held life.

We stopped, Athena and Violet needing to take a pee break. I was talking to Athena, about the vast array of animals we had seen. I noticed something sticking out of her pants pocket. It was a note. I read it, not believing what I was seeing. I ran over to Violet, quickly handing it to her. She began to read:

> *Violet,*
> *Hello. I knew you could do this, would do this.*
> *I assume you are on route 22, headed for The*
> *Pasture. It does exist. I am headed there myself, as*
> *I have been planning my departure from Europa*

the last couple of years. I have simply been waiting for Athena, Luca and Ezra's arrival. Obviously you were part of the plan, and you have done well. My wife, Natalia, and my son Draven are with me. We are several hours behind you. Wait for us. You will find a home, in the town of Baxter, to be a half-way house on your way to The Pasture, near Quebec, Canada. You will know the house when you see it, it is visible from the road. Most likely you are getting low on fuel. You will find more, along with food, water and a place to sleep for as long as you need. This may all come as a shock to you. I am a seer. Arturo is your spirit guide. If you have any questions, ask him. He will have the answers and will help you. Athena is the key. She is gifted as well. Protect her and love her, as if you were her own mother.
Love is always the answer.
Seth

to be continued.........

Boxes

poem

Boxes.
So many boxes scattered
On the carpet.
A carpet stained with our life.
Coffee, pets, children, wine, food.
My home. Our home. A home that I made for us.
I painted each room with vibrancy,
Breathing my love into every corner.
My children grew up here.
Holidays spent here.
Laughter, love, life,
Lived here.
Parties. So many parties.
Friends gathered numerous times
At our house.
Our door was always open.

Everyone was welcome.

Late night campfires.

Sleepovers.

So many children through the front door.

Bouncy houses in the back yard.

Burgers always on the grill.

Someone always in the hot tub.

Wine flowed endlessly.

Newspapers.

So many newspapers scattered on the carpet.

I begin wrapping up what I want to take.

What do I want to take?

I don't even know where to begin.

How do you pack up twenty-three years?

Black and white photographs grace all the walls.

They are my art.

Many of my children.

Many of other children that

I have forgotten the names of.

What do I do with these?

My tears begin to come,

As I pick up items.

Gifts from him.

Drawings from our children.

Wedding photos.

Our china.

Our love.

Once.

I sob. I am paralyzed.
I can't do this.
But I must.
I found an apartment.
I signed a lease.
We both agreed this was best.
Why is it so painful,
So gut-wrenchingly sad?
I go through the motions.
I take some forks, knives, spoons.
Some coffee cups.
A few plates.
I wrap everything carefully in the newspapers.
I lay them carefully in the boxes.
I feel so much sadness.
So much sorrow.
What do my children feel?
How will they cope,
Knowing their mother is leaving.
Packing.
They are in their rooms,
Doors shut.
Can't bear to hear the sounds of newspaper,
Wrapping belongings,
Going into boxes.
Boxes.

Left on Ten, Right on Two

short story

I turn sixty-four soon. How the fuck did that happen? What is the life expectancy now for a man? Is it sixty-eight? Seventy-eight? I know it's higher for a woman.

What's up with that? Shouldn't a man's be higher since he puts up, bows, and says Yes dear to the chronic bitchfest for years? She should go first. Let me enjoy my last few years in quiet and peace and with endless masturbation. She won't fuck me anymore anyway and gets mad if I shake the bed while going to town on my rod. I'm all for twin beds. Let me play with myself in solitude.

By the way, my clock is ticking. My time is running low. Oh, I've done a lot of great things in my life, s'pose. I loved my parents, adored and got along with my sister, went to college, fought in Vietnam, went back to college, got a great job, and got married and had two wonderful children. In fact, my daughter is due to give me a grandson any day now.

I'm preparing to retire. My wife is giddy with excitement over this. She sees a Winnebago in our future, singing show tunes as we careen down the endless highway headed for Yosemite, the Grand Canyon, or some other fucking landmark she has highlighted in pink on the map she just purchased at Bartell's Drug Store. She bought a map and a new pair of readers, so she can actually see where the hell she wants to take me to.

I have no intention of doing this. Zero. *But, honey, she will say, we've talked about this for yearrrsssss!* Correction. You've talked about this for years. I just listened and nodded, not wanting a substantial conversation to ensue with you that could potentially raise my blood pressure, resulting in a stroke, a heart attack, or the dreaded aneurysm. I didn't necessarily want to retire. Correction. I fucking don't want to retire! Why, you ask? Because my job enables me to travel, and I have about five lovers located in various areas across the country. Now, before you go judging me, know this. I am not in love. Not with my wife and not with my girlfriends. I believe if I was in love, I wouldn't be sticking my cock in various snatches.

This is the part where I ask you what is on your bucket list. (Just go with me on this. We're getting there.) Wait, let me guess.

1. Run a marathon.

2. See the Great Wall of China.

3. Go to NYC; see the Empire State Building and Statue of Liberty.

4. Learn a new language.

5. Visit a Castle.

6. Parachute.

7. Learn an Instrument.

Enough. You get the picture. Here's mine.

I. Be in love!

That's my list. Uno. Be in love! Pretty simple, huh? Oddly enough, after scouring others' bucket lists and doing a piece on it for my job (I'm a journalist by the way) no one mentions it ever. Why is that? Is it a given? Mark Twain said, 'A man who lives fully is prepared to die at any time'. Well, I believe a man who loves fully is prepared to die at any time. You still might not be feeling all that sorry for me. After all, I am a scoundrel, a cheater. *Why don't you just leave your wife? You ask. Get a divorce. Come clean. Give her, her own chance at happiness, you two bit, fucking asshole!*

There are a few answers to that question.

I. Complacency.

2. My children would hate me for the rest of my life.

3. Who would want my wife at her age? (Okay, back to hating me for that statement.).

4. I don't want to be taken for all I have worked hard for.

5. My children would hate me for the rest of my life (it was important enough to mention again).

Now, I know what you're wondering. *Then why the fuck did you marry her, you two bit, fucking asshole?*

There are a few answers to that question.

1. I was a young, punk twit.

2. I wanted a virgin (give me a fucking break. I saw it in a movie).

3. My parents loved her.

4. She smelled good.

5. Her breasts were fucking wonderful.

6. See number 1.

So, back to my ticking clock; my time is running out. "Mr. Freeburg, let me just come out with it." I had just left the office of Dr. Stephen Laurent, Gastroenterologist, extraordinaire. According to the good doc, my chances of living another five years are less than five percent. I have stage three pancreatic cancer. "Now, let's go over our plan of attack. Would you like to have your wife come down and we can discuss this process together?" Fuck no. Hell no.

I left, the good doctor trying to persuade me to stay and talk about my options. "Carl, I understand your anger." Oh, really? Do you have cancer? Were you just told you wouldn't last long enough to possibly see your grandchild enter the world? I've never even been in love! So there! Go fuck yourself!

I think he could tell I wasn't planning on staying and going over our plan of attack. "Call me as soon as you have let this sink in, and we will discuss your options," he shouted after me, his glasses sitting on the bridge of his nose. Reminded me of a professor I once had. "Carl, I think you are capable of more than this trivial bullshit you have turned in." He would glance at me, glance back at my paper, back at me all through tiny readers that sat on the bridge of his nose. "My fifteen-year-old writes better dribble than this, in her journal!" he added. Yeah, and I am sure you read it, you cock-sucking, mother-fucking prick! I wanted to shove those tiny readers straight up his ass.

I don't plan on discussing some strategic plan of attack (sounds like a huddle in 'Nam) with Doc Dire or anyone else for that matter. I seem angry, don't I? Seething is a better word for it. I am stewing in my own cancerridic juices (it's not a word, but I think anyone given a less than five percent mortality rate can come up with a plethora of whatever the shit they want. It's my fucking prerogative).

I am still shaking as I strap myself in my car and start the engine. Scratch that. Fuck the seatbelt. At this point, a quick death from a head-on collision resulting in decapitation sounds much better than having my organs go through complete failure. I turn on the radio. My favorite station, Jack FM. All hits, all the time. The best of the 70s, 80s, and 90s. They play current hits but don't know what to call the first decade of the twenty-first century. I am perplexed by this. This gnaws at me still. We as a group, you as well, have all tried to come up with something. The oughts. The noughts. The double 0s. The zeros. Please, someone, anyone! Let's figure this out. Please, God, Please! Before I die!

I pull over to the side of the road. I grip the steering wheel, both hands clenched on it. *Left hand on ten, right hand on two.* That's how my Dad started me out. *Total control of her, son. Left on ten, right on two. Don't be one of those smart ass kids, one hand on the steering wheel, the other smoking, drinking, or fingering his girl. Two hands, son, two hands!*

Dad. I miss you, Dad. Dad, I'm scared, Dad. Simply fucking terrified, Daaaaddyyyyyyyyy!

I pull back into traffic, left on ten, right on two. A quick glance in the rear view mirror. I shouldn't have fucking done that. I don't look so hot. I find the nearest gas station, pull in, buy a pack of Camel lights, ('cause lights are better, right?) and a bottle of Rolling Rock.

"Soree, sir, you nee' buy fo' sex-pack."

"No," I say, throwing down a ten.

"Yez, yez! I no sell u lie dis! Sex onle!"

"Listen, motherfucker. It's not sex; it's six! And you will sell me one because I am dying and probably won't be around long enough to drink the fucking sex pack!"

I walk out of the store, not waiting for my change.

"Learn English, mother-fucker."

I drive out of the city. Left hand on ten, right holding beer. I hear my mother, whispering to me from the backseat. *Carl, I won't tell your father about this. Not this time, Carl. Just promise me, honey, you won't do it again. You're such a good boy, Carl. Now, why would you want to go do something so foolish, anyway?*

Mom. I miss you, Mom. Mom, I'm scared, Mom. Simply fucking terrified, Mommyyyyyyyy! I see a field we used to play in as kids. Wow. I have driven by it so many times but only really realized just now how unchanged it is after all these many, many years. How it had managed to stay the same, dodging the bulldozer and another Stepford wives-looking, sorry ass, cookie-cutter neighborhood. Untouched, virginal. I parked on the side of the road and got out. It was eerily quiet. And humid.

I remember back years ago, I was driving with my girl and we came upon a field similar to this. "Look, honey," she said, "it looks like the perfect meadow." We got out and had only taken a few steps when we realized how fucking quiet it was. No birds or trees rustling, anything like that. And it was humid. We kept walking because that's what teenagers do and came upon an underground cellar. "Well, go ahead, Carl. Open it. No, Carl, what the fuck are you thinking?"

I'll tell you what I'm thinking. I don't want my girl to think I'm some mother-fucking panty-waist, that's what I'm thinking, so I pulled open the latch, the door oddly heavy. It creaked loudly. Again, silence. That creaking sound would have set off a murder of crows if there had been a murder of crows in the vicinity. The smell hit us first. It was the smell of death. As our eyes adjusted and more of the sunlight hit the dredges below, we saw what we realized were at least twenty dead dogs and cats hung by their necks from a badly assembled barrage of rafters. The screaming from my girl hit the back of my neck like a dislodged loogie sliding down my throat. I dropped the door so fucking fast and screamed, "Run!" After I got the car started and we sped away, the screaming subsiding, the words devil worshipers slipped out of both of our mouths. I didn't want to be anywhere in the vicinity when they grew bored of animal sacrificing and moved onto humans.

Anyway, this field was just like that. Sorry if you were looking for more regarding that story. Notice how when you're upset, or in my case told you could fall dead at any moment, random, stupid ass thoughts start entering your mind. You start thinking about stuff. Unimportant stuff, trivial stuff. Life stuff. Stuff to take the edge off. Anyway, it was eerily quiet. I continued to walk, still holding my Rolling Rock and my pack of smokes. I got to where I thought seemed the middle of the field and sat down, the tall grasses swallowing me a bit. I lit up a smoke and thought. About shit. About my kids, about my life, about my wife. I mostly thought about dying. I clearly had decided I didn't want to. I wasn't ready. What the fuck does that mean anyway? But I'm not ready yet! There are soooooooo many things I haven't done yet!

Quit your punk ass, whiny, crybaby bitching, Carl. Buck it up, buttercup. God, this tobacco tasted good. Notice how before an execution, they will have the decency to ask you what you would like before they shoot you between the eyes or strap you down before sending high voltage through your body? I would like a filet mignon, cooked medium rare and a baked potato with all the fixin's. While that is digesting, I would like a cigarette. Is it pushing it for me to ask for a quick blowjob?

Now I lie down, still smoking my cigarette. The sky the bluest of blue with wonderful, puffy clouds moving slowly. My sister, lying next to me. *Look, Carl, it's a tiger chasing a puppy! Carl, look, it's a lamp!" She was so good at picking out shapes of the clouds. "Carl, look, it's a unicorn ramming its horn into ... never mind!*

Denise. I miss you, Denise. Denise, I'm scared, Denise. Simply fucking terrified, Deeeeennnnisssssssse!

I sat up. Snuffed my cigarette into the dirt. I got up and trudged back through the field to my car. I got in, starting the engine. I drove away. *Left on ten, right on two. Good boy, son. Now you're getting the hang of it! That's it! Good!*

I pulled into my driveway. The house looked different. Inviting. Charming. Warm. Cozy. I walked in, the screen door letting the whole god damn neighborhood know I was home. *Nothing some good ol' W-D 40 won't take care of, son. Details, son. Git 'er done!* My wife appeared suddenly in the hallway, her hair wrapped in a turban, wearing my old, green, terry cloth robe. What the fuck? I bought her a lovely, satin jobby last

Christmas. Why does she insist on wearing mine, stinking it up with her White Shoulders perfume?

"Carl, how was your doctor's appointment? Everything go okay?" I looked at my wife. I mean, really looked at her.

"Yup. Great, no worries," I lied. "Hey honey," I said, surprising myself at my upbeat tone, "let's go look at Winnebagos."

My wife's face lit up, kind of like when I asked her to go steady light up. Yup, same look. "I would love to, honey. Let me dry my hair real quick and put some clothes on. Just give me a sec."

She rushed off to our bedroom. *You're such a good son, Carl. We are so proud of you. Yes, way to step up and be a man, son.*

We headed down the road toward Ken's Kampers, my wife smoothing down her skirt. I slipped my right hand between her thighs.

"Carl," she said, "Whatever are you doing?"

Left on ten, right fingering my girl.

The Art of Peeing Standing Up

short story

I have three brothers. They are all so completely different from each other. So completely distinctive. I always thought it to be so odd, how we could all be raised together but be so entirely unparalleled from each other. I am the second oldest. It goes Zane, me, Esme then Holden. My mother was constantly pregnant it seems, beginning at the age of 22, so we are all close in age. If you were to ask me if I had a favorite I would quickly be stern with you and say "I love them the same." And I did, but the love of each had its own originality. The love was unrivaled. There were things about Zane that I admired that gave our relationship its own uniqueness.

Zane, the brilliant one in the family. Innovative, athletic, beautiful, smart, funny, yet so emotional, quick to anger, but the first to apologize if things went wrong. Zane, class president, class clown. He had a 4.0 all through school and would go on to get appointed by our state senator, chosen among thousands to be one of the few to attend the prestigious Annapolis Naval Academy in Annapolis, Maryland.

Esme, the brooder. Genius in his own right. An artist that could draw your face and make it look like a photograph. He used pencil, but mostly charcoal. I think at the age of seven he could draw most anything you asked for. He was also an amazing drummer and was self-taught. I was in awe of his talents. Maybe even a little jealous. He would sit in his room for hours, drawing, drumming and listening to the Beatles. He was tall, lanky, poetic, with the face of an angel. Painfully shy, not liking to be spoken to, to engage in conversation of any kind. Not even with us. He was called the black sheep of the family and I still don't know what that really means. I loved him dearly, but I just didn't understand him. Not at that time anyway.

Holden, the youngest. We got along the best, or should I say I had the most in common with him, for a while. Holden was the most striking of the brothers. Charismatic, athletic to the hilt, social, outgoing and loved by everyone; stoners, jocks and the unpopular sect alike. His body was so perfect, he was chosen among hundreds of entries to be our high school mascot. When you think of mascot, you think of a beaver or a duck, perhaps a hunk of cheese. Not our high school mascot. It was an Indian. And as we know, Indian warriors were scantily clad, other than a headdress, moccasins and a loincloth of sorts.

Watching Holden crash through the gymnasium doors, tomahawk in hand, to begin a pep rally was an image one could never forget. His grace, his beauty, his incredibly muscular legs, chest and arms, enticing women and men alike as he performed his pre-game warrior dance, bringing the student body to their feet, screaming and cheering for more. The one thing you would like most about Holden, was that he didn't know it. None of it. He lived in his own world, not realizing the girls loved him and the boys envied him. He would give you the shirt off his back, the morsels on his plate, the last coins in his pocket, if you needed it. He was the giver, the peace maker, the sensitive one. He cried easily and he loved hard. He would go on to play college football. He was given a scholarship. His high school girlfriend dumped him their first year of college and he would be forever changed by that.

I learned a lot from my brothers. First, there were the physical things one learns. Like how to run insanely fast when one would chase me with a mouse or some other unlikely creature they would pluck from the earth. When Esme wasn't drawing or drumming, he would play basketball with me. We constantly played the game 'horse' and I became so good at free-throws I won two free-throw competitions when I was eleven. I played basketball in sixth grade much to my father's excitement but that was short lived. Esme made me stilts out of coffee cans one summer and I learned balance. Zane was always in a tree, reading a book. If I wanted to be near him, which I always did, I learned how to climb.

I also learned the art of reading. Oh yes, there is an art to it. I would watch Zane's eyes as they would shutter back and forth like a type-writer, consuming the words so fast as he rapidly turned pages. He would teach me how to read like that, fast. Of course, I never really learned to read that fast. I mean I could, but I would find my mind wandering so quickly, I would have to re-read the previous sentence. It was Zane that introduced me to the illustrious Stephen King. He would become my favorite author of all time.

I learned how to ride a bike, but not just on the road. My brothers would ride their bikes through all sorts of terrain and I had to keep up with them. Holden was the fastest and most daring of all of us. He has a few scars and battle wounds to prove it. I became fast. I became fearless. I constantly wore bruises on my knees. Had all my front teeth knocked out riding a tricycle too fast and hitting a bump in the sidewalk. I could do back bends, flips and the splits.

My greatest feat, however, after all of this, was that my brothers had taught me how to pee standing up. How to stand a certain way and spray the urine so it didn't run down my legs. This took a lot of practice but I got it. It came in handy when camping as I was able to avoid the feared, smelly, dank and ever deep outhouse. On car trips, when we had to pee, I was able to go by the side of the road with my brothers, much to my mother's dismay.

After all, having three boys, she was hopeful that she could raise 'a lady.' That she could have some femininity in the house. That I would learn how to cook and bake. I never did. She insisted on me wearing dresses. Insisted my hair be in braids. Hoped I would play with the neighborhood girls. I did, but the girls treated me poorly. And when I was with them, I would long to be with my brothers, much to my mother's dismay.

I wanted to play football in the back yard with the boys, taking my shirt off like they would. Or just simply running around the neighborhood spying on everyone. I wanted to play in the slough with them. The slough was a magical place. We made up fictitious monsters or crazy people that we would imagine to be chasing us. My mother made my brothers promise to not take me down there. But they did, almost every day. Things began to change after one fateful day. We were all climbing out of the slough. I was wearing a skirt and saddle shoes, my usual uniform. I think my mother insisted on that just to keep me from doing anything crazy.

Zane was in front, Esme and Holden behind me. They would make sure I wouldn't lose my footing. Zane usually holding my hand from behind his back. The side was very steep, full of vines and loose dirt. I lost my footing and as I began to slip, a vine reached out, cutting my face from my temple to my chin. Holden grabbed at me, keeping me from falling altogether but the damage was done. Blood

The Art of Peeing Standing Up

was trickling down the side of my face and onto my blouse. My brothers began to freak out. Facing my mother was one thing, but since this involved blood and it was on my face, they feared the wrath of my father.

After all, I was daddy's little girl and he was very protective of me. The moment we got into the house, my mother began screaming, my father carrying me to the car. I was taken to the hospital, the cut now bleeding profusely. I felt horrible for my brothers. I was sure they were sent to their rooms without dinner and were told they would be further punished when their father got home. I felt incredible guilt and sadness, my mistake costing them dearly. I cried all the way to the hospital. The cut, once cleaned, wasn't as bad as they thought. It wasn't deep enough to require stitches. It was promptly cleaned and bandaged. I looked awful, the bulky bandage almost covering half of my face. My father was so angry he couldn't even speak. I knew when we got home my brothers would be thrashed. After that day, things changed.

My brothers began to shy away, fearing I would get hurt. I was crushed to not be included except for a few silly games like 'no ghosts are out tonight' and 'olly olly oxen free.' I resorted to my room, reading and writing in my journal for hours.

I went through the change rapidly. I had my period and a C cup in the 6th grade. My moods were so up and down that Holden and Esme began to ignore me. Zane had his own problems and pulled himself away from me. I think he had started seeing one of my friends which changed the dynamics of our relationship. I found I could have my pick of any boy. I replaced my brothers with a new kind of attention. I found him the first day of seventh grade. His beauty struck me like a lightning bolt. I had never seen him before and after inquiring, found out he had moved up from California. One look and it was all over. We were together for four years. He would be one of the greatest loves of my life but this story isn't about us.

It's about Zane. My brother Zane. We would all grow up, lead lives very varied from each other. Zane left for a prep school in Rhode Island and then entered the Naval Academy one year later. He wrote the most beautiful letters to me while away. He talked of his loneliness, his challenges following orders, and how much he missed me. Desperately, he said. I left our small town, striking out on my own in a big city. I never saw Zane much. He graduated from the Academy, met a girl, married and stayed in Virginia. I had lost him for good. A woman had taken him away. No one in my eyes was good enough for Zane. Or Holden and Esme for that matter. Holden would eventually marry as well. Esme stayed the crazy single artist that he was.

I saw Zane only a handful of times over the next thirty years. We mostly talked on the phone. One summer he had arranged for a family get-together. It was our parent's 50th wedding anniversary. Zane demanded everyone to be there, paying for their airfare if he had to. And we all were. He had rented a beautiful log cabin for the weekend. We all brought our children. My parents were ecstatic, children and grand-children all under the same roof. I clung to Zane that weekend, trying to make up for lost time. He made me feel I didn't need to. For him, no time had passed. Our love was deep, golden and we could look at each other and know what the other was thinking. I never saw Zane again.

He died a year later. Unexpectedly, suddenly, and all our lives would be shattered. My daddy lost his best friend. My mother, her firstborn. Holden his idol. Esme his muse. Me, one of the greatest unconditional loves of my life. He taught me more than he could ever know. He taught me passion, fire, the love of reading, writing, forgiveness and grace. Oh, and the art of peeing standing up.

My Man

poem

He is a man,
He is a God.

He is simple,
He is complicated.

He is smart,
He is brilliant.

He is handsome,
He is beautiful.

He is sexy,
He is sensuous.

He is loving,
He is a lover.

He thrills me,
He exhilarates me.

I think of him often,
I think of him every moment.

I love men,
I only love him.

I want him,
I lust for him.

I dream of him,
I fantasize of him.

He is something,
He is my everything.

Freefall into Us

short story

It is a beautiful March morning. I open the French doors in my two-bedroom apartment in Seattle. I stand out on my balcony and breathe in the crisp winter air. I feel like I am back in New York again and I am instantly happy, gratified, consoled for a moment, hopefully longer. I sit down on my couch, stretching my legs out. My kindle is playing Damien Rice's melancholy voice, soothing me further. I have just washed my face. I have started the dishwasher and wiped the kitchen counters down. I have my strange concoction of lemon juice, cayenne pepper and water. I am trying to cleanse, trying to remove the disdain and toxicity of the muck that is running through my bloodstream. The events of February twenty-sixth caused me to drink excessive amounts of alcohol for the next few days. Now, today, I start afresh. I made an appointment with my therapist for tomorrow. Rent has been paid. My daughter fed breakfast. I nestle my laptop on the tops of my legs. I burrow myself further into the corner of the couch. I take a deep breath, a swig of my drink and begin this painful story, going something like this. *When love is not madness, it is not love ~ Pedro Calderon de la Barca. And we all know love is a glass which makes even a monster appear fascinating ~Alberto Moravia*

The day I met him started like any other day. We met by sheer odd odds. Actually, I think the chance of me winning the lottery was more likely. It was late July and hotter than holy fuck. I was working away at my laptop on my first book. It was hard for me to work under these conditions. I excelled and was most happy when the sky was a sad gray color and there was a steady stream of drizzle hitting the rooftop. The sound caused a tremendous amount of words to flow. The greyness of the day caused my artistic side to become fully engorged, like an erect cock. In the heat and blue sky, I was easily distracted. I meandered over to social media to check on the usual bullshit.

A dating site, Hatch.com popped up on my screen. This wasn't a rare thing by any means. It happened most every day (this would be the reason my lottery chances were better. Because I didn't do dating sites and I judged those that did). But on this day, at this moment, I actually looked at it. A voice in my head urging me to check it out. *No fucking way.* I had my own kind of relationship troubles. My marriage of over twenty years was disintegrating. We had been separated for three years, though still cohabitating.

You know, for financial reasons, or maybe we would somehow pull through, though we had definitely moved our minds and hearts into our own places. My place was my writing. His was music. If anyone tells you that it is hard for two artists to live normally, happily, they would probably be right.

My heart had moved on years ago, and I believe his head had. I closed my computer and padded around my kitchen. I poured cold coffee into a cup, the heating element on the coffee maker having turned itself off hours ago. I opened the refrigerator and debated cleaning it. I looked at the dust that was gathering on table tops. I knew there was gardening to do, bathrooms to be scrubbed. It was normal for me to get up more than a dozen times on a typical day of writing. A small distraction, a quick 'doing' of a few household chores. Sometimes I would masturbate, or take a bath. Sometimes both.

I returned to my computer. Upon opening it, the dating site popped up again. That voice returning, even stronger. *GO ON IT, GO ON IT, GO ON IT!* I felt it was my brother talking to me. He had died almost a year ago. It was July, the day before what would have been his 51st birthday. I felt him with me. In fact, I was sure of it. As sure as I had heard him shortly after his funeral. He spoke to me in a dream. He urged me to continue writing, when I was too grief-stricken to even think of it. He told me I was good. That I had things to say. He told me not only would I write my book, but it would be picked up by a publisher. I got up and wrote for the next year. I was on fire. The words coming so quickly I could barely keep up. Now, here he was, again. Urging me to go on a dating site. Why? *You will meet someone that will change your life.* I quickly grabbed my credit card and signed up. I put in a dubious silly profile, a photo, and I was set. Within seconds, there he was. According to Hatch.com, we were 93% compatible. *Jesus, what about that nagging 7%?* I laughed to myself even thinking it. He was beautiful. It was instant. He must have felt the same. He messaged me right away. The playful banter back and forth had begun.

Hi. My name is Aiden, and you are beautiful.

Thank you. You're too kind. I'm Rowan. You're gorgeous.

I was in fact so sure Aiden was *the one* that I asked for his email. I then deleted my account with Hatch, not wanting to be on there in the first place. Besides, I knew now why I had been urged. It was to meet him. I sent him an email, telling him that I felt he was the one and that I had left Hatch. He couldn't believe it. I am sure he was surprised at my honesty and hunch. I certainly was. We didn't rush to meet. Frankly, I thoroughly enjoyed our phone conversations, our texts and emails that we would exchange over the next few weeks. He was busy. I was busy.

Then, a date had been set. We would go see a movie. I would meet him in a grocery store parking lot. Of course I was nervous. I had never met anyone this way. We had both agreed that if there wasn't that chemistry between us, we would simply be honest with each other and part as friends.

Yea, you know that doesn't work. We would just part.

He parked next to me and got into my car. It was instant.

His smell hit me first. Clean, somewhat musky with ivory soap undertones. He wasn't a big man. In fact, very slight and my height. He made eye contact right away, touching me on the arm. His smile lovely and contagious. I was happy. I drove us into the city. We were an hour early for the movie as I knew we would be, so we parked on the street, in front of someone's house. I pulled out wine and crackers that I had purchased earlier. He was surprised and seemed elated I had done this. Conversation came easily to us. We found much to talk about. His laugh was wonderful. We munched on cheese and drank wine, exiting the car after forty five minutes of chatter. Once in the theatre, as the lights began to dim, he grabbed my hand and held it tight against his knee. I felt like I was sixteen again. He made me feel so alive. He whispered something funny regarding a scene in the movie and we giggled about it off and on through the film. Those around us probably thought we were complete idiots.

When the movie was over, we parted so he could make a phone call and I could use the bathroom. I didn't see him when I came out. I walked onto a balcony, my eyes searching for him in the lobby below. Then, there he was. Across from me on the other side of the balcony. He was staring at me, and then he smiled. That was the moment I knew he was mine. We saw each other over the next couple months, bonding quickly. So much in fact I had this urge to bring some of my things to put into his apartment. I asked him if this would be okay and his response was quick. I would love that, he said. I also knew at that moment we were a couple, that he had left the dating site and was no longer searching.

He invited me to meet his family. His parents, his children. He wanted to make plans for the holidays, involving me with Christmas and New Year. Things were moving rapidly. I wasn't getting any writing done. He was constantly on my mind. When I wasn't with him I longed to be, and when I was with him I didn't want to leave. All thoughts were of him and my writing began to suffer. I had a deadline of December 31st to meet. This would not happen if I continued on this path.

I began to pull away. He seemed to change, as if he could sense things were no longer going as he desired. I couldn't tell him that I lived and breathed him. I couldn't tell him my productivity was deteriorating because of him. I didn't want to end it, I just wanted to put it on hold for a bit. I decided to send him an email explaining this, but somehow I had written the wrong words. Somehow I had told him I wanted to end it, that he wasn't right for me. Was I game playing, seeing how he would react? After I sent it, I realized it wasn't what I meant. But, it was too late.

It was as though I had stabbed his heart. He emailed me back asking what had he done, what had he said, to make me change so quickly. He was beyond hurt, he said, and told me he was going to go away for a while, to lick his wounds, that we would talk later, down the road. I felt my breath come back. I felt grounded again. I had come off of my high with him and was grateful for some space, some breathing room.

I re-focused and over the next couple months I wrote with gusto, the words coming back in rapid fire. Though he was still constantly on my mind, I felt as though I had gotten his intoxicating smell out of my skin. His lips could no longer bite mine, his lovemaking so animalistic, causing bruises on my body. It was like nothing I had ever experienced with a man and I was certain every man after would never please me as much as he. He had in fact moved me so much I felt inspired, grateful for the time I had had with him because he made me see things differently, made me see how some things didn't matter and what was important in life.

His apartment was sparse and my things had brought life into it. I felt as though I had made him feel the same way. Alive. I began to feel remorse and sadness for what I had done. It wouldn't be the first time I had acted foolishly and childishly with a man that I truly wanted. Had I cut off my nose to spite my face, or whatever the hell the saying was? I felt as though he should have fought for me. I felt as though he let me go too easily. After all, I hadn't heard from him for well over a month. I knew I would never meet anyone quite like him. I wanted him, so why had I pushed him away?

It was December 30th. I was at Starbucks, writing away on my laptop. An email came through. It said, *Hi, how are you?* I thought it strange that the email came from a phone number. I ignored it. Then another came through from the same number. It said, *I am in Loma Linda, Ca.* I then wrote back. *Who is this?* Another came through, on the heels of the other. I read the words, *I have stage four lung cancer.*

I wrote back in caps. *WHO THE FUCK IS THIS?* One word came back. *Aiden.* I stared at my laptop in utter disbelief. Tears began to well up into my eyes. Aiden. Aiden. Aiden. I closed my laptop, my body began to shake. I picked up my phone and walked outside. I called him. He picked up. The moment I heard his voice I began to sob, horribly. He went on to tell me that he had gone into the hospital with a temperature of 104. That he had started chemo. Radiation. That he felt horrible. We talked for an hour. I don't remember the conversation. Only bits and pieces of it. I certainly remember him telling me they were giving him until April to live.

I didn't hear much after that. He told me to stop crying, please. He said he couldn't bear to hear it. I begged him to let me come and see him. He said no. He would be back to Seattle soon. We would be together again, soon. I hung up the phone, walked back into Starbucks a different woman. A woman forever changed. I packed up my stuff. The barista asked me if I was okay. I said no and walked out the door. I cried the whole way home. Guilt began to set in. Guilt for what I had said to him. Guilt that I should have been the one to drive him to the hospital. That I should have flown to Loma Linda with him. Guilt for the game I had played with him. For the lie I had told him. Guilt that I had stripped my art from his apartment walls. My books, my blankets, movies. Guilt. Lots of fucking guilt.

I told myself I would never ever challenge a man's feelings again. That I would never toy with him or play hard to get. I had learned my lesson. I also started praying. I had left my Catholic religion years ago, but now I begged for it back. I begged for God to hear me, to heed me, to cure him, please. Please. Just this once. I will be good forever. Just give him back to me. Don't tell me you've never done that. Begged for something with a promise of forever being a do-gooder.

The next few days were a haze of emotions, the most powerful one being sadness. Profound grief. Anguish. First my brother, now Aiden. Oddly enough, when the anniversary of my brother's death had arrived Aiden was there by my side. Holding me, comforting me, telling me that my brother would always be with me. Now Aiden was dying, and who would comfort me through this? How would I even get through this? I would fall apart. Surely I would.

The next couple of months consisted of phone calls and texts between us. He told me they had decided to remove both lower lungs. He told me how the health care system sucked. He told me how sick he felt and how ironic he thought it was that he was comforting everyone around him when he was the one dying. He also got angry with me. He told me he wouldn't talk anymore if I didn't stop crying. Said he couldn't bear to hear it anymore. He asked why I had left him. He said stripping my things out of his apartment was cruel. Did I really mean it when I told him that he wasn't right for me? I told him emphatically, no. I didn't mean it. I just needed to take a break, that he was overwhelming me, that he was all I thought about and my productivity had all but ceased. I told him I wanted to be with him every moment, every second. I told him that I was wrong. Wrong to do it that way. I told him that I loved him. That I needed him. That he was the best thing to ever happen to me.

I cried, and he hung up on me. I never spoke to him again. He texted me a couple of weeks later and told me he was unable to talk. That breathing was like breathing through a straw. That both lower lungs had been removed and that he was having a hard time recovering from surgery. That he had lost all hair on his body and that he was down to one hundred and twelve pounds. He hated being sick he told me. Sick of being sick. Couldn't remember the last time he felt good. His words seemed full of anger, resentment and great sadness. Why him? He wondered. Why now? He asked if I wanted to be with a dying man. I said emphatically, yes. Yes, I want to be with you. Then he said, *it is too late now. See what you have done? It is too late for you. Much too late baby, too late for us.* His words cut into me. His words filled me with the most intense anguish and guilt I had ever felt. Why was this happening to us? I, he, we, had been a complete freefall into each other, a freefall into us. It couldn't end this way. Could it? But it seemed it would. Over the next couple of months I only got a couple more texts. Then, they ended. There was nothing, though I had texted him randomly at different times of the day, night. I pictured him in his hospital bed. I pictured his family around him, crying, sobbing, full of grief beyond their dreams. I thought of his parents, his children, left without a father. I sunk.

I could feel the end coming near for him. For me. For us.

There were days I was so full of grief I couldn't move, fearing my body would shatter into a million pieces if I did. I questioned why we had met. I questioned why we had fallen in love. I questioned the monster that would take him from me. And then a text came through as I was driving. I knew. I pulled over and read it, my hands shaking, the tears already spilling out of my eyes before I even saw the words. He had died. It was his cousin telling me that he had passed a couple days ago and his body had been cremated.

I lost it. I could barely get myself home. My world had crashed and the hole had swallowed me up. I couldn't get out of bed for a couple days. I had stopped eating. My body was cold and I shivered non-stop. A friend stepped in finally, forcing me to get my shit together. I had my children to take care of, a job to get to and words that still needed to be written. Even my husband was sympathetic and caring during this time, knowing how badly I was hurting. Everyone around me worried. Hadn't I been through enough with my brother's death and the slow dissection of my marriage? I got support from all sides. I even turned to boyfriends for shoulders and they were there.

I was grateful. Over the next few months I reasoned why. And I knew the answer. I felt fate had dealt us this hand, that I was chosen to be the last one with him, his last lover, his last hurrah, if you will. And I felt he had taught me so much. His heart was beautiful. He had treated me like gold. I began to mourn what I felt was the perfect man. The perfect lover. I wrote poetry about his death. I wrote about us, hell I had even written him as a major character in one of my stories. I was thankful that I had read this to him before he had died. He was a warrior with a big heart in the story, as I had perceived him in real life. Full of intense passion and compassion. He was so happy. So proud. So honored.

The next few months after his death, brought significant change in my life. I was encouraged to see a therapist. She would save my life. I found an inner power with her that I knew was there but she had given me the head nod, the assurance that I could do this. To be alone. Alone, without a man, for the first time since I was fourteen. She wanted me single, whole and loving *me*. If I didn't love me, I would be worthless to everyone else. I moved out of my home and into an apartment. It was the hardest thing I had ever done in my life. I feared what it would do to my children. But I knew the damage would be more if I were to stay. It would turn out to be the best thing I could have done. Though I missed Aiden horribly, and thought of him every single day, I felt he had played the role he was meant to play in my life, though it was short, brief. I felt that somehow he was breathing through me. I still had days where I would cry for hours over him, my body aching for him, but they grew less and less.

I was moving on with my life. I was writing again. In fact, I had gotten a major publishing contract from a house that I had grown very fond of and had pursued. It turned out they wanted me as much as I wanted them. My children seemed happier. My husband happier, reaching for his own dreams.

Then, it happened. What were the odds of the event occurring exactly as it did before. E X A C T L Y as before. It was a year to the day that Aiden had died. I was lying on my couch, at twelve-thirty at night, reading a book. A voice whispered in my ear. *Go on Hatch.com, now, you must, you must, you must.* I don't even remember getting up, retrieving my credit card, putting up a profile. I took a small break.

Fifteen minutes later, back on the site again, I noticed fifteen men had viewed my profile. I clicked on the second one. It was Aiden. There were four pictures of him. I stared at each one in disbelief. They were taken in his apartment. I recognized everything behind him. I knew the pea-coat he wore in one of the photos, for I had worn it myself.

My saliva began to dry. I stared, knowing full well this was not possible. Aiden was dead. Had his account not been closed? But surely after a year, it would run out, or delete itself from non-payment? Had someone taken his identity, taken over his account? I knew there had to be a simple answer. My head reeling, I went to bed.

The next morning, I opened my computer, rushing back to the site. He was there. In fact, it said he was online. *Aiden, Aiden*, was all I wrote, quickly sending the message to his inbox. No response. Another voice in my ear. It was loud. *CALL HIS WORK. CALL HIS WORK. CALL HIS WORK.* I quickly googled his work, writing down the number. I grabbed my phone and called. I asked if Aiden Carver worked there. They said yes, and gave me his number. I wrote it down, beginning to feel numb. I looked at the number. It was Aiden's number. I called it. No answer. I called it fifteen times. Nothing. Then I called my girlfriend.

I told her I thought Aiden was alive. I told her to call his work, posing as a niece and saying it was a family emergency. They told her Aiden was in the building and gave her his number. She called me back, confirming that Aiden was indeed alive. I began to come apart. I began to shake uncontrollably. My heart was beating so loud and fast I could hear each rapid thump. I called close friends. I was in utter disbelief. This wasn't possible. Why? Why? The word ran over and over in my mind. Why would he do this? My friends were angry. They had watched me suffer the past year, knowing he was gone. Knowing how I felt about him and he, me. But why would you deceive someone so horribly that you claim to love? I couldn't make sense of it.

After the initial shock wore off, I became elated. He was alive! Alive! I could see him again. I could hold him, kiss him, lie with him. I called him. He answered. His voice. His voice the same, but different. He didn't seem sorry for what he had done. He didn't have answers that I needed. I began to question if even the answers he gave me would be the truth. I spent the next two days talking to him. I told him I forgave him. That I loved him. That I wanted to be with him. He said he wanted to see me. He said he wanted to go away together for a few days. *Could we pick up where we left off?* He also told me that he did in fact have cancer.

Stage three lung, not stage four like he had said. He told me if we were to get back together, I could not ask him about his illness, or how he felt, or cry over him. I agreed. Those closest to me sensed that I had been drawn in by him again. That I was going to go back to him. They were beyond upset about this. Called me an idiot. A fool. Said he was a sociopath and if he had done this to me, what other atrocities was he capable of? They told me they would not support me if I went back. That they would think less of me, that I was as weak and as foolish as they come. These were men that thought this way, that said these things.

My women friends had very different reactions. Some

felt he had faked his death because he didn't want to put me through the long agony of dying. He wanted to make it quick, simple, to spare me so to speak. That I had stopped writing and he was afraid I wouldn't be able to further my words, that they would just dry up and blow away. But hadn't I broken up with him for that very reason? So I could take a break from us? Why had he just shared his news on that cold December night? The questions just kept coming at me. I was in a daze for a week. I could think of nothing but us. I was falling again. Falling into him. Falling into me. Falling into us.

A friend called me one night. He said, Aiden didn't love you, you know. You don't do that to someone you love. You don't hurt them like that. He played God with you and that wasn't right. Learn from him. Learn from this past year. Take this as one of the most gratifying experiences of your life. He taught you how to love, passionately. He taught you the greatest of pain. He made you come alive, really alive. He made you strong. He made you bold, fearless. Leave him now. Say goodbye.

And I did. And I have. Nothing is ever easy. We can't learn if it is easy. We can only learn if we break. We can only learn if we feel that we can't go on. We can only learn if our heart splits in two. And now, now I go through the steps of feeling whole again. There is no ending to this story. Not as long as he walks the earth and so do I.

The Reveal

poem

I saw your picture splashed on my
computer screen,
stupid ass dating site.
Not possible, nope. Can't be.
My heart dropped, dropped to my bowels.
I felt it there, heavy and I
wanted to take a shit.
I wanted to throw-up.
Throw-up my last meal of kale and spinach salad,
sprinkled with sunflower seeds.
I called my friend, A.
I called J.
I called M.
I called P.

I called S.

I called T.

Stumped as shit they were.

Yup.

Stumped like me.

Who the fuck does that?

Who?

It can't be so.

Oh, motherfuckers, but it is.

I got the shivers.

I paced the floor.

I took off my bra.

I took off my pants.

I walked around the apartment, my ass exposed.

I took a piss.

I smoked a cigarette.

I let my hair down.

I called A. Again.

Come over here. Come over now.

I am falling apart in the middle of my
kitchen.

My legs began to shake.

I felt the burn climbing from my
stomach, into my throat.

I threw-up.

No kale, no sunflower seeds.

Morning coffee, staining the porcelain.

Some splashed on the floor.

Some in my hair.

I am falling apart.

I looked at my balcony.

I wanted to leap, head first.

I wanted to take the dive.

I wanted my heart to pop out of my asshole

hitting the pavement, splattering.

I wanted it out of me.

I wanted it gone.

The pain is too real

And I just can't do it right now.

Can't face this.

Can't fathom this.

Can't understand this.

Can't, can't, can't.

I hung up the phone.

A was on her way.

I looked at him again on my

computer screen.

I wanted to fuck him.

The Boogeyman

poem

T hey lurk.

They wait for you.

They hide behind masks of beauty,

Intelligence, calm and grace.

But not always.

Sometimes they are strivers, motivators,

Innovators, brilliant.

They feast on kindness, love and generosity.

They dine on your body, your mind,

Your soul.

They make you think

You are the one.

You fall for them.

You fall for the beast, the devil, the boogeyman.

He is dressed well.

His smell intoxicates you.

It is nectar in your senses.

His skin entices you.

The softness, the honey color.

His eyes, penetrate you, adore you,

Tell you it is you. I have found you.

His sex is the best you

Have ever had.

See how he works?

If you look closely, you can see his markings.

If you listen, you can hear his lies.

If you put your head to his chest,

You can hear his heartbeat.

It is fast. It is calculated.

It plots, it waits, it deceives.

He holds you like he will never let you go.

You won't know what hit you.

You won't stop and think,

Because he has blinded you, seduced you.

You are at his mercy.

If you should hurt him, deny him, insult him

Or not let him ravish your body at his will,

He will get you.

He will destroy you.

He will crush you.

He will mutilate you,

And watch your blood pour

Out of your pussy,

Your mouth,

Your ass,

Your every pore.

You are muck.

He will paralyze you.

You want to get up,

You see him walking away.

Your body won't let you.

You are weak.

And he has won.

He will turn and look at you,

Not seeing your tears,

Your blood,

Your sadness.

He will laugh at you

And then he will move on to

His next victim.

The Rage

poem

It took me in the middle of the night.
It woke me from a deep sleep.
It shook me, rolled me over
And slapped me in the face.
It crashed over me like a wave.
Get up you fucking moron.
Come to your senses now you
Stupid bitch.
The rage took hold,
It held fast.
I called him.
I screamed.
I was relentless.
I fought.

I fought for me for a change.

I fought for breathing rights.

I fought for integrity, self-worth,

Self-preservation.

I fought so I could be whole again.

I fought because I deserved to love myself.

Wasn't that my problem in the first place?

No self-love.

No fucking worth.

I usually loathe me.

No more.

I told him things I hope

To God I never have to say to anyone again.

Ever.

Horrible things. Mean things. But things

He deserved. He deserves it all.

Karma's a fucking ass bitch, baby.

Now walk the fuck away....

Forgiveness

poem

I know what you did.

I don't know why.

Will I ever?

Fuck no.

I don't care

What you did.

I want you back.

You didn't mean to.

You were confused,

Your life mayhem, a cluster-fuck.

Jesus, I made excuses for you.

I told my friends you were sorry.

I told my friends that you had a mental breakdown.

I told my friends that I still loved you.

They thought I was crazy.

Have you gone mad? They asked.

What is wrong with you?

You are smart, funny, artistic, gifted, beautiful.

You are a friend, a mother, a daughter, a sister.

You would forsake that

For a broken, sick, fuck of a man?

But you didn't hear him on the phone.

You didn't hear his voice.

It cried. It begged for forgiveness.

It told me it loved me.

Just like old times.

So like old times.

I craved him again.

I yearned for his body to take me.

I longed to smell his skin, his scent,

Intoxicating.

My friends said,

Can you not see through that?

Look at what he has done to you.

He has played the cruelest of the cruel tricks

One can ever play.

The cruelest.

He is not capable of love.

He is not human.

Please, don't do this.

Don't go back.

I must. I shall. I need him. I want him.

It will work out. It will pass. We will be fine.

I forgive him.